Where the Bright
Lights Shine

Where the Bright Lights Shine

Anne Nall Stallworth
author of *This Time Next Year*

The Vanguard Press, Inc.
New York

*For my sisters, Mary and Margaret
and for my children, Carole and Clarke,
in consideration of love.*

Part One

1

IN THE MID-AFTERNOON of a day in early June, Snow Berryhill and his wife, Callie, stood in the shade under the wide limbs of a sycamore tree, arguing. The tree stood in the front yard of their new house, and its leaves were still the thin, translucent green of spring; they had not yet turned the darker green of summer.

They were fussing about the best way to unload their furniture from the pickup truck parked at the curb; the Negro man who owned the truck sat on the curbstone smoking a cigarette and waiting for the argument to end so that he could untie the ropes and help unload the few belongings.

Snow's face was red because he was angry and because the day was so hot. He fanned with his straw sun hat, only to slap it back on his head and take from the hip pocket of his overalls a faded blue square of handkerchief to wipe the sweat from his forehead. Callie glared at him, hands on hips. She wore her Sunday clothes, a pink voile dress fastened at the neck with a brooch set with many glass stones that flashed in the sunshine. The brooch had belonged to her mother and was her dearest possession.

It was 1939, and after nearly twenty years on the farm the

Berryhills were moving to a place in town called Magnolia Hills. The name of the community pleased Callie, she thought it poetic, but she had found that it was not descriptive: there were no magnolias to be seen anywhere.

The street was wide and tree-shaded, and though the old frame houses were large, they seemed shrunken under the white glare of the sun, and vacant too, with their window shades pulled against the heat. It seemed as if everyone had moved away except for the women and children, who had crept onto their porches, puffy-eyed from their naps, to watch the new people move in. Later, when they were not so sleepy, they would remember how old or how new the furniture was, whether the stove was gas or wood burning, and pass judgment as to the financial condition of their new neighbors.

There was no movement anywhere except that far up the street a tall girl ran racing down the sidewalk, her dark hair whipping around her shoulders, her long, skinny legs poking like sticks from beneath her too-short dress. Exhausted with her running, the soles of her bare feet blistered from the hot concrete, she dropped onto the grass in the front yard and lay on her back. Her father and the Negro man were struggling to get the iron stove off the truck; her mother stood close to them, motioning, directing their labor.

After a while the girl's back began to sting in the dry grass and she sat up and pushed her long hair to the top of her head; she closed her eyes and sighed with pleasure as the faint, sensuous breeze cooled her neck, bringing with it the warm sweet smell of privet hedges in bloom. She opened her eyes and, with her chin resting on her knees, watched her father and the Negro man named Olan Calvert as they puffed up the front steps, straining with the weight of the stove.

Her father was a big man with broad shoulders and powerful arms; she thought him handsome with his long face and bright blue eyes; his once coal black hair was streaked with gray. Always, she was proud that people said she favored him, had ways like him. Sometimes she awoke in the night scared he had died, and after she had tiptoed to his room to check his breathing to make sure he still lived, she lay in her bed and worried that one day he would die. For he was growing old: today was his forty-fifth birthday. She could not imagine living in the world without him.

A long time ago he had loved her too. He had taken her to the fields with him, let her help pull the weeds away from the cotton and ride in the wagon when he hauled corn. But that was before Jo Anna got big enough to tag along after them. It wasn't long before he stopped loving her to love the baby sister; it was as if he couldn't love more than one person at a time, he had to take from one to give to the other. At first, she didn't understand why he loved Jo Anna; she never stayed long in the field but always left after a few minutes to go home to play dolls on the front porch. Then she decided that he loved her because she was so pretty, with her golden-brown hair and her fair skin. When she compared herself to Jo Anna, she supposed she could not blame her father; he could never love someone so tall and skinny, so plain as she.

She lay back in the grass again and stared up into the blue, blue sky; she stared without blinking until she felt as if she were floating and falling upward. She thought that if she concentrated hard enough she could will herself back to the farm, hoped that when she opened her eyes she would be far away from this tiny patch of grass and back in the field. It was there her father had loved her, carrying her on his back when it was time to go to the house for dinner.

Last night, as she lay in bed next to Maribeth, she listened to him snore in the other room and was angry that he could

5

sleep away their last night at home. As she lay awake, she memorized the night sounds she would try never to forget: the wind blowing down the chimney with a sighing, whooshing sound and in the deep quiet of the night she could hear the McCrary dogs barking from far away. There was the chooga-chooga-chooga of cars going down the dirt road, and once the cow's hoof clanged against the metal feed bucket her father left sitting in the middle of the stall. He had left it there because when he fed the cow he was drinking with Olan and had forgotten to put it away. He'd stayed in the loft with Olan until bedtime and it wasn't long after he'd gone to bed that she heard him snoring. Once, she nearly slept too, but she licked her fingers and rubbed her eyes with spit so that she could stay awake. She had done that several times until the room was light and her mother called them to breakfast.

"Mama said to tell you not to run any more, Lee Rose," Jo Anna said, sitting beside her in the grass. Jo Anna had come from the house, where, with their sister Maribeth, she'd been helping to arrange the furniture. "Mama said the neighbors are watching you, and Maribeth's embarrassed because we're all acting so country and they're staring at our furniture and everything—"

Lee Rose shrugged her disinterest and crossed her legs, resting her right ankle on her drawn-up left knee.

"Put your legs down, Lee Rose," Jo Anna said, "I can see your underpants and Mama said you'll get a whipping if you don't quit acting so wild and all, running up and down the sidewalk that way—"

"She knows I won't stop running and she knows that she won't whip me," and Lee Rose yawned to show Jo Anna how little she cared about her mother's threats. She was fourteen and her mother would never whip her again.

6

The last time was over a year ago when Maribeth told on her for skipping church. It was a warm morning in early spring and she knew she could not sit still to listen to the preacher tell how soon the end of time was coming, how any day now God would destroy the world. She did not believe the world could end on such a day and she went to run with the boys in the churchyard. It was a day of fairest blue sky and shiny black grasshoppers that jumped in a wide arc from the white daisies that covered the ground.

None of the boys could run as fast as she, and when she had turned cartwheels until she was dizzy, she went home where her mother was waiting for her. She was not mad at her for skipping church, but she was mad that she'd shown her underpants in front of all those boys. Her mother whipped her hard, striping her legs with a limber green hedge switch. Afterwards Lee Rose had crawled far under the house and hidden behind a brick pillar.

She stayed there all afternoon, crying, huddled in the dark. There were the sounds overhead, footsteps walking back and forth, the scrape of the broom as someone swept the floor. Toward dark, when she had finished crying, she crawled out and went for a walk and knew that she would never let anyone make her cry again. She passed the McCrary's house and somebody had forgotten and left the gate open. All the dogs had run out at her and chased her up the fence post.

It was full dark when they found her. Jo Anna and her father appeared out of the dark calling her name. Her father laughed when he saw her squatting on the post, the dogs lying there keeping guard over her. He yelled at the dogs, throwing a rock at them, and they ran away. But she hated him for laughing at her. She didn't know anyone around there who wasn't scared of those dogs, they were so mean. Walking back home, she decided her mother would never whip her again. Lee Rose never told her, but somehow her mother had known that she'd better not ever touch her that way again.

"The air's hot enough to bake biscuits," Jo Anna complained irritably, wiping the sweat from her forehead.

"I like it hot," Lee Rose said. "In a minute I'm going to run and run until my blood vessels burst and I fall over dead on the sidewalk." She smiled and closed her eyes, waiting to savor the objections that were sure to come.

"No you're not, Lee Rose," Jo Anna said, leaning over her, pulling open the lid of one dark blue eye. "I'll tell on you."

Lee Rose rolled the open eye heavenward.

"You can go tell but you *know* I'll run anyway, nobody can stop me from running."

When she ran there was a power came up in her, there was a joy that she felt at no other time; her body was light, buoyant. She felt as if her feet scarcely touched the ground, that she would leave the ground altogether to soar in the air currents as the hawks did, the wind in her face.

"In just a minute I'm going to run down that sidewalk all the way back home and I'll never come back here, I'll live in the woods back of the house and just come out at the full of the moon to turn cartwheels. People will think I'm a ghost or some kind of a werewolf that walks on its hind legs...."

Jo Anna tried to look unconcerned, but she was worried, and Lee Rose was enjoying it. Poor scary Jo Anna believed all the things she told her. When Jo Anna was little Lee Rose even made her believe the hot-water bag that hung on the back of the bathroom door was filled with gas and that if she pulled the stopper it would explode and the house would blow up. Jo Anna was too smart for that now, but Lee Rose had lately convinced her there was a nigger man hiding under her bed at night and that if she got up to go to the bathroom he would reach out and grab her legs, pull her under the bed and kill her. Sometimes Jo Anna wet the bed because she was afraid to go to the bathroom. Lee Rose listened to her mother fuss at her as she changed the wet sheets in the middle of the night, but Jo Anna never told on her, never told she wet the bed because she was afraid to get up in the dark.

Lee Rose squinted her eyes at the sun and thought there was plenty enough daylight left for exploring. It was not a day for staying in a tacky front yard so small that when she stretched her legs her feet were in the neighbor's yard. She'd start exploring in the alley; she'd already been there once before when her mother brought her and Maribeth and Jo Anna along to look at the house. Lee Rose had left them, bored with Maribeth and her mother exclaiming over the flowered wallpaper and their talk of where to place the furniture. Jo Anna was jumping in and out of closets, pouncing on people as they passed by, and Lee Rose was bored with that too.

So she went to the back yard, and outside the wire fence was a narrow dirt road. She went out the gate to see where it led and it was a new world, nearly as good as some of the places back at the farm. She pulled off her shoes, and the gravel cut her feet, but she walked all the way to the next corner, looking in strange back yards that had clothes flapping on the lines and flowers of all colors bordering the fences. She'd never seen so many back yards at one time. At the corner she stood looking away up the long road and she knew that one day she would follow it as far as it went to see where it led.

When she was back at her own gate she noticed for the first time tiny bits of glass sparkling among the gray slag. She knelt and scratched around with her fingertips until she found two pieces of glass that especially pleased her, one red and one green. She held them in the palm of her hand like jewels and took them back home with her and wrapped them in a piece of toilet paper. She hid them in the dresser drawer under her socks.

A young boy left the group of children who sat next door on the front steps watching the moving of the furniture. He sat down with Lee Rose and Jo Anna.

"My name's Sammy Tancretti," he said.

"So?" asked Lee Rose.

Jo Anna glared at her for being so rude, and in her politest voice said, "My name's Jo Anna Berryhill and this is my sister, Lee Rose Berryhill. At least I *think* she's my sister. Sometimes I think Mama and Daddy adopted her, the way she acts. Nobody else in our family acts like her."

"I'll cut your goddam head off, Jo Anna, if you *ever* say that again, Daddy's little baby," Lee Rose said. She sat up, her blue eyes turned nearly black with fury.

It had been her secret fear since Jo Anna was born that she was indeed adopted and that this might be another reason for her father's rejection of her: at last, he'd had his own baby, he no longer needed the homely, lanky Lee Rose. She never thought of whether Maribeth was, or was not, adopted. Maribeth was her mother's favorite and so she never considered her in connection with her father.

"You're not supposed to curse since we joined the church, Lee Rose," Jo Anna said. "You promised Mama faithfully after you were saved that you would stop cursing."

"I did not promise, *she* was the one that said I'd stop, *I* never did. I have not *once* felt Jesus in my heart, I don't even believe there was such a person, or a God—"

Sammy Tancretti gasped when she said the blasphemous words and crossed himself.

"Well, you needn't act so holy, Sammy whatever-your-name-is," Lee Rose said. "It's perfectly obvious *you're* a Catholic and worship idols and statues and kneel down to ordinary men and kiss their rings. I've heard about people like you in Sunday school."

The thin, spindly-legged boy's face flushed and he picked at the grass, sifting the pieces through his fingers. He had large pale eyes and pale blond hair; he wore winter corduroy knickers with long socks and high-top shoes. His long-sleeved blue flannel shirt was buttoned all the way to his neck.

"Why do you run so much on such a hot day?" he asked Lee Rose.

"If it's any of your business, I run because I like to. Why do you dress for the middle of the winter on such a hot day?", and she mimicked his thin, reedy voice.

The boy shrugged as if he were used to the question.

"Because I have asthma and I can't let the wind blow on me. If it does I have an attack or get pneumonia. Last winter I had pneumonia *twice*," and proudly he held up two fingers to emphasize his point. "Probably I won't live to get grown," and he watched their faces to see the sympathy that was sure to be there, that was always on grown-ups' faces when his mother told them about poor Sammy.

"Phooey," Lee Rose said, and jumping over his outstretched legs she ran away up the sidewalk. The children who still sat on the steps jumped up and ran after her.

"Why *does* she run like that?" Sammy asked Jo Anna.

"Because she *feels* like running. Are you jealous? You have a jealous-looking face."

The boy smoothed his silky blond hair back from his forehead. His face was so pale that Jo Anna knew if she touched his skin it would be cool to her fingertips.

"Yes, I guess I'm jealous. I wish I could run like that."

She was surprised that he admitted it, that he was not mad. Always she was furious if someone called her jealous, it was the supreme insult, the last put-down.

"Do you like the movies?" he asked.

"I don't know. I've never been. My big sister Maribeth and my mother went to see *Gone With the Wind*, but she wouldn't take Lee Rose and me. Lee Rose hollered and screamed and stomped her feet to go, but still Mama wouldn't let her. Mama said there were curse words we shouldn't hear. There's not *any* curse word Lee Rose shouldn't hear. I guess at one time or another I've heard her say them all."

"Maybe sometimes you can go with me to the movies."

"Maybe so."

"Maybe your mother will trade at our grocery store and all of us will get to be friends."

"Maybe so."

"How old are you, Jo Anna?"

"Eleven."

"I'm thirteen."

They sat without talking, and under the trees the shade was black, solid. Then Jo Anna stood up and, making a visor of her hands, peered up the bright sidewalk. At first she didn't see Lee Rose and she was afraid, her heart fluttering under her ribs. Already Lee Rose was dead; she had run and run and even now lay on the sidewalk, her blood vessels burst. Then through the shimmering heat waves, all the way to the corner, she saw her surrounded by a crowd of children, all of them a head or more shorter than she.

"I have to go play with my sister now, Sammy," and, waving and calling to Lee Rose, she ran off up the sidewalk.

Sammy watched her, and his legs twitched, urging him to run after her. But instead he watched the flattened blades of grass where she had sat pop up one by one.

12

Snow Berryhill cursed as his fingers scraped the edge of the doorjamb.

"God damn it all to hell," he said, and dropped his side of the dining room table to rub his bruised knuckles.

He saw the disgusted look his wife, Callie, gave him. He was embrarrassing her in front of the neighbors who were gawking at them from their front porches. He was glad to embarrass her, it was small punishment for her not cooking breakfast this morning. Toast, all he'd had all day was toast; he was so hungry the sides of his stomach scraped together, churning and growling. She'd packed the dishes last night deliberately, just so she wouldn't have to cook. Callie hated to cook and if she had her way she'd starve him to death.

He sucked at the salty blood oozing from his knuckles and thought that nobody remembered today was his birthday. He was forty-five years old and nobody remembered. He raised the lids of his eyes to look at Callie. *You're a good-looking woman, but you're getting on up there like me.* If he was forty-five, then she was forty, though she could pass for thirty any day. There wasn't a streak of gray in her light brown hair, not a wrinkle in her face. Her hair was thick and shiny and sometimes he wanted to reach over and touch it, feel the softness of it on his rough hands. But he would not dare to touch her, it would make her mad. He had not touched her deliberately for years.

He fought the move to town. He told Callie he wouldn't come, that he'd stay there in the old place by himself, but she kept right on packing. She told him she didn't care if he stayed, she was taking her furniture and her girls to town. He didn't know how she came to have sole claim on the girls and on the furniture, but she did. And she had money now to back up her threats. Her brother Royce had been killed by a taxi running a red light in St. Louis and since he'd never married and didn't have any family but Callie, all the insurance money was paid to her. And that was two thousand dollars.

Callie had cried off and on for a few days after the funeral, but then she'd sat dazed and dreamy, folding and refolding the check the insurance company had mailed to her. She dressed in her best clothes every morning for a week or two and went into town, but she wouldn't tell anybody but Maribeth where she went. Finally, one afternoon she got off the bus, crossed the road to the house, and sent Jo Anna to the field after him and made her announcement. She had found a house and they were moving to town, she said; she didn't ask any of them if they wanted to go or who shot John or anything else; the next morning she just started in packing. Snow came along because there was nothing else to do, he didn't have the stomach for batching it and he hated to start all over again someplace else all by himself.

Maribeth came out the front door and she didn't look at him and she didn't say anything as she brushed past him. She walked with her left foot turned slightly inward and shook her brown hair around her face. He was an embarrassment to her too, and he thought how much like Callie she was; she didn't look like her so much, wasn't nearly as pretty, but she had her mother's ways. She had freckles where Callie's skin was peaches and cream and at sixteen she seemed completely grownup. Snow never had known what to say to the girls when they started getting big so he just didn't say anything. He'd never been around girls much and sometimes he felt guilty because he wished so bad that they were boys so they could hunt and fish together, work the fields together. If they were boys there'd be things to talk about.

14

Snow looked at the sky and saw the top rim of the sun was just behind the white-skinned sycamore that grew in the front yard. It couldn't be more than four o'clock, just about the time he used to leave the field and come to the house for supper. He was worried about his cotton, it broke his heart to go off and leave it there in the field with nobody but Olan to take care of it; it was tender as a new-born babe this time of year and ought to be hoed every day. He could feel the sun warm on his back, and there was the smell of the moist black dirt as he chopped the weeds; his fingers twitched as the black dirt crumbled in his hands. That's where he ought to be, in the field chopping his cotton. But it had been a good day for Callie when old Royce got hit by that taxi and hit his head on the curbstone. . . .

"Come on in with the table, Snow," Callie said dryly from inside the screen door, "I don't expect a scraped knuckle will kill you, I don't think the Lord is ready to call you home."

"No, I don't expect I'd be that lucky," he said, and he picked up his end of the table and, nodding to Olan, they angled it through the front door.

2

THE HOUSE WAS quiet and dark except for the yellow square of light shining through the bathroom transom into the back bedroom. Callie lay on her back next to Jo Anna; Snow slept in the other iron bed across the room. He was snoring and in a minute she would have to tell him to turn over on his side.

She was too excited to sleep, too keyed up. For the first time in her life she slept in a house that belonged to her. The day she first came here she knew she had come home at last, a feeling of familiarity sweeping through her; she thought she must have lived in this house before but, of course, knew that she had not. She had walked through the high-ceilinged rooms and was not surprised that there were two bedrooms, one bright with sunshine because there were many windows, one only half light because there was only one window; there was a door that led from the back bedroom onto a latticed back porch.

The house was old, but it was sturdy, there were no rotting boards in her house. She had made certain of that; she was not dazzled by the new wallpaper or the fresh paint put there by the real estate company. She had even gone down on her hands and knees and with the real estate salesman's flashlight examined the foundation under the house. He had found that she was no fool.

When she had walked in the back yard that first day, she stood under the huge walnut tree that grew there and stared in awe at the flowers growing in the yard next door. There were flowers of every description, there was no grass, only flower beds with just enough room to walk between them. It was the most beautiful sight she'd ever seen in her life, the pink and yellow spikes of gladiolas, red poppies and the pink thrift that crawled over the rocks edging the flower beds. One day her yard would look like that, after Jo Anna grew up and Lee Rose stopped being such a tomboy. One day she would not need a lawn for children to play on and she would turn the whole back yard into flowers.

Jo Anna sighed and turned over, her arm resting across Callie's throat. Callie smiled and gently moved her arm, shifting to make more room for her. Jo Anna had slept with her since she was born because Callie did not sleep with Snow any more. She did not want any more children so she did not let him make love to her. When she first refused him, he was furious and told her it was her duty as his wife, that he fed and clothed her, kept a roof over her head. But after a while he didn't ask her any more and he quit fussing; she heard talk from the colored who came around the house that he had a nigger girl he was sleeping with who lived on Olan Calvert's place. Callie pretended she hadn't heard a thing and she took her girls and went to church and held her head high; nobody held it against her what Snow did, she was still respected, well thought of.

On the farm her hatred of him was diffused, he was only a part of the fabric of all the things she despised: the raw fields, the bleak, lonely winters, the black nights with not even a neighbor's friendly light to see when she looked out a window. But today, when she watched him unloading the furniture, her hatred condensed and was suddenly concentrated solely on him: he was a symbol of the old life, a reminder of all she wanted to forget. She wished with all her heart that he had not come, that he did not now lie snoring in her bed between her new sheets.

She turned on her side and through the open door saw the ghostly criss-crossing of the latticed back porch. There was the smell of honeysuckle matted with morning glory vines that climbed the lattice; she could see the circle of lights that ringed the golf course a block away and she sighed with pure bliss. Lights, lights, all she had to do was open her eyes and even late at night there were lights shining everywhere.

Restless, she turned onto her back and wondered if somewhere her mother knew that tonight she slept in a house of her own, that in only ten years she would pay off the mortgage. She was five years old when her mother died, but she remembered things about her, the sound of her voice as they sat around the fireplace at night while she read scary stories out of the Bible to her and Royce. She read to them about the flood and Jezebel and how Lot's wife was turned into a pillar of salt for disobeying the Lord. She remembered too the strong soap smell of her mother's skin and the long white aprons she wore over her dresses.

She could remember her father better because she was twelve years old when he died. He was a slightly built man with brown wavy hair; after supper every summer night he went to the yard and carved out gourds for the birds to build nests in. Then he hung them in the trees and all around town people smiled and nicknamed him "Gourd." She didn't remember him being a drinking man, but one afternoon he took the notion to leave the field and go up the road to have a drink with Mr. Underwood. When he came back home he cut across Mr. Underwood's vacant lot and fell through a hole in the rusted tin cover of an old dried-up-well.

When he didn't come home, toward dark Royce went to look for him and found him in the well with his neck broken. A few days after the funeral she and Royce were sent to live in Opelika with their daddy's sister. Their aunt had a lot of children of her own and she and Royce could tell she didn't really want them there. Royce was sixteen and didn't hang around long; he left one night after supper and it wasn't until after she was married to Snow that she heard from him. He wrote her a penny post card in care of her aunt and the aunt sent it on to her. He told her he was living in St. Louis and one night he got to studying about his little sister. He wrote, *You know how Mama always told us if we got to studying about someone we ought to get in touch with that person, so that's what I'm doing. Sometimes I'd like to hear whatever happened to you. Yours truly, Royce Braden.*

She was tickled to hear from him and was going to write him at the address he put on the front of the card, but before she had the chance a letter came from her aunt telling her he'd gotten killed. It was strange, thinking back on it, how he wrote to her after all those years, and she wondered if he'd had some premonition that he would die and wanted to get in touch with her one more time. She wrote to her aunt in Opelika and told her to have Royce sent back home and asked her to come to the funeral because there were so few who remembered him, there wasn't anyone much to come. But her aunt didn't even answer the letter; she had never forgiven Royce for running away like he had.

Snow snorted and groaned in his sleep.

19

"Turn over on your side, Snow," Callie called softly to him, trying to wake him without waking Jo Anna.

The bedsprings creaked as he turned over and Callie pushed the damp strands of hair away from her face and wished it was not so hot. She thought that if it were not so hot she could sleep, though even the heat was not so bad when suffered in the city. Still, she did not like to be awake when all the rest of them slept; it made her feel lonesome.

Once, a long time ago, when the girls were little, she'd caught the Greyhound bus and gone back to the old place where she and Royce had been children together. Though her father never owned the house and land, she was excited to show the children where she once had lived. When they got off the bus and stood at the top of the hill everything was the same except there wasn't a house any more. The chinaberry tree was still there where the front yard used to be, but everything else was weeds and half-grown trees. She ran down the hill, and the children were crying after her, their legs too short to keep up with her, but she wouldn't stop for them, she kept on running, certain that any minute the house would appear, would blossom like magic before her eyes.

She found the spot where it had stood; beneath the weeds she found the crumbling stones of the foundation and she sat down under a tree while the children played there. When she lay her head to rest against the trunk of an old white oak tree, she saw high in its branches a gray and weathered gourd swaying in the breeze. Her father had put it there years ago, and, excited, she called the girls to come and see.

"Look," she said, pointing to the gourd high in the branches, "your grandfather Braden hung that gourd there for the birds to make nests in I don't know *how* many years ago."

They looked to where her finger pointed, but they were not

much interested and ran back to play their game among the stones. She wondered why her father had climbed so high to hang the gourd, then realized that the tree had grown tall in the years since he had put it there.

She sighed and shifted, wanting to sleep, needing to be rested for unpacking the cardboard boxes tomorrow. Maribeth would help her, always she could count on Maribeth who liked things nice the way she did. Maribeth had been as happy as she was to move away from the farm, that they were buying their own house. Callie was sorry it took Royce dying for them to get the house, but if he had to die, she thought he would approve of the way she was spending the money. She thought that he would be proud, and her father and mother, too, that finally someone in the family owned land. She thought the three of them stood impatiently on the banks of the Jordan waiting for her to cross over and tell them how it felt to be a property owner.

She had taken Royce back home to bury him. She had his grave dug in the church cemetery on a grassy slope up from the Coosa River where he could lie at the feet of their mother and father. She was happy for them all to be together; when she wanted to visit one, she could visit all. It was a spring day of clear blue sky and yellow butterflies that she had the funeral. The preacher at the Primitive Baptist Church came to read the service, and the wind blew off the river, flattening the tall grass that grew in the cemetery. She cried for her brother, but she cried mostly for herself that her family was all gone except for her. It had been too many years since Royce had been a part of her life to be really sad that he was gone.

When they had left the cemetery, were almost back to the road to wait for the bus, she turned to look back and saw an old man coming over the hill. She went back to the grave and the old man was Luke Underwood. She took his hand and told him who she was. He looked much the same as he had when she was a child except that now his hair was gray and there were more wrinkles in his face. He was nearly blind, he said, and he stared into her face and nodded that she was correct, she was the person she said she was.

"It's been a long time since I saw you, but you're Braden's baby girl, I can tell," and the tears ran down his face when she told him it was Royce they buried that afternoon and that she was the only member of her family still alive.

He put his arms around her when she told him good-by, she left him standing by Royce's grave with his hands tucked under the bib of his overalls.

Far across the railroad tracks, past the Magnolia Hills business district, the tank factory blew its midnight whistle and still Callie was awake. She stretched, and though she was tired, exhausted from the long day, she felt young and strong, the years still before her rising like golden stairs into heaven. If the tight bud of her youth had opened into the full-blown flower, she was still pretty, even the years of hard work and doing without had not aged her. Last week, she had blushed with pleasure when the president of the First National Bank had complimented her: *You are a pretty lady, Mrs. Berryhill, a fine example of Southern womanhood,* and he smiled at her and the cool air of the bank cooled her face and there was the smell of the thick, black ink as he stamped her papers *Warranty Deed and Land Title.* When she bragged that the president had complimented her, telling Snow what he said, Snow said it was because she was buying the house from the bank, that he was greedy and wanted her money. But she did not believe him, the president was a nice man, a kind man . . .

Someone moved in the door of the bedroom, there was the shadowy figure of a person silhouetted against the dim light that shone through the transom. It was Maribeth or Lee Rose going to the bathroom, Callie thought, but then the figure moved across the room to Snow's bed. Then she heard the low murmur of whispered words.

"Who's there?" she asked, sitting up in bed.

The whispering stopped and it was Lee Rose's voice she heard.

"It's me, Lee Rose, Mama," she said.

"What are you doing out of bed?" and anger spread through her, causing her to tremble in the hot night. She was furious that Lee Rose had secrets with Snow, that she told him things she wouldn't tell her own mother. It was not the first time she had come to his bed. When she was little she sometimes walked in her sleep, got into bed with him, and did not remember the next morning what she had done.

"Answer me, Lee Rose, what are you doing out of bed, what were you whispering that I shouldn't hear?"

"I wished him a happy birthday, nobody remembered that today was his birthday."

Snow sat up, Callie could see him straining toward her in the dark.

"Leave the child alone, quit nagging at the child—"

"She's not a child, she's nearly a grown woman. Don't you have any secrets with my girls; if you don't walk the chalk line I'll put you out of my house. Your name is nowhere on my deed, Snow Berryhill."

When Lee Rose left the room, he sighed and lay back, and Callie took a deep breath and lay on her back. She had remembered that today was his birthday but she would never let him know she did. The time was past for that, remembering other's birthday and having celebrations was for people who loved each other.

Behind the golf course, a train blew its whistle as it crossed the trestle and started the long climb up the hill. It was morning, light was already coming in the window before Callie finally closed her eyes and slept.

3

THEY SAT in the movie theater, the three of them together, Lee Rose, Jo Anna, and Sammy. Jo Anna sat with her eyes closed, oblivious to the crumpled popcorn sacks that flew around her head; she was enthralled, unwilling to break the spell that held her. It was the happiest day of her whole life, nothing that had happened to her before, not even the train ride last year to Mobile, could equal it.

There were three movies that Saturday afternoon: *Boston Blackie, The Lone Ranger Rides Again* and the serial called *Jungle Girl.* Finally, there were the *Previews of Coming Attractions.* It was a show she would never forget. A popcorn sack hit her on the back of her head and she opened her eyes and wondered how the children could play, why they were not transported as she had been. Even Sammy was throwing wadded sacks and scuffling with Lee Rose for one that had just been thrown from the colored balcony. She closed her eyes to shut out the torn seat covers and the popcorn mashed into the spilled drinks that smeared the floor; she wished she could see the movies all over again.

The doors opened and late afternoon sun shone pale and weak against the yellow electric glare of the theater. Lee Rose stretched and stood up.

"Open your eyes and let's go home, Jo Anna," she said. "I'm hungry."

They stood up and inched their way into the crowd of people shuffling toward the rectangle of sunlight. A dark stream of Negroes flowed down the stairs from the balcony, going toward their own side door. The blacks were not allowed to mix with the whites inside the theater. When they passed the ticket taker who stood holding open the door, Jo Anna cringed, embarrassed all over again at how Lee Rose and Sammy had tried to get Lee Rose in on a child's ticket.

Walking to the theater, they had decided that if they could get Lee Rose in on a child's ticket, they would have fifteen cents left over for candy—Callie would give them no extra money and Jo Anna was against their plan from the beginning; she told them she didn't like the sound of it, but they paid no attention to her. They planned for Sammy to buy the tickets and for Lee Rose to stand behind Jo Anna to the side of the ticket office, bending her knees to look short.

They had gotten by with it at the ticket office, and Sammy and Lee Rose had smiled wisely at each other; already they could taste the creamy chocolate center of the Milky Way candy bar, could feel the smooth caramel sticking to their teeth. But when they got to the ticket taker, bristling with importance in his bright blue uniform with the gold braid trim, he looked at the ten-cent ticket and then at Lee Rose.

"How's the weather up there?" he asked, sarcastic as could be.

Lee Rose grinned and shrugged.

"Raining," she said, and spit a stream of spit next to his foot.

"All *right*," the boy said, his pimply face red with anger, "that was real cute, shorty. I could call the manager and have you thrown out for that. If you want to get in on this child's ticket you'll have to go home and get your mama."

He handed the ticket back to her.

Lee Rose wasn't the least bit embarrassed, she just went back and bought a grown-up's ticket. Sammy had shared his popcorn with them.

On the sidewalk, the white and colored lines merged, and some of the boys, white and black, began to taunt one another.

"Chocolate-covered peanuts," a white boy yelled.

"Snowball, snowball," a Negro boy answered.

"Smoked meat," said the white boy.

"Paleface."

"Nigger."

"You call me a nigger?"

"Yeah, I called you a nigger."

The big Negro boy, dressed only in faded blue overalls, pushed through the crowd toward the white boy. He was not tall, but he was broad, the thick muscles of his upper arms criss-crossed with large veins. A crowd gathered to watch the fight making up, forming a circle that was half white, half black.

Jo Anna pressed forward to see. The only fights she had seen were in the school yard, but those fights were mostly a lot of shoving and rolling around in the dirt. This had the look of a real fight, a mean fight.

"You say you call me 'nigger'?" the black boy asked again, crouching low, his big hands curled into fists.

"Naw, I called you *jig*aboo," the white boy laughed and ran back into the half circle of whites, fading into the crowd.

"Go on back over the railroad tracks where you belong, niggers," someone hollered, "get on back down by the packing house where you belong and quit stinking up our movie house."

The circle began to close, and no matter how hard she

tried to turn around and go the other way, Jo Anna felt herself being pushed forward. She looked around for Lee Rose but didn't see her. She was close enough now to the Negroes to smell their strong, musty odor, to see the drops of sweat swell in beads on their foreheads, then burst and run in streams down the sides of their faces. She struggled to free herself from the crowd, thought she was smothering, tried to scream and could not.

These people were black, but they were not like the Negroes back at the farm. They were not like the children who were led by their mamas into her yard to play while their mamas worked for her Mama; they were not like Olan who nodded his head politely when he came around the white folks.

Jo Anna looked straight into the eyes of a black boy and through her terror saw the yellow cast of his eyes, the wide flare of his nostrils. They stared at each other and it was strange that here was a black face that looked at her with no smiling benevolence or tender solicitude; this black mouth had no smile, no flashing gold tooth or kind words for her. This was the dark something that hid under her bed, the familiar face distorted with hatred, cold and hard. Panicked, she tried to run, but was wedged in and could not even move her feet.

"Lee Rose," she screamed, and a hand grabbed her arm, dragging her back and back until finally she was out of the crowd.

"How come you just didn't come on, Jo Anna?" Lee Rose fussed. "I *told* you to stay right behind me and the next thing I look back and you're not there."

Jo Anna's knees trembled as she walked, her heart thumping, jumping around. Sammy was at the corner waiting for them. Far away there was the thin sound of a police siren; the crowd in front of the theater broke apart, black and white running in every direction. A few minutes later a police car pulled up to the curb but everything was quiet, there was no one there to arrest.

"That's the scaredest I ever was in my *whole* life," Jo Anna said as the three of them crossed the street. "I thought I was a goner for sure, I thought one of those niggers was going to kill me."

"Don't say 'nigger,' " Sammy said, "it's not nice."

"Why not? It's what they are," Jo Anna said.

"I don't know, they just don't like it, that's all. Let's go home through the sewer," he said, abruptly changing the subject.

"*What* sewer?" Lee Rose asked.

"Down the block there's a place you can crawl through down into the sewer and you can go all the way home underground. It's lots of fun."

They crossed the street and halfway down the block there was the dark opening of the sewer.

"That's it," Sammy said, pointing to a flat, concrete bridge that ran across the middle of the street. There was the faint, hollow sound of water.

"Okay," Lee Rose said without hesitation, "it looks like fun to me."

"Well, it doesn't look like fun to me," Jo Anna said. "I've had all the fun I want for one day. You didn't nearly get killed the way I did."

Sammy and Lee Rose knelt by the opening of the sewer.

"Come on, Jo Anna," Lee Rose said, "let's have some fun; we haven't had any fun since we moved to this place."

"What about the alley? We've had fun in the alley, Lee Rose, you know we have," Jo Anna said.

"Yes, I guess so," she admitted grudgingly, "but that's no reason we can't have some *more* fun."

"We better go straight on home, Lee Rose, the way Mama told us to, or she won't let us come to the movies any more," and Jo Anna could not bear the thought of that. "Let's go home and go looking for glass in the alley, you *know* you like to do that a lot, Lee Rose."

Lee Rose sat back on her heels looking thoughtful. She was tempted, Jo Anna could tell, she was always ready to get the cigar boxes and go searching for glass. Sometimes they sat in the back yard looking through the pieces of glass, turning the world all different colors; once Lee Rose emptied her box over her head and the glass fell around her like colored raindrops.

"I believe we have time to do both," Lee Rose said. "We have time to go home through the sewer and still look for glass when we get home. It's not more than five o'clock, there's plenty of time before dark. Mama won't ever know, she doesn't know how long the movies lasted."

"*Okay* then, I'll go, but I don't like it, Lee Rose, not one little tiny bit."

"I'll go first since I know the way," Sammy said, strutting around the opening of the sewer, happy that for once he was the leader, that these two strapping girls off the farm had to stand back and follow him.

He sat down and slid along on the grass that sloped to the sewer. He dropped into the round black circle, disappearing as if he had never existed. Then his voice was calling to them, ghostly, echoing.

"We're going to get our dresses dirty, Lee Rose," Jo Anna said; "you remember when we left, Mama said, the *last* thing she said, was for us not to get our dresses dirty. We have to wear them to church Sunday."

"Well, we look stupid, we just look stupid. We were the only ones there dressed in Sunday clothes. I hate this dress any-

30

way, I will always from now on and forever after hate this dress."

She wore the white dress she had been baptized in. She had not wanted to join the church, she wanted to stay home and sit on the porch with her father, to prop her feet on the bannister and talk to him. He did not go to church and had certainly not been baptized.

One hot night last August, during revival, Callie had made all three of her girls march down the aisle to dedicate their lives to the Lord. The next Sunday afternoon, right at sunset, the preacher led all of them who had been saved down to the banks of old man Cunningham's lake. He had blistered them for two weeks with the words of the Lord, engaged in a mighty battle with the devil for their souls; wearing a white robe and a perpetual smile, he waded waist deep into the water. He told his lambs huddling on shore that the water was a symbol of the grave, that they would die to rise again in Christ. One by one they followed him into the watery grave, one by one they followed him into the water and gave testimony. There was an old man, a child, a young woman and a deputy sheriff. The sheriff said he had his badge in his pocket to be baptized along with him, that he wanted his badge to be made holy to keep him safe when he went after niggers and bootleggers.

"Say 'Amen,'" the preacher shouted, and, obediently, the people on shore said "Amen."

Lee Rose's turn came and the preacher told her to give testimony. But she wouldn't say anything, she just stood staring at her wavering reflection in the murky water.

"Come on," the preacher said, "tell the people standing there how you and me come to run that devil clean on out of your life," but she still would not speak.

"You make the devil grin when you won't witness for the

31

Lord, daughter," and, still smiling, he folded the white square of handkerchief over her face and pushed her under the water and baptized her. She knew that he had held her under longer than he had the others, and she was ashamed because her breasts were outlined under the sodden voile of the dress as she walked through the slippery mud back to the bank where her mother and sisters waited for her. Jo Anna and Maribeth had witnessed as they were supposed to do, but she did not believe the muddy water of Mr. Cunningham's lake had washed her sins whiter than snow.

Now she crawled down the slope to the sewer as Sammy had done and vanished through the black hole. It was Jo Anna's turn and she took one last look up the warm concrete sidewalk that was calling her home. The sun was low and red behind the trees, the street lay in long afternoon shadows. Halfway down the block a man indolently pushed a lawn mower, the blades gently whirring. The doors and windows of the houses were closed against the heat; after dark the doors would open and the people would come out like nocturnal animals from their dens. They would sit on their porches, rocking and listening to the radio turned up loud so they could hear it through open windows.

Lee Rose's head popped up through the hole.

"Don't just *stand* there, Jo Anna, come *on*," and once again she sank from sight.

Reluctantly, loath to leave the bright sidewalk, Jo Anna sat on the grassy bank and slid to the opening. At the edge, she peered down at Lee Rose's and Sammy's faces, pale in the gloom, staring up at her. Dank air blew in her face and she could see a mossy green wall. She drew back, unwilling to surrender herself to the dark and gurgling sewer.

"You just come on back up out of there, Lee Rose, I don't care *what* you say, I'm not going to do it. You come on up out of there and let's walk home on the sidewalk like Mama told us to and if you don't I'm going to run home and tell on you."

"Well, just run on home then, Daddy's little baby. Why can't you come on and let's have some fun? My goodness, what's wrong with having some *fun* once in a while?"

"Come on up out of there, Lee Rose, or I'll tell."

"*Please*, Jo Anna, come on and just *see* what it's like. I promise if you really don't like it we'll all go back up and walk home on the sidewalk. Just come on down and see what it's like, you can't tell standing up there, for goodness sake."

Lee Rose was begging and she was never one to beg. The vein in her forehead was swollen, pulsing with blood; Jo Anna knew it would not be long before she got a headache. If Lee Rose wanted to go home through the sewer bad enough to get a headache, then she could not refuse her. But first she would extract some payment from her; she was tired of Lee Rose always bossing her around.

"What will you give me if I do?"

"What do you want?" Lee Rose's voice was resigned. Jo Anna had the advantage and knew it; she would not give in without a bribe of some kind.

"I want the red piece of glass that looks like a ruby that you've got hidden in your sock drawer."

"You've been rambling in my drawers again, Jo Anna; I'm going to come up out of here and knock the living daylights out of you—"

"If you dare touch me I'll tell Mama and I'll tell her you went down in the sewer too—"

"You can have the damned old red glass, just shut up and come on before it gets any later."

Jo Anna loosened her grip on the sides of the hole and slid the rest of the way in, Lee Rose catching her as she dropped. Ahead of her the tunnel stretched as far as she could see;

33

there were bare electric bulbs all along the ceiling that lit the way poorly, the floor dark between the lights. Out of the corner of her eye she saw something move and when she jerked her head to see what it was, a lizard flicked through a crack in the wall. Water ran down the gutters on each side of them, the concrete where they walked was treacherous with thick, green slime so that their steps had to be slow and cautious to keep from falling. They clung to one another, the three of them, holding up one another. In the corner, a spider was dead in his own web, his dead eyes staring, waiting for prey that never came. The air was cold but suffocating with the smell of sulphur.

"This is fun, isn't it?" Lee Rose asked. "See, I *told* you it was going to be fun, Jo Anna."

"It's not one bit of fun, Lee Rose, and you know it," Jo Anna said, her teeth chattering.

They walked along and when they came to a crossroads, a place where the tunnel branched in three different directions, they stopped and Lee Rose and Jo Anna looked at Sammy for directions.

Sammy fingered the buttons of his shirt.

"Which way?" Lee Rose asked.

"Well—" he said, hesitating, "I *think* we go to the left, but then it could be to the right—" and his voice slowed with uncertainty.

"You *think* we go to the left," Lee Rose yelled at him, "you damn well *bet*ter know which way—"

"Lee Rose," Jo Anna said, "you promised Mama you wouldn't curse any more—"

"Don't you know which way we go, Sammy?" Lee Rose asked, her voice ominous with sweetness.

"Well, *act*ually, I've never really been home this way, but the Levi brothers have," he added quickly when Lee Rose snorted. "They told me just the way to go and it *seemed* like I'd been home this way, but they didn't tell me about these crossroads—" and his voice trailed away.

"You are a liar," said Lee Rose, "a stinking, filthy liar that lured me and my little sister into this stinking hole of hell—"

"Lee Rose, you're not supposed to curse any more; you told Mama you wouldn't curse—"

"Let's go home," Lee Rose said, but when she whirled around to start in the direction they had come, she slipped down in the slime and banged her elbow on the concrete.

"You are a son of a bitch," she yelled at Sammy as she lay sprawled on the floor, "you are a son of a bitch and a liar and I've fallen down and ruined my dress!" And she searched her mind for more ways to curse him, tried to remember all the swear words she'd heard her father and Olan use when they were drinking up in the barn loft.

"Bastard, prick, son of a bitch," she continued, pausing now for breath.

Sammy looked at her with disbelief.

"If I talked like that," he said, "I'd have to go to confession and the priest would make me say at *least* three hundred Hail Marys and I don't know how many Our Fathers—"

"Bastard," Lee Rose yelled and, slowly crawling to her feet, she stood up and wiped away the slime that ran down her arms, that had soaked her Sunday dress. "Son of a bitch, prick and bastard," she repeated, her voice fading away decrescendo like a symphony that was ending.

It was quiet, there was no sound but the trickle of water running through the gutters. Sammy stared at the floor, the toe of his shoe pushing at the slime. Then, without speaking, they all linked arms and turned around, heading back the way they had come.

They had walked about half the distance when there was

35

suddenly a sound like a donkey braying; the sound came from Sammy, and when Lee Rose and Jo Anna looked at him his face was dark blue, nearly black, the muscles of his throat tight and bunched as he strained to breathe. He slumped to his knees, his fingers clawing at the collar of his shirt.

"He's dying, Lee Rose," Jo Anna screamed, and Lee Rose's face turned as white as her dress.

Lee Rose stooped and grabbed him under his arms, pulling him toward the wall. She slipped and nearly fell again, and when she looked at him his jaw was slack, his breath rattling in his throat.

"He's going to be dead, Lee Rose," and Jo Anna dropped to her knees and began to pray: "Our Father who art in heaven, hallowed be thy name, thy kingdom come—"

"Shut up and help me get this bottle out of his pocket, Jo Anna, can't you see he's trying to get this bottle out?" Finally Lee Rose was able to pull a small, squat bottle filled with dark amber liquid from his pocket. The bottle had attached to it a rubber bulb and Lee Rose cradled his head on her arm.

"Spray it in his nose, Jo Anna," she yelled, her voice echoing, bouncing off the sewer walls.

A brown gopher rat, big as a cat, ran down the gutter and into a hole in the wall.

"Don't be scared, Jo Anna, just don't pay any attention," Lee Rose said, "remember how they used to be like that in the loft? They won't bother you, so spray Sammy's nose." Jo Anna began to squeeze the rubber bulb, her hands trembling so that most of the yellow liquid ran over his mouth.

"It's no use, he's dead, Lee Rose." She took the bottle away from his face.

"Spray it in his throat, Jo Anna, while I hold his mouth open." Lee Rose pressed his jaws, forcing open his mouth.

Jo Anna sprayed and sprayed, and finally she said it was

no use, he was already dead. But then there was a rattle in his chest and he coughed and strangled, struggling to sit up. Gradually, the blue faded from his face. After a while he opened his eyes. The three of them sat for a long time, their backs against the cold wall, but not noticing that it was cold. They were quiet, as if sitting on a warm afternoon with their backs against the garage trying to decide what game to play next. When the faint pink color was in his cheeks they stood up, and Sammy turned his collar up around his neck and tucked in his shirttail.

"I'm very sorry to do that," he said, and once again they began to walk back the way they had come.

"I guess that was an attack like you told us about," said Lee Rose.

Sammy nodded that it was and nothing else was said about what had happened. When they were back at the opening, through the small round hole overhead they saw that it was nearly dark, the first pale stars already out. They climbed the iron ladder out of the sewer and rolled onto the grass that was wet with dew.

They walked home slowly because Sammy could not go fast, and they could not leave him to walk alone. In the cool of early evening, porch rockers creaked, children played tag, running from yard to yard. When they turned onto Sammy's street, they waited under the streetlight until he went inside; then they continued to walk slowly, in no hurry now to get home to see what their mother would say when she saw their wet and dirty clothes.

When finally they climbed the steps to their porch, Maribeth was sitting in the rocking chair, watching for them.

"Boy, are you all in trouble," she said, cheerfully. "Mama got dressed in her best clothes and went all the way down to the Delmar looking for you all. She's steaming mad, and not only that, Daddy hasn't come home from town yet, either. Mama thinks he's been drinking—"

They didn't answer her or wait to hear the rest of what she was telling them, but went on inside the house, too tired to care what punishment Callie had planned for them.

4

THE NOON WHISTLE BLEW at the Betsy Ross Bakery. Snow had been standing in line since seven o'clock that morning. There was a job open on the bread-wrapping machine and he had gotten there as soon as the bakery opened, hoping he would be first in line, but he was not. In fact, the line stretched all the way down one block and turned the corner at the next; it was only in the last half hour that he had turned the corner and could see the glass window of the employment office.

He twisted around slightly to see his reflection in the plate glass window of the bakery. He straightened his tie and thought his gray wool suit looked shabby even in the dim reflection of the glass; his gray felt hat was out of shape. His face was old like his suit. Years of working in the sun had aged him beyond his forty-five years. Still, when he was farming he had never thought himself old. With the sleeves of his shirt rolled above the muscles of his upper arm he'd felt as young as when he first married Callie—Callie, who now wouldn't even let him touch her.

"Okay, that's it," the man said over the loudspeaker from the employment office. "That's all the applications we're taking today."

The man he had hired to run the bread-wrapping machine on the graveyard shift turned and grinned at the men behind him. He was the lucky one, the one who got to work all night and the next day too if the boss told him to. The pay was fourteen dollars a week and nothing extra for overtime.

"Shit," Snow said, turning away from the window.

It was the third time this week he'd missed out on a job. He'd worked at the Sno-Brite Laundry for two weeks before he got fired for cursing the foreman. He'd asked for a two-dollar advance on his pay to buy some beer on the way home; he hadn't had a drink for a month or more.

"What do you think we're running here, a loan company?" the foreman had asked him, and Snow had told him where he could stick his red hot ironing machine. The foreman had told him to check out and not come back, and now he couldn't find another job, not for love or money.

He walked slowly down the sidewalk, grumbling and muttering under his breath. Hell of a lot of good it had done him to get up at the crack of dawn to polish his shoes and cut out new cardboard for the insides. He thought he was better dressed than the man they had hired for the job; at least he wore a suit and even if his shoes were old and cracked in the creases, they had a Griffin wax shine. If he'd gotten to that window first they'd have hired him for sure and he'd have been the one to turn and gloat at the line of men strung out behind him. Thirty minutes sooner and he'd have been the one on his way to fill out his employment papers, the one on his way to see the bread-wrapping machine and to meet the foreman.

"Shit," he said again, and took off his hat and rubbed at the red crease on his forehead where the band was too tight, had pressed into his flesh making his head ache.

He stood there fanning with his hat and in the July heat

there was the smell of bread baking and, faintly, the smell of his own sweat. The men who had stood in line flowed around him, bumping him and glaring at him for blocking the sidewalk where he had wandered aimlessly, wondering what to do now.

He strolled to the corner, his hand in his pocket, fingering the five-dollar bill Callie had given him that morning. That five dollars had to last him until the first of the month, had to make do for carfare and smoking tobacco, too. It was the bitterest gall to think that all the money he had was what Callie gave him. She ruled the roost, forever telling him she'd put him out of her house. Instead of being a man and telling *her* what to do, he slunk around like old man Garrett's hound dog, scared to stand up on his hind legs and holler. Hell, he ought to be home right now telling her what to cook for supper, make her step around like his daddy had his mother.

"God damn it all to hell and back," he said, and a passing woman looked at him, hurried on by, then looked back over her shoulder at him.

"Screw you, lady," he said, and turning the corner walked toward the center of town.

He had no purpose, no plan as to where he was going, only the vague idea that he was hungry. He was not supposed to spend Callie's money on food, she expected him home by lunchtime. She would have a cheese or a baloney sandwich with a glass of New Yorker ginger ale for him. If there was anything in this world he hated, it was a sandwich, especially a cheese sandwich. What he wanted was vegetables, string beans cooked all day long until they were dry, nearly scorched, on the bottom of the boiler, and fried corn and cold buttermilk to wash it all down with.

"Screw you too, Callie," and he turned into the cafeteria with the sign over the door that said "Pandora's."

41

He stood at the end of the line and with the saliva flowing under and around his tongue, read the menu on the wall behind the steam table. There was salmon loaf and roast beef, fried liver and steak, and too many vegetables to ever decide what he wanted: okra, sweet potatoes, cabbage, turnip greens, squash. It was food to put his own mother's groaning board to shame. He felt his heart pumping with excitement at so much food.

"You're losing your mind, Snow," he muttered and grinned, thinking this must be the way you got just before they took you away to the loony bin. "Yeah, doc," he'd say, "I've been getting real excited over vegetables lately," and he laughed aloud as he thought of it.

"Is it a private party or can anybody join?" a voice behind him asked.

He jerked around to see who had spoken to him, embarrassed, his neck hot with anger. A young man looked at him, grinning, his thumbs hooked loosely in his trouser pockets. He wore a brown tweed suit with cap to match. The suit looked new, not worn out at all; his brown hair around the edges of his cap was clipped neatly, not shaggy around his shirt collar like Snow's. The boy's smile held up under Snow's hard look at him. He was only being friendly so Snow shrugged, no longer angry.

"Yeah, I guess that did look pretty funny, me just standing here laughing like hell. I was all excited about coming in here to eat, excited at the sight of all that meat and vegetables. I thought I must be about ready for the loony bin if that's all it took to get me excited."

"Well, I've heard of people that get excited about a whole lot less," the boy said.

"You see," Snow said, turning all the way around to face the boy, "my wife don't like to cook. When she *does* cook it's usually just a pot of something, butterbeans or something like that, and let me tell you that's a *good* day. Most days it's sandwiches, and if there's anything I hate it's sandwiches."

"Why won't she cook?" the boy asked. "Wives are supposed to cook, I thought. Of course, I don't know, not being married, but my mother is a good cook. Hot meals every night."

"You sure are lucky," Snow said, envying the boy who got a hot meal every night. "My wife's a yard woman, she stays in that damn yard all the time, hardly ever comes in before dark. Improving her property, you see. And I do mean *her* property. She inherited some money and bought herself a house. Lets me live in it as long as I act right. Acting right means keeping my mouth shut and getting a job, and so far I haven't been able to do either one. She says she's going to put me out of her house."

"That sounds like hell living with a woman like that."

All at once Snow realized that some of the people in line in front of him had turned to stare at him, were rubbernecking and gawking at him. He stopped talking and took a good look around the restaurant for the first time.

This was a high-class place he was in, the tables covered with white tablecloths, not oilcloths like most of the restaurants he'd eaten in. Over the clinking of china was the soft sound of music. The people eating in here did not look shabby and poor, as he did. He was embarrassed and thought that everyone was looking at him, hating him for coming into their restaurant. He should never have come in here, he should be home this very minute biting into the cheese sandwich Callie had made for him. This boy here with the fine suit of clothes was making fun of him and he was country dumb to fall for it.

He turned abruptly and elbowed his way past the line of people who snickered at him as he passed. In a blur, he wound his way through the tables and past the painted lady who played the organ for the noontime diners; he went past the cashier who half rose from her high stool behind the cash register calling him back to pay his check. Then he was on the sidewalk and gasped as the July heat hit him in the face. He turned toward the streetcar stop that would take him to Callie's house.

"Just a minute there, sir," a man called to him.

Snow turned to see a short, fat man in a dark suit and red tie running after him.

"Just a minute there, sir," the man said, puffing, "you haven't paid your check."

"Well, goddamn it, I didn't eat anything," Snow said. "I left because I didn't like the looks of your goddam restaurant or the smell of your food."

The boy he had talked to in the restaurant hurried out and grasped his arm.

"This man is my friend," he said to the man in the red tie. "He didn't eat a bite and I can vouch for it."

"All right," the man said, looking doubtful, "but it's only because I know you, Mr. Bradley. This man cursed me and I don't ever want him in my restaurant again," and he walked back down the street.

"Now what do *you* want, son," Snow asked the boy. "Why don't you go on back and eat your dinner? Didn't you have enough fun there in the restaurant? Don't you have anything better to do than spend the day making fun of me?"

"Why do you think I'm making fun?" the boy asked. Snow saw that the boy really was puzzled.

"Ah, I don't know, I guess maybe I'm just touchy. No offense. Thanks for telling the man I didn't eat. I might be on my way to jail now if you hadn't come out and explained."

"You don't need food, anyway," the boy said, "what you

44

need is a drink. Let's you and me go down on Morris Avenue and get a drink."

Snow hesitated.

The boy said, "If it's money you're worried about it's my treat."

"Now why in hell would you want to buy me a drink?" Snow saw the number 23 streetcar half a block away that would take him home. He took a step to run for it, then turned back to the boy.

"You mean you'd *pay* for the drink?"

The boy nodded that he would.

Snow watched his streetcar turn the corner heading north. He'd missed it and there wouldn't be another for at least a half hour, maybe longer if it got held up at the train crossing. His mouth was dry and his Adam's apple came up to swallow the cold, bitter beer that bubbled in his mouth, came up to swallow a beer he didn't have to pay for.

"How come you'd pay for it? Why would you want to buy me a drink?"

"Well, because you look like you'd be fun to have a drink with for one thing, and for another I'm not twenty-one and it's easier for me to get a drink if I'm with someone older. Usually, they don't ask questions if I'm with someone older."

Snow realized now that the boy didn't look to be any older than Maribeth.

"Where do you get the money in this day and time to go around buying strangers drinks?"

"My daddy gives me some money. He owns the lumberyard over on the north side. It's a living." And he shrugged, pushing his hands deep into his pockets. "Come on," he said, cuffing Snow playfully on the shoulder, "let's go have something cold."

45

"What's your name?" Snow asked abruptly.

"David Bradley. What's yours?"

"My name's Snow Berryhill," and he held out his big-knuckled hand to clasp the soft, slender hand of the boy.

"What do you do for a living?" Snow asked, and the boy took his arm, urging him along to make the green light as they crossed the street.

"I go to school."

"What school? You might go to the same high school my two girls go to."

"I go to college—Southern Prep, on the west side. Do you know it?"

"Your daddy must really have money to send you to college. No, I don't know the school. I've been living in Alabama a long time but this is my first time in Jones Valley. We come from way up in the north of the state. Alabama's not my home, though. I'm a Georgia cracker."

They walked past slick, glass-fronted department stores that let out through their doors rushes of sweet-scented cool air from the perfume counter. It was a street of expensive stores with windows filled with furs and strings of pearls, mannequins in silk dresses and feather-plumed hats. For the second time that day, Snow's reflection in the plate glass window showed him how shabbily he was dressed, how poor he looked in spite of his freshly shined shoes and the suit that Callie had steam pressed for him last night. He was not at home here, was embarrassed to be in this fine section of town.

"Let's hurry along, son," he said, and they walked faster, pushing through the crowd of early afternoon shoppers.

They walked another two blocks and then turned south onto the brick-paved street called Morris Avenue, where the stores weren't fancy any more. There were fish markets and cheap hotels and produce stands, the flies and yellow jackets swarming around the cantaloupes and peaches; turnip greens and collards wilted in the hot sun. Some of the hotels were air conditioned and on their front doors had big pictures of polar bears, snow dripping from their heads. The signs said Twenty Degrees Cooler Inside.

Close to a railroad track the Perfection Mattress Company blew its one o'clock whistle and Snow's stomach cramped and curled with hunger. He'd eaten no breakfast because he'd gotten up early enough so he could walk to town and save the seven cents' carfare.

When he walked the three miles and saved the money Callie was so pleased she was nice to him for a while. The first time she was nice he followed her to the back bedroom and when she bent to get something out of the bottom dresser drawer he reached around her and grasped her breast. Her softness shocked him. He'd forgotten how soft Callie's breasts were, had half thought they'd be hard and cold like the breasts on the statue of the Winged Victory that stood in the lobby of the State Employment Agency. He laughed now, wondering if she had a wad of gum stuck in her navel like the statue did.

"You old fool," she said, her voice whisper-soft with contained fury, "don't you ever touch me again," and she left him standing alone in the half-light, shadowy bedroom.

Morris Avenue was crowded, but Snow felt at home now, relaxed because it seemed familiar to him with the pickup trucks parked at the curb, loaded with tow sacks of onions and potatoes, the farmers wearing faded overalls and wide-brimmed sun hats. He grinned and nodded as he passed them and was puzzled at first when they looked at him with closed faces and did not return his smile. But then he realized that wearing a suit of clothes and walking with this rich boy, they did not know he was one of them, had no way of knowing he envied them and would like nothing better than to spend

47

the day jawing with them. Hell, what he really wanted to do was crawl on the back end of one of those dusty old pickups, strike up a friendly conversation, and after a while tell some jokes.

The sidewalk burned through the cardboard soles of his shoes; the top of his head was soaking wet where no air penetrated the winter felt of his hat. He felt lightheaded, detached from himself, as they walked closer to the railroad tracks. He wished now he had not come with this boy, wished he were with the bunch of farmers across the street leaning on a truck, laughing and joking and sharing an R.C. Cola.

"How much further to this place we're going, son?" he asked, and felt in his pocket to make sure the folded five-dollar bill was still there, half afraid the boy had already picked his pocket.

"We're here," David said.

Snow turned around and directly in front of him was a door with a champagne glass painted on it, bubbles floating upward. Underneath, in pink letters chipped and fading away, was written Pink Elephant Lounge. Two pink elephants danced drunkenly on each side of the letters. Snow grinned. He was excited again, the way he was earlier at the restaurant, and again his stomach curled, only this time it was from anticipation.

"Let's go in," David said, and Snow followed him through the door.

The sudden cold after the burning heat of the street shocked him, taking away his breath and turning the sweat clammy beneath his shirt; he pulled back because he could not see in the gloom of the bar. Snow never drank in the dark unless he knew exactly what was going on and who he was with. Oh, he'd drunk often enough in the moonlight or in the back of Olan's barn with him and the other Negroes back on the

48

farm. If he drank too much to walk they'd carry him home to his own barn and he'd sleep in the hay until daybreak.

Gradually, his eyes adjusted to the half-light and he saw two or three men at the tables drinking; from the radio behind the bar came the low shriek of Clyde McCoy's "Sugar Blues." Snow took off his hat and sighed as the breeze from the air conditioner cooled him.

He whispered to David: "I'll be goddamned, I believe I *am* twenty degrees cooler," he said, laughing softly at his own joke.

David led him toward the bar, pushing chairs aside as they weaved their way through the forest of small round tables. They sat on high swivel stools at the bar. A paunchy bartender with a short bull neck and black wavy hair stood up from the chair where he was reading a Superman funny book in the pink glow of the lights. He came to where they sat.

"What'll you fellas have?" he asked, and Snow said he'd have a Schlitz and his son here, he said, winking at David, would have the same.

Snow felt good now that he was cool; he was no longer light-headed and his feet didn't burn. This place, except for the pink lights and cool air, was almost like the truck stop he went to down on the highway. As he relaxed he became expansive, jovial. He drank his beer, and because no one had spoken for a long time and because to him silence was offensive, an affront to friendliness, he leaned close to David.

"Did you hear the one about the country boy come to town and brought his girl friend to a place just about like this one?"

"No," David said.

"Well," Snow said, "seems this country boy come to town and brought his girl to a bar. Seems the country boy hadn't ever been to a bar before and he didn't know exactly what to order, but he was trying to impress the girl friend, see."

The bartender moved closer and Snow turned to include

49

him in the telling of his joke, flattered that he wanted to hear.

"This country boy brought his girl to a bar, see," he said, tapping the bartender's arm. "Well, he looked over all the bottles lined up on the shelf behind the bar and he spotted one that said Pluto Water. You all know what Pluto Water is, don't you?" and they nodded.

" 'Well,' the boy told the bartender, 'the little lady here will have a ginger ale, and me, I'll have a bottle of that Pluto Water.' He was trying to be a big shot, see. He didn't know what he was drinking, but he sat there with his girl and they drank their drinks and after a while they left. They got in the boy's Model T and drove around for a while, the boy squirming all around, looking more uncomfortable all the time. Finally the girl said, 'If you don't mind, sugar, I'd like to run down the street to the A and P.'

"With that the country boy stopped the car, jumped out and said, 'That's just *fine* with me, sugar. You go on down to the A and *pee*, I'm gonna jump behind this here bush and take a *crap*.' "

Snow laughed and clapped his knee and turned up his bottle of beer, draining the last golden drops, happiness flowing with the beer through his body. The bartender laughed and David laughed and Snow repeated, " 'I'm gonna go behind this bush and take a crap,' that's a good one, isn't it?"

The bartender and David laughed again and Snow, gratified, felt lazy and heavy in the warm pool of their approval. They liked him, they didn't mind that he didn't have a job, that he had holes in his shoes.

"Ah, it's good to be here. I'm real glad I came with you, son. This is the only fun I've had in months. It's a shame I never had a son. I can see now the good times I've missed out on not having a boy to pal around with. Don't misunderstand," he added quickly, "I love my three girls. It's just that to have a son really would have been something. A son to go rabbit hunting with and drink with . . . go fishing with."

"You poor son of a bitch," the bartender said.

"What do you mean, 'You poor son of a bitch'?" Snow asked, half rising off his stool, his hands already closed into fists.

"Ah, don't fly off the handle, friend. I meant it's tough to be one man with four women. Hell, man, you don't stand a chance."

Snow sat back down, the muscles in his back relaxing. He twirled the empty beer bottle on the counter, idly picking at the damp label.

"Well, you're right, women gang up and stick together, but it's mostly the girls' mammy. She's never been happy like most women. She nags all the time and tries to wear the pants. But I tell you something, I always kept her fed and a roof over her head. There's lots of men can't say that."

The three men huddled together beneath the pink lights and agreed if your wife's never been hungry she can't complain. The boy bought Snow another beer and another. Snow knew he was drunk. Not falling-down drunk yet, but on the way. The lights were blurred pink moons and when he went to the bathroom his legs felt light, of no substance as he picked them up and put them down. He splashed cold water on his face and the sink rose to meet him; he leaned against the wall of the john and laughed and laughed at the moving sink, trying it again and again, making it rise to meet him. He went back to the bar, and David had started on another Schlitz.

"Come on, David, let's go," Snow said. "Let's go while I can still walk and get on the streetcar and get home. Callie's gon' be mad as hell and I'll have to lie all night and listen to her bellyache. She is *one* woman that don't have to fuss *with* anybody, she can carry the whole goddam argument all by herself."

"You poor bastard," David said, clasping his arm, pulling him to the stool. "Sit back down and let's have one more beer. Just one more."

Snow saw that the boy was just as drunk, if not drunker, than he was.

"I can't pay for it," Snow said, "I can't pay for any of this. That's my wife's five-dollar bill in my pocket. You sure *you* got the money?" Fear licked in the pit of his stomach.

The bartender was friendly enough now, but just let him not be able to pay and Snow knew how quickly he would turn mean, might even call the police. He was no stranger to the inside of a jail. He'd been there once when somebody slipped him a mickey and stole his pay when he was in the three C camp in 1937. They came and threw him in jail and when he'd asked to go to the bathroom, his bladder nearly bursting, they'd told him to pee on the floor. Pee on the floor, the sheriff said, and that's what he did, peed on the floor. Wouldn't even let him go to the bathroom. Callie showed up the next morning to get him out, but when they got home she spoke not a word to him for the three days' leave he'd had before he went back to camp. Callie's silence was more terrible than the bawling out would have been.

"I got the money, Pappy," David said. "Re*lax*. Sit," he said, pointing to the bar stool.

"You know, I feel real bad letting a boy like you get drunk. You're only a boy," he said, sitting down. "I wouldn't like it if it was my boy some old man was letting get drunk."

"Hell, you're not old, Pappy. Another Schiltz, bartender," David said, and another beer, frosted, steam rising from the neck of the bottle, appeared before Snow.

52

Snow drank and the numbness crept over him, stiffening his lips so that he had to say each word slow and easy to keep it from slurring. He told jokes to the soft-cheeked boy and the bull-neck man and he quit worrying about going to jail or what Callie was going to say. He didn't feel the least bit worried about his cotton that surely was, by now, choked with Johnson grass. He was euphoric in this dark room with the pink lights; his new friends, insubstantial as shadows, were the whole world. He drank to the bottom of the bottle and he knew he was past standing up and walking back up that hot street to go home.

The bartender leaned close and the thin, gold rim on his front tooth winked in the dim light. Snow patted his friend on the arm.

"You are the best goddam bartender in the whole world. Every time I get drunk I'm coming *here* to get drunk," and he began to sing, *When the mill wheel turns, Mary, I'll be coming home to you.*

"Yessir," Snow said, clasping the beer bottle with both hands, "the best bartender in the whole goddam world."

The bartender put his arms around Snow and David, drawing them in close to him.

"There's a little something upstairs," he whispered, "if you fellas are interested."

"What?" Snow asked.

"A coupla girls. They're special just for our friends. I think the girls might be willing to give you and the boy a little something," he said to Snow.

Snow had not been with a woman for months, not since he moved away from the farm. He had not been with a white woman since Callie stopped sleeping with him.

"Are they white?" he asked.

"Hell, yes, they're white. What kind of a place do you think

53

this is anyway?" The bartender shook his head, disgusted with his new friend. "This town is segregated, if you didn't but know it. You must think you've moved to one of those *northern* cities."

He took away the empty bottles, setting them under the counter, still muttering and shaking his head.

"Well, what do you say, Pappy?" David asked.

"It won't hurt to have a look, will it?"

"Let's go." The boy took Snow's arm as they followed the bartender through a door behind the bar.

Snow's stomach burned and he thought for a moment that he was going to throw up the sour beer. White electric light jabbed his eyes from the hallway, stairs leaped upward to the floor above; Snow saw now that the bar was in a hotel. He climbed the wooden steps, his feet so light he held tightly to the bannister to keep from leaving the floor altogether and thought it peculiar that still he could feel his heart beating hard from the effort of climbing.

At the landing they walked down a dimly lit hall. The walls were dirty gray and looked as if they'd been whitewashed with lime water. Brown-and-gold flowered carpet covered the floor, the flowers worn away down the center but brightening at the edges where no one ever walked. The bartender knocked on a door at the end of the hall.

"Velma, you and Jeannine in there?" he called.

There were muffled voices from inside the room and after a while the door inched open.

"Yeah?" a husky, female voice asked.

"I got a coupla good friends of mine here could use a little. You think you and Jeannine could take care of them?"

The door opened wider and Snow could see a short girl with short black hair and dark skin. She wore no makeup and looked as if she had just waked up. She looked Snow and

54

David up and down, the clack of her chewing gum ticking off the seconds; then she moved back and opened the door all the way.

"It's okay," she said.

The bartender winked at Snow, motioning them in.

"See you later," and he walked back down the hall and disappeared down the dark stairwell.

Snow followed David through the door. There was no rug on the floor; twin beds covered with rumpled white chenille bedspreads stood in opposite corners. It was late afternoon and the room glowed rosy red from the sun shining through wine-colored draperies that covered the window.

On the bed in the far corner, the other girl, Jeannine, lay resting. The room was close and hot after the air-conditioned bar. Stockings and girdles lay limp over the arm of a pink-flowered chintz chair. Enthroned on the chair were two stuffed animals, a blue plush rabbit and a white teddy bear wearing a pink ribbon. They were still covered with their cellophane wrappers. On the wall between their beds was a picture of Jesus, a heavenly light shining round His head.

Velma closed the door and pulled her pink seersucker robe closer around her thin body. In the dim light of the room she looked young, not more than twenty, and Snow thought she was pretty. The girl on the bed raised up, propping on one elbow, watching them. Snow could not tell how old she was or what she looked like from across the room; her bed was outside the circle of lamplight. Already, David had taken off his coat and was unbuckling his belt. Snow stood by the door uncertain which girl was for him.

"Come on over here, sweetie face," the girl on the bed called, patting the mattress. "Come on over here and meet Jeannine. Come *on*, I don't bite, that is unless you *want* me to," and she giggled.

55

Snow walked slowly over to her bed and as he got closer he saw the grotesque mound of her body, saw the swollen, doughy breasts half spilled from the pink rayon slip. Puffy eyes, slits in the full moon roundness of her face, watched as he sat down beside her.

"My name's Jeannine, what's *yours?*" she asked in a lilting Betty Boop voice; she rolled slowly onto her back.

Her stomach was soft and bulging, the hem of her slip scarcely covering the dark triangle of pubic hair; her legs were creased and dimpled, tapering to amazingly small, dainty feet tipped with purple-tinted toenails.

She pushed her hair, blond and dry as straw from too much peroxide, away from her face.

"Okay, sweetie face, I'm ready any time you are," and she took his hand and placed it on the warm fuzzy dampness of her crotch. She lay waiting for his lovemaking.

Snow knew he should kiss her but he was sickened by the sweet, rancid odor of her sweat. The pores of her nose were clogged and oily with dirt; brown powder was streaked in the flare of her nostrils and in the parenthesis lines of her mouth. From the other bed came the sighs and grunts and muted sounds of David and Velma making love and Snow closed his eyes and there was the dusty smell of the hayloft and the dark body of the girl he made love to. Against the pale, washed blue sky of summer, white clouds floated past his barn loft window and he shuddered as he fell exhausted into the hay.

"Hey, what's the matter, sweetie face?" Jeannine asked. "Can't get it up?"

"I'm sorry," he whispered, not looking at her, "I don't feel good. I think I drank too much beer."

"Yeah, I can smell the beer all right," and she wrinkled her nose daintily. "Don't worry, sugar, *I* don't care whether we screw or not. I get paid right on, whether we do or whether

56

we don't. Prob'ly you shouldn't drink right before, sweetie. Drink *after* and then at your age you got somethin' to celebrate. *Sure* you can't get it up?" and she patted the fly of his pants.

"You're right, sweetie, it's flatter'n a popped balloon."

She sat up and the springs sagged and creaked as she slowly swung her legs over the side of the bed.

The sun had set behind the hotel, the fire in the draperies had gone out. David moved in the shadows, pulling on his pants. Snow thought he had never been so tired. He didn't feel drunk any more, only tired.

"Ah, if you think that'll be all," Jeannine said, "you'd better be going. Your friend's ready," and she nodded toward David.

Sadly, Snow reached in his pocket and brought out Callie's five-dollar bill. He handed it still folded to the girl and she tucked it between the twin mountains of her breasts. He sat waiting for his change.

"I need three dollars' change," he said.

"The price is five dollars, you son of a bitch," she said. "Honey," she added.

"But I didn't get anything," Snow begged. "That's all the money I have. I have to catch the streetcar."

"Like I said, sweetie face, it don't cut no ice with me one way or the other; you got problems, I get paid right on. You come up here to get something, I deliver. I don't deliver, you don't pay. You can't get it up, I get paid just the same. Now get on out of here."

Snow leaned over and picked his hat up off the floor and when he straightened, waited for the room to stop spinning. He left the room with David, pulling the door shut softly behind them. They went back along the hall and down the steps onto the sidewalk. It was going-home time; office workers

57

and department store workers were heading for home. Snow pressed his fingers against the throbbing pain behind his eyes and considered going to the gutter and throwing up the beer that roiled in his stomach; he swallowed back the bile that burned in his throat.

They left the hotel and walked back uptown to Snow's streetcar stop.

"Well," said David.

Snow held out his hand and they were polite with each other as if they had just met.

"Goodby, thanks for the beer. Say," he laughed, trying for the light touch, "brother could you spare a dime for the streetcar? I sure don't feel like hoofing it." He looked up the street, hopeful that already a streetcar was in sight.

"Sure thing," David said, and reached into his pocket. He gave Snow a dime.

They shook hands again and David crossed the street, turning once to wave to Snow. Snow leaned against the Title Guaranty Building and watched him walk away, and knew without a doubt that the boy had set him up for the fat girl while he had sat there, a dumb country fool, and let her take Callie's money. A police car cruised around the corner and Snow stood straight, breathing hard with the effort.

"If there's anything I hate it's a goddam cop," he said, though there was no one on the corner to hear but himself. "If there's anything in the world I hate it's the sons of bitches of the world that think they've got the right to big-mouth me," and he closed his eyes, remembering the way the officers in the army swaggered and ordered him around. His hands hardened into fists as he thought of the smirking face of the sergeant who ordered him out of mess one morning to shave. By the time he shaved and got back it was too late to eat. He'd never forgotten that man, still dreamed of running into him on the street by accident. If he ever did run into him, he would beat him into the ground.

Sometimes he thought what he'd do, *knew* what he'd really like to do was just walk off someday, walk off down some dusty road and never look back, just walk and walk and walk, going nowhere. There'd be nobody holding him, nobody telling him what to do. He went to the curb and saw number 23 streetcar in the next block loading passengers, its white, electric numbers blurred. Number 23, Magnolia Hills, would take him home to Callie.

Hands in pockets, he stood at the yellow painted curb and waited. Soon the streetcar scraped along the tracks in the middle of the street stopping at his corner. A boy and girl holding hands ran from across the street and pushed in front of him. He waited for them to climb the steps and thought that never in his life had he been so miserable. His head ached, he was sick at his stomach, his beer-filled bladder felt as if it would burst; his five dollars was gone and he had no job. Worst of all, he had to go home and face Callie.

Weary, he climbed the steps behind the young lovers and gave the conductor his dime, took the three pennies change and sat down in a seat next to a window. He rested his head against the cool glass, but when he saw the conductor watching him in the mirror above the driver's seat, he sat up straight and looked out at the bright lights of the city.

5

ALL SUMMER SNOW LOOKED for a job but could not find one. His name was registered with the State Employment office, and finally one morning when he went down to hang around the office with the other men out of work like himself, to laugh and make jokes with them about the WPA, he was told he had a job. The man who handled his application said it was not permanent, that it would last only about three weeks, but Snow was glad to get it. That postponed for a while having to work on the WPA or being laughed at and the butt of all those jokes about WPA workers leaning on their shovels.

He was at work by seven o'clock every morning, mixing and pouring concrete, repairing the brick street on Morris Avenue. The bar where he and David had gone was on the corner, but he had not gone in because he had no money. Since he had lost Callie's five dollars (she thought he spent it all getting drunk) she would not give him more than carfare and tobacco money.

Once again, he worked shoulder to shoulder with a black man, stirring the mortar while the other man poured the water, but it was not like working with Olan in the cotton field. This man said nothing as he sloshed the water into the wheelbarrow, but it was not a friendly silence like the silences he'd shared with Olan. He and Olan had worked as one man, chopping the cotton, stopping to rest at the same instant, each knowing what the other was going to do before he did it.

Snow knew how to work niggers, all right, he'd worked niggers all his life, but he had not been able to work up a friendly comradeship with this man. His jokes had brought no velvet laughter from that black face. Sweat dripped off both of them, splotching the warm, red brick like drops of blood. Snow had never worked so hard with so little pleasure, his neck and shoulders aching at the end of the day like an abscessed tooth. The job paid thirty dollars for the three weeks' work and that was damn good pay. He endorsed the check when the job was done and handed it over to Callie; it was enough to make two payments on her house.

He never had seen her so tickled, could not remember having done another thing in all their married life that pleased her so much. She smiled at him as friendly as could be and cooked him a boiled dinner of potatoes and string beans, scorched down to the bottom of the boiler, just the way he liked them. He ate the dinner and was grateful for it, thanked her politely, but he did not make the mistake of touching her again. Later they sat on the porch and talked and if it hadn't been for the streetlights they might have been back on the old front porch at the farm.

The day after the job ran out, he took the carfare Callie had given him to look for a job and caught the Greyhound bus and made the two-hour trip back to the farm. Before he lost his mind, before he went clean out of his head, he had to get away from concrete for a while. He wanted to see woods and dirt, let his eye wander as far as it could without a building jumping up in front of him, cutting off the wide expanse of sky, and the smoky blue rim of mountains in the distance.

61

When he was nearly there, when the turns in the road were as familiar to him as his own face, his palms began to sweat, the soles of his feet sweating, too, inside his wool socks. It was early September but still hot as midsummer. He wished he could afford summer shoes like the man at the employment office wore, two-tone brown wing tips, with webbed netting that let the air in to cool your feet. Never had he been able to afford different clothes to suit the changes of seasons; he just took off his underwear or put it on, according to how hot or cold it was. When he looked for a job he wore his suit and he had to wear it today because Callie thought he was looking for a job.

Snow pulled the cord that rang the buzzer for the bus to stop. He asked the driver if the weather was hot enough for him and jumped down the steps to the highway. As the bus pulled away he took off his jacket and, hooking it on his thumb, hung it over his shoulder as he crossed the highway to walk the last half mile to the old house.

He did not mind walking, would rather walk the road that wound around by his fields, that would lead him, finally, right up to his old front door. It was a small house, not big enough to turn around in, Callie had complained over the years they'd lived there; but it was big enough to eat and sleep in, and in the days when she would let him, to crawl into the bed and make love to her. He did not see what more was needed in a house.

Funny thing how women were about houses, though, always cleaning them, forever dusting and mopping, putting doilies on the sofa and chairs and then telling him not to sit on them unless there was company; then Callie would make him put on clean clothes and come sit in the living room and talk to whoever it was who came. He didn't like being inside the house, had never in his life since he was a kid spent a whole day inside; even on rainy days he didn't hang around the house but stayed out in the barn with the colored, drinking and telling jokes.

He walked along, happy with the sun hot on his shoulders, pleased that the brown wax shine of his shoes was dulled with dust. Hell, he hadn't had dirt on his shoes since he left here He went around the last curve and there was the line of cedars that grew along his fence; his ditch was still lush with Johnson grass. All at once he stopped dead still, not believing what he saw.

To the right, his cotton field bloomed in the glow of after-noon sun, the bolls turned golden as if they had felt the Midas touch.

"Yonder it is," he breathed, "yonder's my cotton."

It was not dead, dried and shriveled on the ground from lack of care, but standing crisp and straight without a weed in sight that he could see. He raised his arms like a preacher giving benediction on Sunday morning.

"By God, it's true, I'm not dreaming it, it's really here," and he dropped his coat in the road and jumped the ditch.

He knelt to plunge his arms in the cotton, cradling it to his bosom like Jesus carrying the baby lambs.

"Hey, there now, you, what are you doing in my cotton?" a voice called from the road.

Snow stood up and there was a solemn-faced farmer in dark blue bibbed overalls and faded blue shirt. His hair, black as a crow's wing, was parted in the middle, one cheek pouched out with a twist of chewing tobacco. Parked in the road be-hind him was a sagging Ford pickup truck. He was a young man, no more than thirty, and envy struck hard inside Snow. He didn't grudge the man the golden field of cotton that he and Olan had planted and he didn't grudge him the truck, though he'd often longed for a truck to haul his corn. But he did grudge the man his head of black hair. A man with a head full of black hair had all the time in the world, could do anything he wanted to do.

"How old are you?" Snow asked.

"Now, what has how old I am got to do with you trespassing in my field?"

Snow stared at the young upstart standing there in the road as if he owned all hell and beyond. The man stared back.

"You're a city man?" the farmer asked.

"*Hell* no, I ain't no city man."

"You *look* like a city man," and he shifted the wad of tobacco from the right cheek to the left, spitting into the ditch of Johnson grass. The brown liquid juice beaded and ran down the wide leaves.

"I'm a farmer same as you," Snow said. "Got shanghaied to the city, that's all. This here I'm standing in used to be my field. It was me and my hand Olan Calvert planted that cotton you're so all-fired quick to claim."

"You're Snow Berryhill, then," the farmer said, reaching out his hand.

Snow jumped back over the ditch and they shook hands, grinning at each other. Snow picked his jacket up from the dust and brushed it off, slapping at it with the palm of his hand.

"My name's Leonard Abney," the farmer said. "Sorry not to be more friendly but I didn't know who in the hell you were there in my cotton with that suit and tie on. I bought that land, you know, all twenty-five acres of it. That's mine clear on back five acres into the woods."

Snow nodded.

"That's what I always wanted to do, buy at least ten acres of the cotton land, but I never was able to scrape enough together to do more than rent it. From the looks of that cotton, this year I might have made it though."

"Hell, man, you don't need land. Folks around here still talk about how you struck it rich and moved to town seeking fame and fortune."

"*I* didn't strike it rich, my *wife* did. She's the one with the money. She wouldn't give me a dime to buy *one acre* of ground."

"Well, to me it's all the same, a man takes what his wife's got, it's only right. Come on to the house and meet the wife and kids," he said, opening the door of the pickup for Snow.

Snow climbed in and the farmer got in beside him on the driver's side. He mashed the ignition over and over with his left foot and worked the choke. The truck whined, and just when they had decided it wouldn't catch, that they would have to get out and push, the motor caught and they were bumping and tilting down the wagon-rutted road.

They rode along, and for the first time since he had left here Snow was happy, the warm, dusty air blowing in his face; through the hole in the floorboard he saw the red gravel road streak along beneath his feet. After a while they came in sight of the white frame house, its front porch nearly hidden by the deep green leaves of the trees.

Leonard Abney parked his truck at the front gate and Snow thought how strange everything looked, familiar but strange, too, like things seen in a dream. Of course, it could be the fresh coat of white paint made the house look different, but Snow didn't really think that was it. It was like he'd died and his soul come visiting.

They went inside and he met the timid, blushing Mrs. Abney and the four little stair-step children. The oldest girl, about Jo Anna's age, led Snow from room to room as her daddy told her to, but none of it seemed real—the mohair chairs in the living room, the giant mahogany bed with the carved cherubs on the bedposts. Snow had been gone from here for four months but it seemed more like four hundred. He tried to bring it all back, the red-faced babies lying in bed with Callie when they were born, the time Jo Anna nearly died from blood poisoning and they'd sat all night long in the kitchen soaking her foot in hot salt water. But all those years seemed as if they had happened in an afternoon; it was all over; he couldn't bring any of it back. He heard his father's voice saying, *What is, is, son.*

After he'd seen the house he went to the barn and drank corn whiskey with Leonard. It was then Leonard told him Olan was dead.

"By the way," he said, wiping his mouth on his sleeve and handing the jug of whiskey to Snow, "Olan Calvert died, I guess you heard."

Snow stood with his mouth gaped, wanting to hit the man for telling him such a thing in so offhand a way. When the shock passed, sorrow washed over him and he asked Leonard Abney how it happened, Olan was all right four months ago. A man didn't just die in four months.

"He had a heart attack, I believe that's the way it happened," Leonard said. "I don't know for sure, though."

Snow hadn't known when Olan waved at him and rode away in that truck they'd rented the morning they'd moved, that it was the last time he'd ever see him. He'd planned on seeing him lots of times but it was hard to get away, him being so busy looking for a job. He blamed Callie for that, him not ever seeing Olan again.

He said good-by to Leonard and walked the two miles to Olan's house. He cut through the woods and came up in the familiar, clean-swept yard; chickens scattered, cackling and fluttering their wings; a skeletal dog ran under the house. Exa, Olan's wife, sat on the porch, smaller and even more shriveled up than the last time he had seen her. Her tiny feet barely touched the smooth, scrubbed boards of the porch, the gray kink of her hair was pulled into tight, cruel squares of plaits all over her head. Her mother, Mattie, sat next to her in another rocking chair.

Mattie was eighty-four in the spring but she looked younger, her skin smoother and less wrinkled than her daughter's, twenty years younger. Both of them wore long print dresses and white aprons. Exa leaned forward in her chair, squinting at Snow. He was almost to the steps before she recognized him.

"Law', if it ain't Mista Snow; look, Mama, it's Mista Snow. Come on up and set, Mista Snow. Us is sho' glad to see you."

Snow sat on the steps and patted the brown dog that slunk up to him. The dog fell on his back, so limp with joy at the unaccustomed petting that yellow drops of urine trickled down his stomach. Mattie smiled and touched Snow's shoulder, patted him, her old hand fluttering like a moth over him.

"Tell me about Olan, Exa," Snow said. "The man who bought my old house said Olan died and I don't believe it."

Exa told him about Olan, and as she talked, the tears ran down her face, gathering in the deep wrinkles at the sides of her mouth. Snow marveled at how those two had loved each other. He'd never known any married people, black or white, who loved each other the way they did. If they ever fussed, Snow had never known about it, and through the years Olan was as faithful to Exa as the day they married.

"Y'all been gone about two months, Mista Snow, when Olan passed. He shucked corn and he dug potatoes all day that day, he didn't quit. He come in the house complaining

67

he don' feel good. He say he reckon he don' have any right to feel good, hard as he worked that day. He say he reckon he lay down and rest. I cain't even git him up for supper."

She wiped her eyes on the hem of her apron.

"He wake me up in the middle of the night, choking and gasping for breath, he say he got the bad pain in his chest. I sent Lora Lee; you don't know Lora Lee, Mista Snow, she stay with us now, she my sister's girl. I sent her to git old man Jack Crocker, he the white man live on the other side of the bottoms. You know Mista Jack?"

Snow nodded that he did.

"Mista Jack, he come with his car and he gits Olan in the back seat with his head on my lap, but he gone before we hardly git to the highway. I know when he go, Mista Snow, he just stare up at me and say 'Exa' and he gone. It was his time to go. I'd have sho' come for you, Mista Snow, if I know where you stay. I sho' would."

Exa went in the house and brought back a picture of Olan lying in his coffin wearing a white robe. Snow looked at it and handed it back to her; that was not the way he wanted to remember his friend, but he could not hurt Exa's feelings.

They sat without talking in the shade of the porch. The dry corn stalks, almost ready to make into shocks, rattled in the wind. Outside the door were pots of crepe-paper flowers Exa had brought home from Olan's funeral.

"Olan, he talk a lot about you after you go, Mista Snow. He say you be around to see him befo' long. He mighty disappointed you didn't never come to see him."

"Yes, well, I came to see him today. I've been looking for a job, it's hard to get away when you're looking for a job . . ."

Snow looked across this land that Mattie owned. She even owned the three-room shack they lived in. Mattie's mother had bought it over fifty years ago, had paid twenty-five dollars for the five acres of ground. The white people didn't like the colored owning land, especially the white people who didn't own any land themselves. Once some men came and told Mattie they'd buy the land from her for a hundred dollars and when she wouldn't sell they came back that night and burned a cross in her yard and dragged Olan off down in the woods and whipped him. Snow wished even now, more than fifteen years later, that he could find the sons of bitches who whipped Olan; he'd kill every yellow-bellied dog one of them.

"Some mens come about two weeks ago, Mista Snow," Mattie said. "They say the gov'mint send them to whitewash our house, that we be arrested we don' let them whitewash our house. They come inside and look around and find thirty-five dollars Olan got off the spring crop. They took the money and splashed some lime water upside the house and then they go. We ain't got money lef' now to buy flour and sugar. We ain't got money for nothin'."

"Why'd you let them in, Exa?" Snow asked. "How come you didn't send for the sheriff?"

"Law', Mista Snow, you know better'n that, you know that sheriff over in Lewisburg be as big a crook as them two mens," Exa said. "We told them to git away from our house but they walk pass us like we ain't even here. There ain't *nothin'* we can do. Them mens ain't from around here, we ain't never seen them befo', ain't never gon' see them again. If Olan livin' he do something, but Olan he gone. Yessir, he gone and I ain't never gon' see him again in *this* life."

Mattie closed her eyes. Her thin lips, a legacy of some long-ago white man's lust, began to move. "*Amazing grace,*" she sang, "*how sweet the sound, that save a wretch like me . . .*"

Exa's wavering voice joined hers, "'*I once was lost but now I'm found, 'twas blind but now I see.*'"

"Exa," Snow said, "you and Mattie got to have a man

around here. Don't you have a brother in Opelika? You got to have somebody to come work these fields and look after you and Mattie. Olan will come back to ha'nt me if I let anything happen to you or Mattie."

"Mista Snow, you kin stop worrying," Exa said. "Me and Lora Lee, you don't know Lora Lee, we kin get in the little bit of crops we need to keep us fed, we kin sell a little. That's all we need, it's more than most folks got nowadays, but I thank you kin'ly and if Olan be here, he thank you kin'ly, too. Lora *Lee*," she called, bending around the chair to call through the door into the house, "come on out here, quit hidin' inside."

Turning back to Snow, she said, "She be the skittiest, scariest girl I *eva* saw."

A young girl, about seventeen years old, stepped shyly onto the porch, her hands behind her back. She leaned against the wall, smiling. She was light, like Mattie, with large, round eyes and there were dimples in her plump, little-girl cheeks. Her red dress was too short and too tight, the white buttons straining across her breasts. Snow started to stand up but stopped himself. White men did not stand up for nigger girls.

Mattie, rocking slowly, began to sing again and Snow leaned back against the slick, peeled pine post that helped to hold up the roof, and sang, too. He sang in the tenor voice that Callie loved so well when he first married her. Callie even used to tell him he ought to go on the radio. In the warm glow of the September afternoon they sang, calling for the sweet chariot to come and carry them home, and they sang to brighten the corner where you are.

They sang until the porch and yard were in full shade, the sun low and red behind the trees; then Lora Lee led Snow through the cornfield and down the hill to the colored churchyard that lay next to the white frame church. They stood, one on each side of Olan's grave. Snow took off his hat and told Lora Lee that he had never had a better friend.

"Did they ever tell you how scared Olan was of tornadoes?" he asked her. She said that they had not.

"One time a tornado came across those fields," Snow said, pointing down the road in the direction of Olan's potato field. "It dipped and skipped over the field. Olan said he could see it coming a mile off. He ran to the house, sure that tornado was fixing to grab him any minute and blow him right off the face of the earth. When he got to the house he grabbed his Bible and sat down in the chair by the fireplace. I ran in from the other side of the field about the same time and I can tell you I was mighty impressed with a man that could sit there and read the Bible while all hell broke loose outside.

"Then I remembered Olan couldn't read and when I looked closer the Bible was upside down. I pointed it out to him that the book was upside down and we both started to laugh, laughed like hell the whole time it sounded like the house was coming down. Olan said that was the last time he'd ever run from a storm and I guess he never did, either, least not that I ever heard of."

Lora Lee smiled at him, then looked at the ground unable to meet his eyes. She leaned down to set right a vase of spilled flowers and Snow saw the round, dark curve of her young breasts.

"Exa ever tell you about the time Olan thought he got bit by a mad dog?" Snow asked her.

She shook her head no, still not looking at him.

"Olan was walking home from my place just after dark one night and old man McCrary's dog, you remember what mean dogs they always had, came running out slobbering at the mouth and bit Olan on the leg. Sank his teeth all the way through the calf of Olan's leg. The slobber got all in the bite and Olan went home and washed it out good with turpentine, but he was sure he was a goner and he told Exa, 'Exa, I don't know whether that old dog's mad or not, Mr. McCrary said he just took up there a week or two ago. But you watch me real good for the next two weeks and if I get to acting funny you run to Lewisburg and get the doctor.'

"Well, Olan said Exa really watched him and after about ten days and he hadn't shown any signs of going mad, he decided to play a trick on Exa. He got home just about dark from the fields one afternoon and Exa was in the kitchen cooking supper. Olan said he slipped up on the porch and stood at the screen door watching her—she hadn't even heard him come up the steps. After a while he pushed his face up close to the screen and said, 'Exa,' in a low kind of scary voice. She turned around and saw him looking in at her and she said, 'Olan?'

" 'Exa,' Olan said again, grinning kind of funny at her, and then he scratched the screen with his fingernail.

"Olan said Exa threw down the bowl she had in her hand and flew like a bird out the window, hit the ground running and ran screaming through the field to our house. Me and my wife like to have never talked her into going back, and when we did get back to the house Olan laughed until he cried. Then he told Exa he was sorry because she was so mad; she started to cry when she found out it was only a joke."

Snow put on his hat and left the cemetery, Lora Lee following behind him. They passed the church and Snow went up the crumbling concrete steps and inside. It was the first time he'd ever gone in Olan's church and he stood just inside the door, curious about the place where Olan and Exa had come to worship a white God.

The smell of old sweat hung in the air, an eternal reminder

72

of years of shouted hallelujas and amens, the stale memory of people who had come to praise the Lord and pass on, some to Birmingham, some all the way up north and some, like Olan, to heaven.

Wooden benches lined each side of the church with a narrow aisle up the middle that led to the pulpit. There was a piano on the left-hand side, and a blackboard on the wall with the page numbers of the hymns the congregation had sung the Sunday before written in chalk. Behind the pulpit was a life-size plaster-of-Paris figure of Christ dying on the cross. He wore a crown of thorns, dark red blood dripped from His hands and His feet.

Snow did not understand how one man could worship another man, nor did he believe there was a better life waiting for him on the other side of the grave. This life was it, this was all there was. When you died your family could go with you only as far as the grave and could go no further. Sometimes when he was half asleep, just drifting off, or sometimes when he was awakening in the morning, the reality of dying would sweep over him and he would lie terrified that someday he must die. When he was younger he'd read the Bible and gone to church wanting to believe that someday he would see his father again and his mother, too, but he could never convince himself that it really was true, and after a while he stopped going to church. The only thing he knew for certain was that his father and mother and Olan lay molding in the ground.

He left the church and Lora Lee followed him back down the road; when they came to a pine grove he took her by the arm, looking close at her to see if she was willing. He had never forced any woman, black or white. She would not look at him, but she did not pull away, and when he stepped into the grove she followed him.

73

He pulled her to the ground and there was the musky odor of her flesh, the clean, warm smell of starch in her dress; the pine needles pricked his arms and legs as he covered her. He closed his eyes and heard the rush of wind through the trees and felt the first uncomfortable chill of fall in the early evening air. Afterward, he lay next to her and thought that Leonard Abney better get the cotton picked right away, get the field cleared for the winter crop. A late nesting quail flew up not far from where they lay. Summer had lasted so long this year the quails had nested twice, had raised two families. He closed his eyes and dozed and when next he opened them, was surprised that already there were stars in the darkening sky.

They left the grove and walked back through the woods, but when they reached the corn field he left her to walk the rest of the way home alone and he took the road. He did not slow as he passed his cotton field. It was not his any more and with Olan gone there was no one left he cared about in this community. He strode along, and the yellow light of the farms that he passed did not urge him from the road as Olan's lantern light had done over the years, drawing him in to sit by the fire or on the front porch, according to the season; there was no one behind those doors that he passed in the night that he cared about or that cared about him. He would not come back here again.

It was almost nine o'clock when he got back home. From the sidewalk he could see Callie sitting on the porch in the moonlight and he knew that she thought he was drunk, so he weaved and staggered up the steps to have some fun with her. But she didn't laugh when she found out he was sober; she said the neighbors would think he was drunk anyway so he might as well be.

He sat down in the rocking chair next to her and he didn't

74

feel like sharing with her the news about Olan dying or telling her where he'd been. Callie had always hated Exa, had even accused Snow of sleeping with her. She thought Exa was uppity. That just went to show how much she knew about Olan and Exa.

Snow rocked and sang. *Amazing grace how sweet the sound, that saved a wretch like me* . . .

His voice sounded strong and sure, as it had when he was young, and he thought it just possible that Callie might mention his good singing voice, might even tell him he ought to go on the radio; instead she went inside to the living room and turned on "Amos 'n Andy."

Snow sat silent in the dark, listening to the Kingfish's deep voice saying to his secretary, "Buzz me, Miss Blue, buzz me."

6

It was November. Summer was gone, early blooming trees had dropped their leaves at first frost, but now all the trees were bare, their leaves lying sodden under the chill rains of November. Through the branches, the smokestacks of the factories that ringed Magnolia Hills could be seen in the distance.

Farther north, behind Callie's house, stretched a ridge of hills where the rich people lived. The poor people called that section of town "Silk Stocking Road." The houses there were big, most of them built of red brick, though some were two-story frame with white columns; all of them sat perched on high, grassy terraces. The lots were twice, three times the size of the lots in Callie's neighborhood. Crape myrtle trees and cherry laurels shaded the wide verandas; wrought-iron lounge chairs cradled the weary bones of bankers and business owners who, at the end of the day, sat waiting for their wives to come home from taking children to tap-dancing or piano lessons. Nearly all the children on Silk Stocking Road took lessons.

Once a week the women sat on one or another's veranda and met with their church circle. They wore flowery print dresses and sipped iced tea, dabbing at the moisture on their lips with their rosewater-scented handkerchiefs; they sighed, murmuring to one another, so the maid wouldn't hear, about how lazy "uncle" was (they all called their gardeners "uncle"); after church on Sunday they drove to their darkie's house (they all called their maids "darkies"), blew the horn with a white-gloved hand, and left a basket of corn or tomatoes or whatever vegetable was in season.

The Negroes lived about five miles from Silk Stocking Road. Along the railroad tracks and close to the factories stood row after row of three-room houses. Long ago the real-estate owners had quit painting them because the acid in the ashy soot from the trains and from the smokestacks ate away the paint within a few months' time. Everything in nigger town was sprinkled with the gray ash, even the people, who sat on their porches with nothing to do but watch the trains go by, had grit in their hair; their porches and yards were covered with it.

Some of them fought back and painted the trim around their doors and windows bright colors, yellow or green, sometimes red, and people who rode through on the streetcars laughed and nudged one another and said wasn't it funny how niggers loved red. They planted flowers and trees and scrubbed their walls and porches every day; but it was no use, the smoke ate away the paint and sank into the dirt so that nothing would grow. Some of the strongest trees lived, but their blossoms in the spring were gray like everything else in nigger town.

Snow had been in the colored section many times trying to get a job in one of those monsters of hell that grew there, would call himself blessed if he could blister his face and arms at one of their hearths. He was at the point where he would do most anything at all to get some money, but there was no job in the factories. "We're not hiring," they told him time after time.

Sometimes in the summer when he walked through nigger

town he stopped and talked; he'd missed the Negroes since he'd moved from the farm. They sat rocking, unmoving except for the almost imperceptible motion of their fans with the real-estate ads on the front. Most of them, he thought, were lazy; they were not at all like Olan. who, though he was poor, had never sat with nothing to do as these people did, fanning, stuporous in the heat. Some of the men played cards, but they were listless, disinterested, the dealer licking his thumb as he slowly dealt the sweaty cards; they passed a single bottle of beer back and forth among themselves. Snow didn't see why in hell they didn't just pack up and move on, nobody was forcing them to stay here. If they moved to the country they could farm, and at least they'd have themselves a little something to eat.

But on Sunday the factories closed down and not but one train came through—the L&N northbound to Memphis. Then nigger town came alive and on Saturday night almost all the inhabitants bathed and on Sunday morning they were God's children, blooming brighter than His flowers. Men strutted by in white suits, and the women wore flowered dresses and big hats with artificial flowers drooping on the brims. The girls' heads sprouted pigtails tied with ribbons and they minced down the red clay sidewalks in their fluffy organdy dresses on their way to the First Methodist Church or to the First Baptist Church, according to whether or not their mother believed in sprinkling or in baptizing. The whole day was spent in church and all the women of Silk Stocking Road had long ago found it useless to try to get maid help on a Sunday.

Around the perimeter of nigger town, all the way across the park, was where the poor white trash lived. Their houses were on the edge of the brick foundry where most of the men worked, though some of them owned small grocery stores. But

78

being businessmen did not improve their status with the rest of the community because they sold mostly to Negroes, things like goat meat and chit'lings. When the public health nurse came to the school, it was the brick-yard children who were sent home for having nits in their hair and got blue cards saying they had decayed teeth and infected tonsils. Some people said it was even scarier walking through that neighborhood than it was walking through nigger town, especially at revival time when they held their tent meetings. The shouts and the singing could be heard all the way across the park, and on some nights a lot of them became so excited they fainted and rolled in the sawdust on the floor and talked in strange tongues.

Callie's house was in the valley, not more than a mile from the business district. The people on Silk Stocking Road called it the flat land. In summer the neighborhood was bright and pretty under its camouflage of leaves and flowers. Huge oaks, fifty years old or more, their trunks covered with lichens, spread their branches over roofs and porches; shrubbery grew thick and dense around the houses; there was no front yard without flowers, zinnias and marigolds, larkspur and hollyhocks.

But it was fall, and the neighborhood was an old lady taking off her frills, wiping away her makeup. The houses stood naked, stripped of the leaves and flowers that hid their age, the peeling paint, the beginning rot in their boards. The grass of the tiny lawns had yellowed under the weak rays of the November sun.

There were no maids or uncles in the flat land: all the women did their own housework, their own washing and ironing; the men kept the grass mowed and the bushes trimmed. But the Negroes did pass through the alley on their way to Silk Stocking Road, and when Callie was in the back yard working in her flowers, she talked to them, eager for information about the people on the hill.

Rich people fascinated her. When she was little and living with her aunt in Opelika, and after Royce had run away, she sometimes dreamed of having enough money to own a big house. She lay dreaming away whole afternoons hidden among the vines of the scuppernong arbor; it was then that she summoned from the shadows her pretend girl friends, Betty and Jean, who always awaited her call.

She talked to them, told them the things she dreamed of, hoped for; she said things to them that to her sounded wise and mysterious, words like Seven Up Bottling Company Incorporated, and Chesapeake and Ohio Railroad, and the Way of the Silver Fleet. She had seen those words lettered on the railroad cars that passed behind her aunt's house. She'd stand high on the sandy bank and look down into the gorge as the train passed by and read the words, stand pondering as the red caboose flashed by and the railroad men leaned out the back, waving to her.

So when she worked in the back yard, she worked close to the fence to talk to the colored when they passed. They'd lean on her fence and admire her flowers and she'd run to the house and get them a half sack of peas or beans or sometimes a dress for their children that Jo Anna had outgrown. She chopped away with the hoe at the weeds in her flower bed and the Negroes' soft slow voices told her about the rich folks they worked for.

"Mr. Wes' say he gon' marry that white housekeeper he got las' summer, Miss Callie, and his wife she ain't been dead yet a year—"

"Tell me about the new furniture the real-estate man bought, Georgia, tell me about the rugs and the curtains—"

"—she ain't been dead a year and the wash woman say she

caught them in the bed, they didn't hear her for *noth*in' when she come up on the porch, she say that bed was rockin'—"

And so the talk went, and Callie knew what the president of the bank ate for breakfast every morning and how many times a week the real-estate man's wife changed her sheets; she shook her head with disapproval and envy at the ways of the rich people. Sometimes when she lay in bed at night, she wondered if they loved their houses as much as she loved hers.

It was late one afternoon when Snow came home from looking for a job at the steel mill. The foreman still wasn't hiring and Snow was in a foul mood, made worse when he saw that Callie was working in the yard pruning the nandina bushes. There'd probably be no supper tonight, but if by chance a miracle happened and she *had* cooked, it would be a boiler full of something he didn't like, black-eyed peas or rutabagas.

The sky was lit in the west with the setting sun and in the east with the bright orange glow of the cast-iron plant. The swing shift was pouring iron tonight. Up and down the sidewalk, children who should have long ago been in the house and washed for supper still played freeze tag in the twilight. Wives had pushed supper to the back of the stove and stood with their husbands or with their neighbors looking toward the Coxes' house. Mr. Cox sat on his front steps holding a long hedge switch. Lee Rose had been the only one brave enough to go right up and ask him what was he doing, what was the switch for.

"It's to whip Mrs. Cox with when she gets home," he said. "This is the third time this week I've come home from work and no supper cooked. That's no way for a wife to treat her husband," and he zinged the switch against the innocent sidewalk.

81

Chester Cox didn't look like a wife beater. H was short and delicately made, with long, tapering fingers that molded iron into Lincoln's-head bookends and collie-dog doorstops. He had worked at the cast-iron factory since he was fifteen years old. He and his wife, Birdie, had no children.

He sat on his steps rolling the switch back and forth across his palm; he wore a button-up sweater and small, shiny brown oxfords. Every morning he walked two miles to the cast-iron plant and every afternoon he walked two miles back, rain or shine, hot or cold. He carried a black lunch pail with a thermos of coffee and a spiced-ham sandwich. His lunch was always the same.

Sometimes when Callie was in the front yard at sunrise to dig around her shrubbery or transplant flowers before it got too hot, he stopped for a minute to talk with her. He seemed always about to laugh, a smile twitching the corners of his mouth as he talked. When he laughed, the tears flowed and he would take a clean, white, folded handkerchief from his pocket to wipe his eyes.

On the other hand, Birdie Cox was a big woman, not fat, but stout and raw-boned. She was a head taller than Chester. Her house was the prettiest on the block with its white paint and dark green shutters, her yard the one with the most flowers. It was all Callie could do to keep Lee Rose and Jo Anna out of there, they loved it so, with its trellised arbors and narrow paths that wound through dainty flower beds of sweetheart roses, daisies, and blue lace.

"Well, there's Birdie Cox out there working in that itty bitty garden of hers again," Callie said almost every day, peeping through the living-room curtains. "She's bigger than the flower bed, it's disgraceful the way she leans over with her back end sticking straight up to the sky."

When Birdie Cox caught the streetcar to go to town, she

wore her best silk dress and false teeth. She curled her hair, setting it the night before with water and bobby pins. Jo Anna thought she was the scariest thing with her lips protruding outward, stretching across the ivory-colored teeth that clicked when she talked and had to be pushed back in place with her thumb.

Callie had let Birdie take Lee Rose and Jo Anna to the fair last summer. They had ridden the Ferris wheel and Birdie was eating fig bars during the ride. The gummy filling stuck in her teeth and when she stepped off the giant wheel, almost too dizzy to walk, she'd held onto Jo Anna and Lee Rose and wobbled around behind the cattle barn to wash the shiny, pink-gummed teeth under the faucet where the steers were brought to drink.

Snow sat down on the front steps with a big grin on his face. He was surprised that a skinny little pipsqueak like Chester Cox had gumption enough to stand up to that oversized wife of his, but he had to hand it to him—he gloried in the man's spunk. Hell, he'd thought the man was the worst kind of a sissy. He didn't fish and he didn't hunt and he wouldn't take a drink. What kind of a man was it that spent his days making dogs out of iron like a child playing with clay? But damned if he didn't believe the little man was going to show them all, show Callie especially, how a real man acted. He glanced over his shoulder at her where she'd come to sit on the bannister, but he couldn't tell anything from her face. She just sat staring toward the streetcar stop like everybody else.

Snow blew on his hands, warming them. It had been warm when he started out to look for work that morning, but after the sun went down it turned cold. He shivered and thought that a rabbit ran over his grave. The wind blew harder and dark clouds rolled in from the east, blotting out the last streaks

83

of orange sky. Gnat-sized cinders from the steel mill swirled in the air, which had the faint, rotten-egg smell of the outdoor vats.

Finally, through the dusk, the lights of a streetcar shone over the top of the hill; the children's games stopped, there was no more laughter or talking as it creaked to a stop at the next corner. Nothing moved on the whole block except for the figure that stepped from the streetcar into the near dark of the November evening. Even from far away there was no mistaking the bulky figure of Birdie Cox as she crossed the street and started toward home.

Mr. Cox stood up and walked from the steps to meet her, slapping the switch across the palm of his hand. Birdie stopped when she saw him, watched him for a moment, then resumed her stately march up the sidewalk. She nodded her head to each silent neighbor as she passed, a queen acknowledging her subjects, the faintest, fleeting, wisp of a smile curving her thin lips. She passed the Owens' house and the McNabbs' and the Pearsons'. Finally, she stood before her husband, her head bowed slightly to look down at him.

"What's the matter, sugar?" she asked.

"Birdie," Chester said, "I'm teaching you a lesson. This is the third time I've come home from work this week and there's been no supper cooked. I'm going to whip you so you'll remember a wife's duty to her husband. A wife is supposed to have supper on the table when her husband gets home tired from work." He raised his switch to hit her.

"You better not hit me with that limb, Chester," she said. "That is, if you know what's good for you," she added.

Then she laughed and kissed him on the cheek.

"He's my little banty rooster," she announced to the side-walk audience. "He's my little ole banty rooster that wants

his supper. Come on, sugar, and I'll cook you some supper."
Then she put her hand through his arm.

Mr. Cox lowered the switch and grinned as they walked
arm in arm into the house. The streetlights came on and
children began to yell and chase one another; the first drops of
a sullen November rain began to fall as doors slammed and
supper bells rang up and down the street.

"Shit," Snow said, "I thought he was finally going to be a
man but he's just shit. He just stood there blushing like a June
bride. I was right about him the first time, there's not a thing
to him, he's just shit."

Callie went inside and called to him from behind the front
screen door.

"*Shut* your mouth and come inside. The children and all
the neighbors hear your crude talk." She held the door open
for him to pass through, then called Jo Anna and Lee Rose in
to supper.

Maribeth sat at the kitchen table reading the love serial
in the evening paper.

"Well, did all of you get your eyes full?" she asked, as they
came in. "That's the commonest thing I've ever heard of, a
man beating his wife in public and all of you just standing
there watching—"

"Hush, Maribeth," Callie said. "I watched and I'm not
common. There *is* such a thing as a little normal curiosity.
Besides, he didn't whip her at all; she showed him what was
what," and there was admiration in her voice for Birdie Cox.

They all gathered around the kitchen table and Callie set
out the skillet of cold cornbread and the bowl of butter beans
she had cooked that morning.

"Callie," Snow said, "if there was a law passed tomorrow
that you had to spend your time cooking and stay out of that

damn yard all the time you'd be in a hell of a lot of trouble."

"You can leave," Callie said, "if you don't like what's on the table. I'm not begging you to stay, I don't know of anyone here that's begging you to stay." She crumbled cornbread into the beans. "Why don't you go back to the farm and live with Olan Calvert that you love so well?"

"Olan is dead."

At Callie's surprised look, he added, "Olan died back in the summer. I went to see him and he was dead but I didn't see any reason to tell you. It's your fault I never saw him again. If I'd stayed where I belonged there'd be something on this table tonight besides beans, this sorry little bowl of beans."

"Well, I'm sorry about Olan," Callie said. "He was a good man; he kept his place the way you never did, you and the colored girls—"

"Now what the hell does that mean?" and he threw his spoon to the table and glared at her.

"You know exactly what I mean—"

"Yes, I think I do, but I'd like to see if you've got the guts to say it here in front of these children, tell lies about their father—"

"They know it isn't lies, they already know the truth, why you stayed so much up at Olan's and Exa's. Ask Maribeth what she heard on the school bus. You don't have me fooled or these children either—"

When Snow stood up from his chair it fell over backward, banging in the silence as he leaned across the table to seize Callie around her throat. She pulled at his arms, twisting her head back and forth trying to make him turn her loose; her eyes stared terrified at him and he was pleased that she was afraid. Her fear made the anger come up stronger in him and the heat of it burned in his brain, wave after wave washed over him; through a haze he saw himself carried along, helpless, unresisting. He turned loose and shoved her onto the flowered linoleum floor, battered her arms and shoulders for humiliating him in front of the girls, for taking away his manhood. It seemed his father was there, nodding his head, smiling approval at him.

Vaguely, he heard people shouting, saw the yellow bowl of beans fall off the table and spin across the floor, saw crumbs of cornbread in sharp focus scattered across the red checkered oilcloth. Voices were crying, hands pulled at him, and then he heard the front door slam and Jo Anna's voice on the porch—*Somebody come help, please come help, Daddy's killing Mama*—but then she was there again, her arms around his neck, begging him to stop. The sharp rap of knuckles beat against the glass of the front door again and again, and it was then that his head cleared and he picked his chair off the floor, set it neat and straight at the table before he sat back down.

Maribeth and Jo Anna were crying. They helped their mother off the floor, pulled her gently to her chair, caressed her and smoothed her hair that had fallen from its pins. In the shadows behind the stove, Lee Rose stood stiff and straight, her eyes dry, her face pale; there was no color in her lips, her fists were clenched, her arms rigid. The only sound in the room was their harsh, heavy breathing, the crack of raindrops against the window.

"Go to the door, Maribeth," Callie said, her voice low and hoarse, and tell whoever is there that everything's all right, that you children got to scuffling and Jo Anna got excited, that you all were just playing around; go and tell whoever it is, Maribeth—"

Callie rubbed at the red welts on her throat and stared at Snow, her eyes bright and hard, the corners of her mouth

87

turned down with hatred of him. When Maribeth came back from answering the door, Callie told the girls to go into the living room and turn the radio up loud. They left the kitchen and soon there was a blast of music. *Come on chillun', le's dance,* said Kay Kayser's cheery voice. Maribeth sat alone in the dark, but Lee Rose and Jo Anna hid in a corner of the dining room to listen to Callie and Snow.

"Now I want you out of my house," Callie said. "For years I held my head up and pretended there was nothing wrong, that you weren't sleeping around with the colored girls. I made myself believe that Maribeth didn't really know what was going on in spite of the note a boy passed to her on the bus, that had a dirty picture drawn on it. He asked her if that picture was the size of you, how big you are—"

"That's lies you're telling, Callie, that never happened, you're making that up!" He banged his fist on the table, half rose from the chair as if he would hit her again.

"—she came home crying and said they all snickered on the bus and passed the picture around, but there was nothing I could do—I couldn't leave you, I had nowhere to go, no money—"

"I have always done my duty by you and those children, I've kept you all fed, and damn good, and a roof over your heads. You've never been cold or hungry—"

"You disgraced me before, but you won't disgrace me here in my own home, I'm not trapped any more; God sent Royce in front of that truck so I wouldn't be trapped any more—"

"All right," Snow said, "I'll go, it's time for me to go, I stayed too long with you, way too long—"

He listened to the rain falling and knew that he was afraid to go, to start all over again, and was ashamed of himself. Never before in his life had he been afraid to strike out, to

88

hit the open road. Callie had taken his balls, that was a fact. Chester Cox was more man than he was.

Snow thought he was a hard-luck guy, the kind of a man that, no matter how hard he tried, would die without owning a thing. Other people had things, owned cars, had nice new suits of clothes, but not him, never him. The fault was in him, he knew that. Nobody else in his family was restless as he was, never satisfied, always ready to be on the go. If he was here, he wanted to be there, if he was there he went someplace else. Until Callie and the girls, he'd never stayed so long in one place, and he knew that was because of Callie; he wanted to be with her.

"I'm going back home to Clement," he said. "I'm going back over to Georgia and this time I'll stay and I'll never leave again, this time I'll stay until I die and they can bury me there in Lone Oak. This time I won't ever leave again."

"I don't care *where* you go, as long as you go, as long as you get out of my house, because if you ever touch me again I'll kill you, I don't care if you are my girls' daddy. But I'm glad for what you did tonight, they saw for themselves what kind of a man you are—they saw better than I could have ever told them—"

"That was the first time I ever hit a woman," he said, "and I'm sorry for that." Callie just sat there cold and staring at him.

Twenty years ago he couldn't wait to marry her. She was sweet and she was pretty, but he'd gone with lots of sweet and pretty girls and hadn't wanted to marry them. He'd just been passing through Opelika and was stopping only long enough to help her uncle get in his spring crop; he saw Callie going along the road and she stopped at the fence to watch him plow. Her hair was long and wavy over her shoulders and she was slim and straight; she looked just the way he thought a woman ought to look. She smiled at him and he bunched his muscles and strutted along the furrow, pushing the plow straight as a bird dog's point, showing off for her.

He went to prayer meeting with her that night, and every night after that. For two weeks, they went somewhere together, walking in the moonlight or just sitting on her front steps talking. He found out how unhappy she was with that sour old aunt of hers and he held her up close to him and told her he loved her. That was the only time in his life he ever told a woman he loved her; he'd never even said those words to his own mother that he could remember. They got married more than two hundred miles from Opelika. Callie had her head set that she'd be married at Seddon where she was born, at the church her mother had taken her to when she was little. He supposed that was the real reason he married her: she always knew what she wanted. Once she made up her mind to something you could be sure that's exactly what she'd do.

"I'm a fool, Callie, hanging around for all these years when you wouldn't be a wife to me, letting you wear the pants. I'm moving on." And when he said the words, now that it was decided for sure, he didn't feel so afraid. In fact, he felt the first flicker of excitement in his stomach. The burden of this house and all these women slid from his shoulders.

"You're welcome to this house, Callie, every brick and stick of it. I've been a damn fool trying like hell to find a job and get money to help you pay for *your* house. I'm going back over to Clement and work for myself for a change. The next time you see me I just might be wearing an expensive suit of clothes and driving a fine car—" He wanted still to impress her.

"With a nigger girl in the front seat?"

They stared dreamily at each other, strange to one another,

but without the regard of strangers—two people who over the years had become enemies, who now, finally, on this night, shared their hatred comfortably.

"I'll go back over to Clement and I'll plant me some cotton and some corn," he said, "but before I do that, the first crop I'll grow me is a new set of balls—"

The radio blared, dance music filled the room. Snow left the kitchen and went to the back bedroom and packed his square black suitcase. When it was filled and the straps buckled, he went to the bathroom and put on his suit, white shirt, and black tie. Then he combed his hair, dampening the comb again and again until his hair lay slick and smooth. Jo Anna and Lee Rose stood on the end of the bed watching him through the transom. Then he came into the bedroom and they jumped down. Jo Anna began to cry.

"You hit Mama, Daddy, you ought not to have hit Mama, but she doesn't mean it for you to go, she's just mad—"

Snow pulled her close to him, hugged her.

"I'm sorry for what I did to your mama; that was wrong of me to do that, I lost my temper. But she does mean it for me to go. But next summer I want you to come visit me over at Clement, that's where I'll be living from now on. When you come I'll show you the bottoms where your uncle Roy and I used to help Papa in the field. It's the prettiest place you ever saw. Back in the woods there's a pond with willow trees to sit under and eat your lunch and cool off, there's wild turkeys and possum to hunt, the trees so thick you can't hardly see more than a little patch of sky overhead—"

He noticed Lee Rose for the first time.

"You can come, too, Lee Rose," he said. "You know you still put me in mind of my mother. I'd give you the picture I have of her but it's the last one I have. Your mother burned up all the rest, she burned up all the pictures I had of my family. Now why do you suppose she did that? Maybe you can get her to tell you why someday."

He put on his hat and picked up his suitcase. Lee Rose took his hand.

"Please," she said, "don't go, don't leave us—"

Snow was embarrassed; she was way too big for petting and hugging; why, she hadn't touched him for years. She was nearly about as tall as he was. He pulled his hand away from her, brushed it across his mouth, rubbed the back of his neck.

"I'll get to Clement just about in time to help finish putting in the winter crop," he said, and when he went through the front bedroom Maribeth was sitting cross-legged on the bed writing to her pen-pal boy friend she had found listed on the comic page of the evening paper. Her hair hung around her face and she looked up at him, her cool, pale blue eyes polite, remote, as if he were someone she had just met and didn't care to know better.

"So long, Maribeth," Snow said. "You write to *me* now when I get settled over in Clement, that's where I'll be from now on. I'm sorry about tonight and about everything else that's happened. I'm sorry if I ever caused you embarrassment—"

She didn't say anything and it could just as well be he had told her he was going to the corner store for smoking tobacco. He turned away from her and wondered where was the baby girl who once so loved jaybirds that every time she saw one she'd squeal with joy. That's what he'd called her for years, Jaybird, until she got too big for such childish names.

At the front door, he called through the dark rooms to Callie, who still sat in the kitchen.

"I'm going now, Callie, so good-by and thank you kindly for your hospitality, for your room and board. Good-by to all you girls, I'm sorry I've been such a poor daddy." He took his suitcase to the front porch and Jo Anna followed him, crying and pulling at him.

"Come back in this house," Callie hissed at her as she hurried to the front door. "The neighbors are on their porches watching, just itching to find out what's going on over here. Jo Anna, don't you *dare* come in here crying; if you do I'll send you right along with him—"

Jo Anna came back inside and Callie sent her to bed, told her to tell Lee Rose and Maribeth, too, to turn out the lights and get in bed. "We're disgraced enough for one night," she said.

"It's all yours now, Callie," Snow said from the steps, "just like you wanted it all along—all for you, the house, the girls, everything. I hope you'll be happy now."

"Even after what's happened, what you've done tonight," Callie said, "I wouldn't grudge you bus fare on a bad night like this. I can let you have bus fare, it's the least I can do."

"Hell, no, I don't want your money. I'll hoof it and hitch it over to Clement—I'll get there. I made out a *long* time before you got your hands on Royce's money."

Callie went to the front porch and stood at the bannister watching him walk away. It was still raining, a light drizzle that turned the sidewalk into a shiny silver ribbon that stretched away into the distance. At the corner he stepped into the white glow of the streetlight, and the tilt of his hat and the way he looked so tired, leaning with the weight of his suitcase, made her all at once want to cry out to him: *Wait, Snow, don't go.* Then he disappeared into the jumbled shadows across the street and nothing was left but the empty sidewalk and the spot of light, an empty stage, the player gone.

The wind gusted and the shadows moved on the wall, the bare limbs of the trees clacked against one another; finally, she had the things she wanted—the house, the girls, she was her own boss with no one to answer to, to ask her questions. She had all those things, but she was afraid.

She rubbed her hand along the bannister of her house and knew that now she had it to do, the time had come for her to make it alone. She went inside and locked up. Maribeth and Lee Rose were in bed and, softly, she called their names, called good night to them. Then she undressed and climbed into bed beside Jo Anna, crawled up close to the curve of her warm body. The firelight from the grate flickered on the ceiling and Callie was ashamed of herself for being uneasy without Snow in the house, listened for his step on the porch as she always did when he came in late.

She fell into a light sleep filled with frightful dreams she could not remember when she woke up; toward morning a noise brought her full awake and she sat up in bed, her heart racing.

"Turn over on your side, Snow," she said, but in the awful stillness she heard nothing but the tick of the clock, and she remembered that he was gone.

The fire had gone out, the room was cold and dark. She got out of bed, turned on the bathroom light, and put another quilt on the bed; she lay close to Jo Anna and when, finally, she stopped shivering and was drifting back to sleep, there were the screams of cats mating. She wondered if it were true that male cats had arrow-shaped penises that ripped the female when it was pulled from her. She'd always heard that it was so.

The rain was falling hard now, it thundered on the roof, and Callie hoped that Snow had already caught a ride, hoped he was not still on the highway in all that rain trying to hitch a ride to Georgia.

94

7

Snow walked the seven blocks to highway 78 East that led out of Birmingham. It ran past the grammar school and up the hill to Lewisburg. After Lewisburg it was open highway to Atlanta. It was not late, only a little after nine o'clock, yet there were few cars on the street this time of night in Magnolia Hills. He decided his chances of hitching a ride were better if he hoofed it on up the hill past the winking blue light of the tourist home, better to get on the highway and out of the local traffic.

He climbed the hill, stopping now and then to rest, to put down his suitcase and catch his breath. By God, he wondered if there was ever going to be any peace in his life, any rest. Seemed like the harder he tried, the quicker he got slapped down. He took out his handkerchief and wiped his face and neck, wiped away the moisture that was part rain and part sweat.

He began climbing again until finally he reached the top of the hill where Silk Stocking Road intercepted highway 78. From here he could see the lights that ringed the golf course, could see about where Callie's house would be. He never had been happy with her except at the very beginning. For the first few years she was willing to make love, but after the babies started coming she turned bossy, domineering. She was not a meek woman, as his mother had been. After Jo Anna was born she wouldn't let him touch her any more and he should never have put up with that, but he had, and she had the upper hand.

Past the lights of the Magnolia Hills shopping district was the Buffalo Rock plant, and to the right of that the tank factory. Further on was the switching yard. He stared at the lights haloed in the mist below and wondered if he would ever see this place again and hoped that he would not. It was a shit-eating place, this town of factories and mills. He was leaving, and it was good riddance to bad rubbish. He stood on the hill, threw back his head, stuck out his tongue, and gave the whole city the raspberry.

"And to you, too, Callie." And he picked up his suitcase and headed down the dark highway.

Not far ahead, but not as close as it looked, shone the lights of the Silver Slipper truck stop. That was his goal for now, unless by some miracle a car picked him up before he got there. But no car had passed him since he turned off Thirty-fifth Avenue and headed up the hill. He had enough money for a beer and sandwich but not much else. Might as well start the trip with some food under his belt; he had not touched Callie's supper of butter beans and cornbread.

He trudged along, the rain pooling in the brim of his hat and dripping off onto his shoulders. He thought now that he was a fool not to have taken bus fare from Callie. Hell, it was only right, little enough payment for all those years he'd kept a roof over her head and the girls' too, kept food in their mouths. And damn good food it was, too. Not a little paper sack of canned goods from the A & P, but tow sacks full of peanuts and Irish potatoes and corn. But was Callie satisfied? Hell, no. Bellyached all the time about the mud, and how refined she wanted to be. Kept the girls all up in the air, too, especially Maribeth, looking for pie in the sky, telling them about the vaudeville show she'd seen once in Opelika. Well, she had it now and she was welcome to it, but he was shaking the dust of Magnolia Hills off his feet; if he never saw it again it would be too soon for him.

The red and yellow lights that encircled the roof of the truck stop were closer; he could even see the cars parked outside, smell the hickory smoke that rose from the chimney. The sign at the end of the building said Real Pit Bar-B-Q. He stopped and set his suitcase on the ground while he flexed his cramped fingers, the saliva flowing in streams from under his tongue when he thought of the barbecue. He shifted his suitcase to his other hand, the weight of it slowing him hardly at all as he hurried toward the lights. Outside pork, that's what he wanted, the charred outside, black with hickory smoke, too tough almost to chew and washed down with a Schlitz.

He stopped and reached his hand in his pocket. There was the reassuring feel of the crumpled dollar bill and a handful of change, mostly pennies. He thought briefly that it might be a mistake spending his last money on food, but what better way to spend it? It wasn't enough for bus fare, not enough for a lady of the night back at the blue light that said Wayfarers Tourist Court. Anyway, with any luck at all he'd be in Clement by the day after tomorrow.

He walked across the gravel parking lot of the Silver Slipper and pushed open the door to warmth and the smell of onions frying. A pile of hickory logs was stacked in the corner next to the big red juke box that, aglow with lights, was pouring

97

out the whining voice of a cowboy. *Come sit by my side little darlin', come lay your cool hand on my brow* . . .

At the stone pit behind the counter yellow flames curled over and around dark slabs of pork, and Snow felt his spirits lift as they always did when there was the smell of food cooking, the happy comradeship of people gathering to eat.

He set down his suitcase and looked around. Only a few people were at the tables: a young couple sat by the window and an old man in the corner drinking beer. Two men were at the counter and that's where he decided to sit. He just might strike up a conversation with them, just might get to telling jokes, and that would be enjoyable, a diversion, get his mind off his troubles. He hung his hat on the hat rack and pushed his suitcase into the corner where it would be less likely anyone would steal it. Sometimes in nightmares he dreamed he was going somewhere and had lost his clothes and wandered up and down strange streets looking for them.

He smoothed back his hair and cleared his throat as he approached the two men on the stools at the counter.

"Evening," he said, as he sat down. "Cold November, don't you think? Why, last year we didn't have any cold weather to speak of until after Christmas."

He shivered to prove his point.

"Son of a bitch, I don't think I've been really warm since September. You can take this cold weather, if you ask me, and give it to the yankees. I'm as far north as I ever want to be in my whole life."

He smiled at them and the two men grinned at him, bobbing their heads. One man was older than the other, thin and ferret-faced. His hair was gray and he had a wide overlip and colorless gray eyes in a face without much chin. The younger man looked like the older one except that he had brown hair and fuller cheeks. Both of them wore khaki pants and leather jackets with cowboy boots, their high heels hooked over the steel railing of the counter stool.

"You two look to me like you must be kin," Snow said. "Let me see if I can guess; you're father and son."

The older man slapped the counter with the flat of his hand and laughed.

"Did'ja hear that, son? This must be some pretty smart joker here to guess you're my son."

He turned to Snow.

"This here's my son Burke and I'm Croaker Johnson. My real name's George but I guess you can tell from the sound of my voice why they called me Croaker. My mama said from the time I was a little ole bitsy thing I had a voice sounded just like a frog."

Snow smiled, happy that the man was going to be friendly, that he would have someone to talk to while he ate.

"We're chicken farmers on a run to Anniston. I guess you saw my pickup out there in the parking lot?"

Snow shook his head that he had not.

"Don't get much for chickens nowadays, ain't hardly worth the trouble and feed it takes to raise 'em." And he took a long pull on his bottle of Bud, the Adam's apple of his turkey neck bobbing up and down with each swallow.

The waitress came for Snow's order. He asked for a Schlitz and an outside pork and the acne-scarred girl wrote it down without looking at him. Burke and Croaker asked for another Bud. When the waitress left, Snow shook his head at her back.

"Man, what a ugly woman. I don't believe I've ever seen a uglier one. A man would have to be mighty hard up to want a piece of something like that."

Croaker and Burke nodded solemn agreement as they watched her give the order to the cook, watched the girl with dirty blond hair and sharp, winged shoulder blades open the

99

three beers. She set the bottles in front of the three men and all of them took long swallows of the beer, then fell silent and moody.

Snow knew the men had been drinking a long time because their voices were slurred and they opened their eyes wide when they leaned in close to talk. Well, hell, he didn't care if they were drunk. A man and his son come in to have a little fun, drink a little, it was all right with him. They were too quiet, though, too moody. Snow thought he could fix that. He took a stingy sip of beer, careful so that it wouldn't be all gone by the time his barbecue got there. He tapped Croaker on the shoulder.

"Say, did you all hear the one about the white man and the nigger went hunting and they saw two little bear cubs run in a cave?"

Croaker said, no, they hadn't heard it.

"Well," Snow said, "it seems that there was this white man and this nigger man went in the woods and they saw two little bear cubs run in a cave. The nigger man decided he'd go in and get them and they could take them to sell. The white man said he'd keep watch for the mother bear, but after a while he fell asleep and woke up just in time to see the mother bear going in the cave to save her cubs. The white man quick grabbed her tail and put his legs on each side of the hole to hold her back. The nigger man yelled, 'What darky 'de hole, what darky 'de hole?' and the white man yells back, 'If this tail hold breaks loose you'll *see* what darky 'de hole.' "

They all laughed and Burke slapped the counter and said boy, he bet that was one scared old nigger.

"Yeah," Snow said, "niggers are scary all right. I've worked a lot of niggers in my time and I can tell you they're mighty superstitious. One old nigger woman lived on the place when I was growing up was a witch, least all the colored thought

100

she was. That was because she had blue gums; that's the truth, she really did, too," he said when they laughed. "When she smiled—all her teeth were gone, you understand—when she smiled all you could see was those gums, blue as ink. When I was a kid, not more than five or six years old, I'd go home all the way around the cornfield to keep from passing her house.

"Sometimes she'd be sitting on the front porch and if you passed by there she'd yoo-hoo and wave and show those gums. It was mighty scary, I can tell you. I look back on it now and that old witch was enjoying herself scaring the little white children."

The waitress set his barbecue in front of him. The meat stuck from the edges of the bun, dark and glistening. Snow's stomach cramped with pleasure as he bit into the sandwich, savoring each shred of the hard, stringy meat. He washed it down with beer, looked at the bottle, measuring how much was left; he did not want his last bite of barbecue washed down with water.

His two new friends were shuffling about putting money on the counter. They were ready to leave and Snow quickly ate the last of his sandwich, the last bit of his bread that had no meat. There was one good swallow of beer left and he drank it, wiping his mouth on the sleeve of his coat.

"Croaker," he said, "I was thinking there might be room for me to go a ways with you and Burke down the highway. I'm hoofing it and hitching it trying to get back home to Clement. That's about fifty miles this side of Atlanta. I left my wife tonight and I got no place to go but back home to my people."

"Hell, man, you can ride with us as far as we're going. You'll have to sit in back with the chickens, though, there ain't no room in the cab but for me and Burke. If you don't mind riding with the chickens we're going all the way to Anniston before we turn off seventy-eight."

Snow was at the point of refusing the ride after he'd asked for it; he sure didn't want to sit in the back with a mess of chickens, but he looked out the window and what earlier had been only a drizzle had turned into a downpour. He did not relish walking in the rain nor did he relish sitting another two or three hours in this truck stop waiting for it to slack up. He paid for his sandwich and beer. It took most of his dollar but he did not grudge it. Money spent on food was well spent. When his stomach was full, tight and pushing against his belt buckle, he was happy, felt cheerful with a bright outlook on life.

"Beggars can't be choosers," he said, and put on his hat and got his suitcase from the corner.

He followed Croaker and Burke to the door. Snow reached to pull Croaker's jacket down because it wouldn't do for the sheriff pulling into the parking lot to see the bottle of whiskey sticking from his hip pocket. The leather jacket was caught behind the neck of the bottle. Croaker whirled, glaring at Snow.

"You stealin' my whiskey, friend?"

"Hell, no, I'm not stealing your whiskey."

The sheriff ran into the truck stop, stomping and shaking the rain from his clothes.

"That is truth to God a frawg strangler," the sheriff said, and hung his coat, dripping water, on the hook on the wall.

"I was keeping the sheriff from seeing the bottle sticking out of your pocket, but if you got a urge to fight, *friend*, let's step outside."

"Ah, no," Croaker said, playfully pushing at Snow's shoulder. "That was a nice thing you did. I 'preshate it. No offense."

They left the shelter of the Silver Slipper and ran to the end of the building, where Croaker's truck was parked. A tarpaulin covered the open end where crates of chickens were stacked one on top of the other. It kept the worst of the rain off the chickens, but there was the strong odor of chicken mess and damp chicken feathers. Still, it was better than the cold, pouring rain and Snow hoisted himself aboard, crawling under the tarpaulin. On hands and knees he pushed his suitcase as far back as it would go, then pushed a crate of chickens near to the window in the back of the cab. He pulled the awning, wet and heavy with rain, close around his shoulders and sat down on the chicken crate. It was only slightly better than walking.

Croaker and Burke got in the cab of the pickup. Snow pulled the sleeve of his coat over his hand, wiped the rain from the back window, and peered inside the truck. Croaker was in the driver's seat. Snow wished it was Burke driving because he did not seem to be as drunk as Croaker. Croaker started the truck and the wheels whirled and spun and gripped the wet gravel.

The truck lurched forward, bumping and sputtering, its rear end fishtailing; the sleepy chickens' heads jerked from beneath their wings and they squawked as the crates teetered back and forth. As Croaker turned left and headed back up the highway, a crate on the back end of the truck fell off.

Snow peeped over the awning and saw about a dozen white leghorns scattering across the road, flapping their wings, running in all directions. Funny thing, Snow thought, how it came to be that particular crate to fall off, those particular chickens saved from the frying pan. They'd go in the woods and turn wild after a while like the turkeys back in there. When he hunted he'd seen whole flocks of wild chickens.

He thought once he'd knock on the back window, see if Croaker and Burke wanted to stop the truck and try to catch them, but he knew they wouldn't. The crate was broken and it was pouring down rain. Besides, the real reason he wanted them to stop was so he could get off. The way the truck was bumping and sliding he'd as soon take his chances with the rain.

He huddled down, cold and miserable, under the awning. The swaying of the truck kept sending the beer back up into his throat and his stomach burned. The rain had not slacked a bit; if anything, it was raining harder, thumping him on the head through the awning. It seemed to him like they were going mighty fast, but then it could be that riding in the back he felt the wind and the bumps like he wouldn't if he were inside the truck. Looked to him like they could have all squeezed together in the front, made room for him some way. It was a mean thing to do, stick a man back with the chickens.

The truck rocked from side to side. Finally he had to turn loose the awning and hold on to the chicken crates to keep from falling over. The wheels hit mud on the side of the road and the truck skidded, sliding from one side of the road to the other.

"Jesus Christ," Snow said.

He crawled through the crates to the side of the truck and stuck his head out from under the awning; he squinted his eyes against the rain trying to see the road ahead.

"Jesus God Almighty," he breathed.

Croaker was driving straight down the left-hand side of the road, his dim headlights barely penetrating the solid sheet of rain. Water was pouring down Snow's face and into his eyes, but he could see well enough the trees rushing by on either side of him, the shining, sleek road rushing beneath him so fast it made his head spin.

He crawled back to the window of the cab and, still on hands and knees, knocked on the glass, rubbing away the rain as he knocked. The window was frosted on the inside, but still Snow could see Croaker and Burke passing the bottle of whiskey back and forth.

"Jesus Christ, man, what do you think you're doing?" he yelled at Croaker, but neither of the men heard him, or else they did not pay any attention to him.

Snow knocked again, so hard that pain shot through his knuckles. He called over and over to the crazy men inside the truck. He watched Croaker turn the bottle of whiskey up and then let go of the steering wheel entirely.

"Oh, my God," Snow moaned, then yelled, "Stop this goddam truck and let me out!" But they didn't answer or turn around to see his white and terrified face peering in the window at them.

Snow hugged the back end of the cab as if it were his own mother, unmindful of the rain that drenched him to the skin, not even feeling the wind that, sharp as a knife, cut through his wet clothes. His teeth chattered, his body jerked with spasms of cold and fear. The truck rattled and slid through the night and Snow knew they must be going at least a hundred miles an hour. The chickens had come wide awake, cackling and fluttering their wings when the truck bumped, their feathers ruffled against the cold wind that blew under the awning.

Snow crawled back to the side of the truck and looked out from under the awning. He would jump the next time the truck swerved near the ditch. The ditch was filled with long blades of Johnson grass; it looked like a fairly soft place to land. He hooked his leg over the side but when the truck swerved he did not have the courage to jump. The road spun under him and he was so dizzy he fell back into the truck, lying between the crates. The truck rocked and swayed and after a while he crawled once more to the window, beating on it with his fists.

"Stop this truck, you goddam, mother-fucking fools and let me out of here," he screamed, but they gave no indication they had heard him. Through the breath-frosted glass he could see the headlights of an oncoming car.

"Oh, my God, this is it," he whispered, and he crawled once again to the side of the truck. He would jump this time. He would stand no chance at all if they hit head-on. The round, yellow headlights, like two moons, came closer and closer; Croaker turned the wheel lazily, slowly, and the truck drifted back to the right-hand side of the road.

Snow crawled back under the tarpaulin to his place on the chicken crate and covered his face with his hands. He knew now that he would not jump and neither could he make Croaker stop the truck and let him off. He would stick it out, whatever happened, and with the decision came a feeling of calm.

He closed his eyes and did not believe that he was hurtling through the night with a load of chickens and two drunk men. It was only a nightmare and in a while he would wake up and feel the rough wool touch of his old army blanket pulled tight across his back and tucked up high around his neck. High overhead, the rain fell on Callie's twenty-year-guaranteed roof, the light shone through the bathroom transom, lying dim and friendly across his covers. In the half-light of the room, he saw the curve of his iron bed, the shape of his body lying warm under the brown blanket.

He was a damn fool. If he'd had any sense at all he would have stayed and eaten Callie's butter beans and cornbread. If he'd only kept his mouth shut, even now he would be warm and safe, lying in bed instead of counting the minutes before he crashed in this rattletrap truck and died on the side of the road.

Ordinarily, he did not like a policeman or a sheriff or a deputy sheriff or any manner of uniform that said someone had authority over him, who could tell him what to do. That is until now. Through the wind shrieking around the tarpaulin and through the rain slapping on his head, he heard the thin, high wail of a siren. He stuck his head from under the awning, and far behind them, blurred through the rain, was the flashing red light of a police car.

"Thank God, thank God," Snow sobbed.

He was so happy he cried; drenching, salty tears of happiness flowed with the rain down his face. A policeman was coming to save him, his friends the police would save him from the drunk men. He was to live after all, he would not die lying broken and bleeding among glass and twisted metal. He watched the car with the flashing red light come closer until finally he could see the blurred face of the driver through the windshield.

Croaker, too, finally heard the siren through the closed windows of his truck and floorboarded the accelerator. The truck lunged forward flinging Snow onto his back, sent him crashing into the chicken crates. The chickens squawked and beat their wings against the bars, the truck ran off the road, its right wheels clinging to the rim of a ditch. Snow gathered the tarpaulin close around him, pulling it tight over his head and ears. He lay jammed against the crates, and he knew when the truck bounced and slid that they had changed direction and were sliding sideways down the highway.

The scream of the siren was directly behind them and Snow lay on his back, the sound of the siren and the screeching

107

tires mixed up inside his head. He was resigned now to being killed, wished that he could sleep before it happened; he was only faintly curious as to when it would happen.

He heard the pop of a gun and burrowed deeper in his awning cocoon. The policeman was shooting at Croaker because Croaker would not pull over to the side of the road and stop. There was another pop, louder this time, and the truck lurched and screamed, dragging along the pavement on the metal rim of the burst tire; then it slammed into a ditch and lay tilted on its side.

Snow lay without moving, dazed and weak, dizzy from the sudden stillness. He was also sick at his stomach from the burnt taste of the barbecue sandwich that had come up into his throat. The rain had slackened, settling into a slow November drizzle. It was deathly quiet except for the gentle pad of rain on the tarpaulin. Then suddenly there were scuffling noises and protesting voices as the patrolman pulled Croaker and Burke from the truck. After a while the tarpaulin was flung off and the beam of a flashlight shone in Snow's face.

"Well, I'll be damned, ain't nobody back here but you chickens. Come on out of there, or are you too drunk to walk?"

Snow lifted his head and looked into the disgusted face of a deputy sheriff. He crawled to his hands and knees, then holding onto a chicken crate pulled himself to his feet, stumbled and nearly fell.

"Unh-huh, see there, I knew you was too drunk to walk. Crawl on out of there and let me put you in the patrol car with your two drunk friends. I have *never* in all my ten years of patrolling ever *seen* such driving in all my life. It's a thousand wonders ever' one of you didn't mop up the highway. See there—" he said, bobbing his head up and down as

Snow's legs buckled under him for the second time, "—see there, I knew you was as drunk as them other two."

Snow eased off the end of the truck, sliding along on his backside, and sat down in the road. He could not walk, his legs would not hold him up. He had had the living, mortal hell scared out of him, and as he sat there in the wet grass it seemed he was still moving, the truck pitching beneath him. He closed his eyes and then opened them again quickly, because it made his head swim to close his eyes, made his stomach feel sicker.

"Shit," Snow said.

"Now you watch that kind of talk," the deputy said. "This here's the law you're talking to, not them two drunk fools in the patrol car."

"Look," Snow said, standing up and hanging on to the rear end of the truck. "I'm not drunk. I swear I'm sober as a judge. Don't misunderstand, I've been drunk plenty of times in my life, I'm not too good to. But this just happens to be one of those times I'm not. You saw the way those crazy fools were driving. I thought my time had come for sure. I'm hitching it and they picked me up back there in the Silver Slipper. I left my wife tonight and I've got to get back home to Clement."

From the back of the patrol car came the voices of Croaker and Burke laughing and shouting. Snow thought they probably didn't even know where they were, didn't even realize they weren't in the truck any longer.

"Shut up over there," the deputy yelled, "cut out that whooping and hollering. In a minute I'm gon' see how much fun y'all can have in my jail."

He turned back to Snow, the rain dripping off his broad-brimmed hat that looked like the kind the Canadian Mounties wore. He had on a leather jacket like Croaker's and Burke's, wore black jodhpurs and black shiny boots. A gun was strapped to his hip and Snow thought he wouldn't talk so big if he didn't have that gun.

"It's a wonder all of you hadn't been killed," the deputy said. "I wish you could've seen how y'all looked skidding down that road; it was enough to make your hair stand on end."

"Look," Snow said, the specter of jail rising up to haunt him, "I don't know how I can convince you I was just scared, not drunk. You saw how they were driving. It scared the P-turkey out of me, I can tell you. It would've scared anybody, I guess, except you police. You police are just braver than the rest of us," and he grinned, the words sticking in his craw, nearly choking him.

"Let me smell your breath."

Snow leaned close to him and the deputy sniffed.

"Hell, I don't smell no whiskey. Most I smell is chicken mess. You been lying in chicken mess and man you smell awful. You need a *bath*."

Snow's fingers twitched, itching to hit the son of a bitch.

"You are right for a fact. I never wanted to ride with those chickens but I figured it was better than hoofing it in the rain and then not sure I'd catch a ride. But, hell, I'm as wet as I would've been if I'd of just walked and I wouldn't be in trouble with the law, either."

Snow was dizzy again and gripped the cold metal of the truck, trying not to sway, not to tempt the deputy into arresting him. He squinted, focusing on the spindly, twisted apple trees in the grove across the road. It had stopped raining, the clouds breaking up into great white clumps. It was fairing off cold and he was freezing in the wet suit he wore.

Croaker and Burke were fighting in the back seat of the patrol car. They were yelling, "God *damn* you, Burke," and "I'm gon' knock your head off even if you *are* my daddy."

"You two in there," the deputy yelled, "if you mess up one thing in my patrol car you're gon' spend the rest of your lives in my jail."

"As for you," he said to Snow, "I'm gon' let you go. Don't look to me like you've done nothing wrong except fall in with bad companions. If I was going your way I'd give you a lift, but the jail's back that way," and he jerked his thumb toward the west. "Whyn't you walk on about two, three miles on up the highway and there's a diner open all night. Tell Bitsy, she's the one runs it, that deputy Weehunt told you to come. She'll give you a good hot cup of coffee and let you dry off."

"I sure do appreciate it," Snow said, trying to hurry as he went to the side of the truck and hoisted off his suitcase. "Thanks a lot," and he walked up the highway, desperate for the black shadows of the night to hide him before the deputy changed his mind and put him in the patrol car with Croaker and Burke.

He went a short piece up the road, then turned and watched the deputy get back in the patrol car, make a U-turn and head west back down the highway. Snow waved, but he knew the deputy couldn't see him. He watched until the flashing red light was out of sight, then, heading east, he walked down the middle of the road, stopping now and then to shift his suitcase from one arm to the other.

Once, after climbing a long hill, he stopped at the top to rest. On either side there were woods for as far as he could see, but he was not afraid. The dark and being alone had never bothered him; there was no sound but the wind and his own breathing as he rested from the long climb. He pulled his wet coat close around him, continued walking, putting one heavy foot in front of the other.

Every step was one step closer to the all-night diner that would sell him coffee and let him stay long enough to dry his clothes. Every step took him closer back home to his people. And so he walked, staring at the pavement until at last, when he stopped to rest, he saw the lights of the diner shining in the distance.

It was early morning of the fifth day when Snow reached Clement. He had hoofed it all the way except for the one ride in the back seat of a nigger man's car and that didn't take him far, only a few miles past Bitsy's diner. He had walked holes through the thin soles of his shoes and then he had walked holes through the cardboard he had cut and fit inside them. He had changed clothes at the diner, putting on his field khakis and an old wool green sweater. He stuffed the gray suit into the trash barrel and left it there for Bitsy to burn.

He had slept one night in an open field, crowding for warmth close to the broom sage that grew along the fence. He slept that first night at Bitsy's, his head on the table. She let him stay because deputy Weehunt had sent him and because he was company through the long, lonely night. The next morning she gave him breakfast—eggs and sausage and grits—and would not let him pay for it; she told him she just felt sorry for the red-eyed man in the wet suit. It was the last regular meal he'd had since the beer and barbecue at the Silver Slipper. With the change he had left in his pocket he'd bought coffee and doughnuts along the way. He slept the other nights in barns, always careful to be gone before daybreak.

It was a bright fall morning, crisp and cold as a Georgia winesap, when he reached the outskirts of Clement. He walked along, bone weary, sniffing the air like a red-bone hound. It all looked the same, he couldn't tell anything was different, the woods and the white frame church with the tin steeple where the colored came to worship. The pond was still out back where they did their baptizing. He knew if he kept on the road it would lead him finally through the town and then to the big, wide streets of fine houses that went all the way back to the Civil War.

But he would turn off long before then to his daddy's old farm. He walked along and it was as if he'd never left; he felt like a child again; it could be his young-boy barefoot prints here in the dust as easily as his man's big shoe prints, so familiar was the road where he'd played as a boy. But the last time he'd been here was when his daddy died, the year after he and Callie married. He'd come back home for the funeral and afterward stood around talking to his brothers and his sister, but none of them touched the other, not even to shake hands when they said good-by. Berryhills rarely touched one another, and they did not kiss. Neither did they travel far from home; most of his family had never set foot outside Georgia. Funny, there would be none of his family at the old place—his sister was married and living in Tennessee and he hadn't seen her since Maribeth was born; his two brothers, both older than he, were dead. He half expected them to run around the curve in the road, little again, shirtless and barefoot, on their way to the creek to swim, wondering who was the man with the suitcase walking toward them.

He sat down in the road to rest, he was in no hurry now. He knew the house his daddy had built and where he was born was around the curve waiting for him. In his mind's eye he saw the grove of water oaks his mother had planted forty years ago, and the rose-of-sharon bushes that grew close around the porch, blooming white and purple. It was a small house, with only three bedrooms and an attic under a gabled roof, but his mother had raised her four children there. His mother had a root cellar, and he remembered hiding there from his daddy, trying to keep from chopping cotton on burning hot summer days.

It was dark and cool in the cellar, and he hid among the jars of jams and jellies, the jars of canned soup and the barrels of sweet poatoes. Dried herbs hung by strings from the rafters —garlic, strawberry leaves and the cool, sweet smell of peppermint leaves. He could still hear his daddy's voice calling to him down those clay steps, hollow, echoing.

"Come on up, son, I know you're down there. Come on up and get your whipping."

Oh, he knew the house was there, all right, knew just how it would look, and he rested long beyond the time of his need; he would postpone as long as possible the joy of setting eyes on home again after all these years. His two old bachelor cousins lived in the house, owned it even, with money and a deed, but they could never own it the way he did, with memories. He knew now it was the only place on earth he still loved. At last he stood up, picked up his suitcase and looked down that red road, his heart beating fast; he did not understand how he had stayed away so long.

He walked fast, and when he rounded the last curve he saw the cotton field in the distance, the stalks bare and drying until spring. Beyond the field was the colored quarter, and beyond that were the woods where he'd coon-hunted all night one night and moonshined the next; his sap ran high then, his limbs were young and strong, and he never gave it a thought that one day he'd be old.

Off to the right was the house, and his shoulders slumped

with relief. It really was there, painted white instead of the brown he remembered, but it was there. He knew he'd really been afraid that when he came around the curve the house would be gone, that there would be only a few boards and scattered rocks from the fallen chimney. That's the way it was with his granddaddy's house, farther up the hill back of their house.

He used to play there when he was little, poking around the ruins, sometimes finding bits of broken plates and rusted forks and spoons. His daddy would come and watch him play and, looking sad, tell him how it was when he was a boy and lived in the house that now lay scattered on the ground.

Snow took off his hat and, shading his eyes with his hand, looked toward the small house. He was still far away and it was hard to see it nearly hidden by the water oaks; that was the biggest change he saw: the trees had grown huge since he had seen them last. Their branches towered high over the roof, their leaves still fresh and green. They would not lose their leaves until spring, the new pushing off the old.

The sun glinted on the tin roof and a strange feeling of unreality washed over him. He panicked and began to run, his suitcase bumping against his leg. What if all he saw was a mirage, a dream that would disappear before his eyes? But when he reached the front fence the house loomed in front of him, and he knew it was real, and all the years up till now were the dream and had faded from his life as if they never had been.

Part Two

1

CALLIE LEFT the steamy wet wool smell of the First National
Bank and pushed through the swinging door onto the sidewalk. She clutched Jo Anna's hand as people brushed past her,
flowed around her, stared because she stood unmoving in the
middle of the sidewalk. Some of them were her neighbors and
spoke, but she did not answer them. She squeezed Jo Anna's
hand, remembering the disinterested stare of the president of
the bank. *I'm sorry, Mrs. Berryhill, but by the first of the year
you're going to have to make up at least three payments,
you're behind six. I can't carry you any longer than that.*

She stood there at the counter, waiting for the weakness to
pass, looking at the back of the president's bald head, at the
fringe of hair that encircled his head like a gray laurel wreath;
his shoulders were round under the dark blue of his business
suit. *But what about how pretty I am, don't you remember
how pretty you said I am?*

He turned around and when he saw her still standing there,
he said, "Why don't you call your husband home, Mrs. Berryhill? You can't make it by yourself."

She left then, holding on to her thirteen-year-old daughter's
hand to steady herself.

They walked to the corner and Callie lost Jo Anna when she met up with Sammy Tancretti. Callie had taken the quarter from her purse and pushed it into Jo Anna's hand, too tired to argue about how scarce quarters were, too tired to try to convince her it would be better spent for food or to help pay the electric bill. It was foolishness to spend money on picture shows, but it was Saturday afternoon and Callie couldn't remember that Jo Anna and Sammy had ever missed the show on Saturday afternoon. She watched them cut across the street holding hands, running toward the theater.

Jo Anna wore the brown tweed coat that Callie had cut down from one of her own. It looked fairly well except for the square cut of the neck; Callie had no pattern and did not know how to cut lapels so she had simply squared off the neck. The coat was funny-looking with no collar and no lapels, but Jo Anna didn't seem to mind, had even come from school one day to tell her that one of the teachers had admired her coat. Callie thought the teacher was making fun and scolded Jo Anna, told her she ought not to let the teacher make fun of her mother that way.

She watched Jo Anna and Sammy until they were inside the theater and then she walked on down the street, lonely without her baby girl. Jo Anna still slept with her, had never moved into Snow's empty bed. When the fears came in the night she moved close to Jo Anna, clasped her hand and was not so afraid with her there. Callie did not like Sammy Tancretti, was jealous of the time Jo Anna spent with him; she also thought him below Jo Anna's class because he belonged to a family that lived in a house attached to their grocery store.

Callie walked on down the street looking in the shop windows. It was two days until Thanksgiving, almost a year to the day since Snow had left. She'd had one letter from him a month after he'd gone. He told her he would have written sooner but he'd been sick with the flu. He said he was at the old home place in Clement, living with those two old bachelor cousins of his. He told her to go ahead and get a divorce if she wanted it, he wouldn't stand in her way because he'd never be back to Birmingham. She didn't even answer the letter. It made no difference to her whether there was a divorce or not, all she wanted was to be rid of him and she had that. Why spend good money for something she already had?

She stopped to look in the dime-store window and hunched down in her coat as the wind blew through the thin material. It was a spring coat, the color of old rose. The saleslady called it a topper. It was beautiful when she bought it, soft and fleecy with only one button to close it at the neck. It had three-quarter-length sleeves and Callie had admired herself without shame in the mirror of the store. She had bought it in the spring after Snow left, when she still had plenty of the insurance money left. It was warm and the flowers were blooming and she thought that winter would never come again, so she celebrated by buying the impractical coat. But finally the money was gone, spent on house payments, clothes for the girls, and coal for the heater and grates. Jo Anna outgrew her winter coat so Callie made over her own for her and continued to wear the spring coat that could not keep out the wind of the bleak, November day.

She looked at her reflection in the plate-glass window and saw her wind-burned face reflected back at her; her hair was as much gray now as it was brown. She looked at all the things in the window she would like to get her girls for Christmas: the manicure set in the corner for Maribeth, the red wicker sewing box for Jo Anna. She saw nothing that she thought would please Lee Rose.

Lee Rose, her strange girl, the one who did not manicure

121

her nails or like to sew. She hardly ever talked, keeping to herself most of the time. But she was pretty—In fact, she was beautiful with her red lips and black hair. Callie tried to get her to fluff out her hair and to wear some beads or earrings, but Lee Rose told Callie just to leave her alone. She listened to the radio and took walks by herself, but only rarely did she go any more with Jo Anna and Sammy to the picture show. She didn't play, either, had turned no cartwheels the whole summer long. Callie had not known that she would be sad when Lee Rose stopped playing.

She moved slowly on down the street, and when she reached the Piggly-Wiggly grocery store, felt faint with revulsion as she stopped to watch a feeble-minded beggar with no shoes on pour syrup onto the sidewalk and sop it up with light bread. She leaned against the building and, even though she was sickened, watched him pour and sop, pour and sop, the thick brown sorghum spreading in a pool almost at her feet. He looked up at her and their eyes met, and when she saw reflected there her own terror she walked quickly away, went into the Puro Ice Cream Parlor and Sandwich Shop to escape him.

She slid into a wooden booth and when the waitress came to take her order, when she said, "May I help you?" Callie wanted to say, *You can help me, honey, if you can tell me where I can get three house payments by the first of the year, and that's forty-five dollars. Royce's insurance money is all gone, honey.*

Callie leaned her head on her hand, giddy from the warmth and the smell of food cooking. She had eaten no breakfast that morning, could not push the warm oatmeal past the lump of fear stuck in her throat. She had hardly slept at all the night before.

She was embarrassed for the waitress to see her have to look in her purse to see how much money she had left after giving

Jo Anna the quarter for the movie. She should not be in this restaurant, she should be walking home to eat lunch, saving every penny she could. Somebody put a nickel in the juke box and the record began to play: *Come on down to Birmingham, come on down to Alabam', come on down . . .*

Stop, Callie wanted to scream, *stop, don't put that nickel in there, give it to me to save for Christmas for my girls*. For a moment she thought she *had* screamed, and she rubbed her hand across her forehead, rubbed away the beads of sweat. She was too hot now and she struggled out of her coat, the waitress leaning to help her.

"You okay, hon'?" the girl asked.

"Yes, I'm all right, just weak from missing breakfast. I'll have a hamburger and a Grapico," she said, closing her purse. There was enough change for a hamburger and a cold drink. "You look tired yourself."

"I *am* tired," the waitress said. "I worked till twelve last night and was back at five o'clock this morning. But you can't say nothin'. The boss tells you to stay till twelve and come back at five, shoot, that's what you do. A job's a job."

"No," Callie said, "you certainly can't complain about a job." She laughed, embarrassed, the heat rising in her face as she asked, "You know any jobs open? I certainly could use a job to make a little Christmas money."

"Those I-talians across the street need somebody. You know, the ones run the dry goods store? Whyn't you go over there and see if they found anybody yet."

"Maybe I will after I eat. You're sure they need somebody?"

"The big fat mama and her husband was over here yesterday and I heard them talking, and that's what they said well as I could make out. *You* know how funny they talk. Half the time they wasn't talkin' in English. Gives me the creeps the way they do that."

123

The waitress scratched her head with the point of her pencil and left; Callie squeezed her hands together under the table. She did not want to go across the street and ask those people for a job, but she knew she would. She looked out the window and saw that it had started to sleet, tiny particles of ice mixed with a few snowflakes hitting the glass. She could not remember there ever being such bad weather before Thanksgiving except once when she was little and it snowed early in the fall. She had gotten up one morning and seen the red and yellow leaves heavy with an October snowfall. It was strange to see trees still covered with leaves covered with snow, too.

Well, she thought wryly, the honeymoon's over. She'd had a whole year of living the way she'd always wanted to live, with no man hanging around the house to boss her, no worries about money. Somehow the twelve hundred dollars she'd had left when Snow went back to Georgia had seemed like such a lot of money, she thought it would never run out. She had been like the grasshopper, never giving a thought to the future, never dreaming that winter would come, but dancing and laughing in the spring sunshine.

She should have looked for a job as soon as Snow left, should have known that four people could not live forever on twelve hundred dollars. But she was not really sorry, not even now, because she had the memories of the past year. If she lost everything, if she never had another thing, she would still have those memories. She'd taken the girls downtown to see the vaudeville shows, had taken them to eat dinner in the Chinese restaurant. She'd drunk a glass of port and she smiled now to remember the girls' big eyes as they stared at their mother drinking wine. She'd given each of them a sip of the cold wine; even Lee Rose seemed to enjoy herself, had smiled and talked to them. Afterward, they'd gone to the Alabama Theater and seen some Walt Disney movie, she

124

forgot now what it was, and sang along with the bald-headed man who played the big, red organ. Oh, those were times to remember.

On a dish in front of her was a hamburger—round, moist with grease, enclosed in its brown bun coffin; there was a frosted bottle of Grapico, blue as ink, sitting next to it. She had no idea when they were set before her. But there they were, waiting to be eaten. She should not have ordered the Grapico, she should have ordered coffee. She needed a good strong cup of coffee to put warmth and strength in her, to give her courage to walk across the street and ask for a job. If she could get a job, then she could borrow from the bank to catch up on her back house payments. The president of the bank had told her so. She needed a cup of coffee to save her house. If she did not get some money soon, the president of the bank was going to take her house and sell it.

She looked wildly around the restaurant for the girl who had waited on her. Somebody still pushed precious nickels into the juke box, nickels she could take and save into dollars. She thought once again that she had screamed and that people had turned to stare at her, their mouths pouched with food.

"What is it, hon', what's the matter, can I get something else for you?" The waitress was there, her pencil poised and ready to write on the order pad.

"I want to change this Grapico for a cup of coffee." Callie laughed apologetically. "I'm sorry to bother you, but I need a good strong cup of coffee."

"I'll get you a cup of coffee, hon'," the waitress said, sticking the pencil behind her ear, dropping the order pad into her pocket, "but you'll have to keep the Grapico. See," she said, pointing to the uncapped bottle, "the cap's gone and we can't sell it because the fizz'll be gone. You understand."

"Just keep the coffee then, it's all right, I'll drink the

Grapico," and she looked out the window once more at the snow falling heavier now. Already, the roofs of the buildings were white, but the snowflakes vanished the instant they touched the wet street. She watched without blinking until the feeling that she was going to cry left her; she was ashamed she felt like crying just because the girl wouldn't take back the Grapico and give her a cup of coffee.

Callie waited until the girl's reflection in the glass moved away and then she wrapped a paper napkin halfway around her hamburger and began to eat. It was something she always did if she had not washed her hands first. The hamburger had grown cold; the relish and chopped onions stung her mouth, the fumes rising into her nose, causing her eyes to water. She ate, the cold lumps of food sliding down into her stomach. She had not eaten since the night before and her stomach felt pinched and cramped from being without food for so long. She washed the cold meat down with the sweet, burning, grape drink and was amazed, as she sometimes was, that this flesh she held in her hands, pushed into her mouth, was down inside her. It was a revolting idea that something that had once been alive, had felt pain or itched or known pleasure, would become a part of her body.

She pushed the thought from her mind. She must eat or else she could not walk across the street and face those people who could control the course her life would take. She ate slowly, chewing each bite completely before she swallowed, picked up each crumb that fell onto her plate. She drank every drop of the Grapico. When she was through, she sat until she felt stronger, the weakness gone from her legs. The clock on the wall behind the counter said three-thirty, and now that her mind was made up that she really would go and ask for the **job**, she felt relaxed.

126

She left the booth, paid the cashier her twenty-cent lunch check, then went to the ladies' room to wash her hands and comb her hair. She felt sick and shaky again from smelling the pine scent of the rest room and splashed cold water on her face. She patted her face dry with her handkerchief and looked at herself in the mirror over the sink. She thought she looked all right, even pretty in the yellow light, except that her hair was too gray, it made her look old. She had been looking for a job for weeks in the department stores but they had smiled and shaken their heads. They said they did not hire anyone over forty.

Callie practiced before the mirror how she would act when she went in the store across the street. She would try for gaiety, the light touch, make them think she was a woman with too much time on her hands, a woman with three near-grown girls who needed something more to occupy her time. She would not let them know that the president of the bank was about to take her house away. She nodded and smiled, inclining her head at her reflection, her lips forming silent words.

She put on her coat and left the ladies' room, waved to the red-haired girl who had waited on her; she went outside, reluctant to leave the warmth of the restaurant. She pressed back against the door, snow swirling around her. A man pushed past her into the restaurant and it was only then that she moved onto the sidewalk. She was freezing cold; the wind blew so hard it rattled the neon signs of the stores and pelted her with sleet that stung her face and tore at the flimsy spring coat. Tonight, after the sun went down, the temperature would drop even more and she thought how near gone the coal was. Last night when she had shoveled it up, she scraped the hard bottom of the garage floor.

It was nearly dusk. Some of the stores were already turning on their outside lights because it was Saturday and they would be open until ten o'clock. Callie liked Saturday nights; it always gave her a good feeling to know that the lights of the business district were turned on, that shoppers came and went from the stores as she lay in bed. She thought she would be glad if her house were set between the buildings and there would be the sound of the people's voices, the lights shining all around her.

She stood looking at the dry-goods store across the street. Fershea's Mercantile, printed in red neon, winked off and on at her, beckoned her. She trembled, and again her lips formed the words she would say, the Grapico burning in her stomach, bubbling among the onions and relish. She walked to the corner and stood waiting for the light to change, glad it was red, wishing it would stay red and that she could simply stand on the corner, forever waiting for the light to turn green. When the Rapture came she would still be standing there.

But then the light winked from red to green and she stepped off the curb and walked across the street. She stepped up the curb on the other side and thought she would turn around and go home. She did not think that at age forty-two she should have to go in that store and ask those Italians for a job. *Where will you go, Callie, will you write to Snow and ask him to come back, tell him you can't make it without him, or will you take the girls and go to Clement and be cook for those three old men?*

She walked up the sidewalk to the store, stood looking in the window at the saddle oxfords and the galoshes and high-top, lace-up boots. Inside the window, behind the display of shoes, a woman, short and black-haired, smiled at her, bobbed and nodded, motioning her to come in. Callie thought she looked like a puppet, a woman hung by strings, so exaggerated

128

were the gesturing and the smiling red mouth. *She wants my money and I want hers.*

Callie went in the store and asked the woman to show her a pair of black oxfords. She did not have the courage to ask for the job, nor would she give these common people the satisfaction of turning her down. She sat down, and black dots, like swarming gnats, swam before her eyes in the glare of the electric light, and she thought she would faint. The woman pulled up a stool and sat down, measured Callie's foot with a wooden measurer, clucking over her corn.

"You been-a wear shoes too tight. Who feet you?"

Callie shook her head, ashamed to let this woman see the holes in her stocking.

"I want to see the manager," she said.

"Whatsa matta, lady, you mad about something? I can feet you, I done something you not like?"

Callie leaned over, putting her shoe back on. She had to ask for a job but not with this woman staring at her big toe poking through her stocking.

"I want to ask the manager for a job. The waitress over at Puro's said you needed somebody."

Callie did not look up from tying her shoelaces. Her face was stinging with shame and from the wind and the sleet that had reddened it, chapped it.

"You wanta *work* here?"

"Yes. I need some Christmas money. I have three girls, I'm separated from my husband."

The woman looked hard at Callie as she finished trying her shoelaces and leaned back in the chair.

"You meana you divorsa?"

Callie stared at the thick, dark hairs on the woman's upper lip, her lipstick bleeding into the hairs in fuzzy streaks. A straight white swath of a part ran through the coarse black of her hair. The woman played with the rings on her fingers, a diamond one that sparkled with electric light and a plain gold one with no stones.

"I'm not divorced, I'm separated."

"Eetsa no good for husband and wife to be divorsa. Eetsa sin."

"Yes, that may be so, but sometimes it's more of a sin to stay together. Are you the manager?"

"No, lady, the woman's not manager, eetsa my husband, *he's* manager."

"I'd like to talk to him then, please."

"I get heem."

The woman went to the back of the store, pushing aside the dark green curtains that hung in the doorway.

There were no customers in the store and Callie was grateful for that. At least no one had overheard to spread the word through the neighborhood that Callie Berryhill was begging a job from Italians. The voices of the woman and her husband came from behind the curtains, loud at times and then fading away.

"Lei e divorziato. Lo non voglio che lavora una divorziato in questa bottega."

"Che fa che lei e divorziato? Appartiene a la chiesa. E Cattolico? No? Basta, che importa."

"Importa che non voglio che quella donna lavori in questa bottega. Molti vorrebero lavorare qua, non abbiamo bisogno di implegar la."

Callie stood up to leave. She would not stay here and be talked about, insulted probably, in a language she could not understand. Just then the curtains opened and the woman's husband stared out at her. Callie stared back and then the curtains closed. She started for the door when she heard him call to her.

"Hey, lady . . ."

The man beckoned to her. She walked toward him, counters of underclothes flowing past her, pink and white rayon panties and white slips with rows of lace ruching; there were barrels of boots and galoshes, the smell of new leather and rubber bringing back her nausea. The floor, moving beneath her, slid to a stop in front of Mr. Fershea. He wore a white shirt with the sleeves rolled up and a black bow tie. He was so short Callie looked down at him onto the top of a shiny bald head. Not a strand of hair grew anywhere that she could see. He chewed a burned-out cigar, the end wet and slick with saliva.

"Mees Fershea say you look for job. We hire our own—niece, cousin, nephew—we hire them first. You come back in two, there weeks and see ifa we have anybody then. *Bene?*"

Callie turned away, not answering him. The gall of disappointment tasted bitter in her mouth, and she felt humiliated that she had been so stupid to lower herself, to allow these people the chance to turn her down. She would never set foot in this store again, would never buy anything from them. She went onto the sidewalk and sucked in her breath as the cold air hit her.

She walked down the street, her hand clutching her coat to hold it together, to keep the wind from blowing it open. She hoped that something terrible would happen to Fershea's Mercantile store, that it would burn down, and she could stand on the sidewalk across the street smiling to see it burn, would warm her hands at the blaze.

She crossed the street so that she would not have to pass by the bank. Even from across the street, she could see people working late in there and thought that they must be busy adding up her debt to them. A streetcar was coming but as she started to run for it, decided that she would rather walk.

The cold air felt good on her face. She walked for a while before she realized it would soon be night; it was not past four-thirty and already it was nearly dark.

She turned the corner and went past the library. It was a brown-stone building nearly covered with ivy. Carved in the stone across the top were the words, *"The fountain of wisdom flows through books."* She thought she should go in and ask the librarian for the book of wisdom that told how middle-aged women could get jobs and she laughed at the startled look that would be on the librarian's face. If there *were* such a book, Maribeth would know where in that building to find it. Sometimes she got off the streetcar at the library after leaving the high school and stayed until it closed at seven o'clock. Callie fussed at her, afraid for her to come home alone after dark, but Maribeth wouldn't mind her; she sat in that building for hours reading books of poetry.

Callie had come to the tall hedges that fenced in the playground of the Catholic Church called St. Augustine's. Ordinarily, if she were alone, or even if she were with Jo Anna coming home late from a movie, she would walk in the street because she was afraid somebody might be hiding behind those hedges, waiting to rob her. But tonight, she stayed on the sidewalk. If someone wanted to take the trouble to rob her tonight, they were welcome to the few pennies she had in her purse.

She was only four blocks from home now. The drug-store lights shone brightly across the street, *Ice Cream and Sundries* flashing off and on. A half block up the hill was the grammar school, its windows dark. A sign across the street said *Highway 78 East*; Callie realized she had never noticed it before, that as many times as she had passed here she had not noticed this was the road Snow had taken home to Clement. She stopped and stood in the shadows of the hedges and stared up that hill, stared at the sign that said *Highway 78 East* and knew she would rather die than travel that road, follow Snow up the hill that led to Clement. She thought about him and wondered if he'd been humiliated as she had been when he was turned down for a job, and for the first time understood how he must have felt. But her mind slid away from the thought; she would not allow herself to have sympathy for him: it had been his duty to find a job, just as now she had to accept this fact. She would not whine or ask for sympathy.

She turned the corner onto Thirty-fifth Avenue, walking faster, half trotting those last blocks home. She went past the houses, cozy with light, smoke pouring from their chimneys, and could not wait to get to her own house. She came to the top of the hill. Running now, she passed the grocery store, and in the distance could see her own porch light. She was so happy she felt like crying because it was turned on for her. Many nights she left the light on for whichever of her girls was out after dark, but she did not remember that it had ever been left on for her. She ran faster, eager to see her children, desperate for the lights of her own house; already she could taste the coffee that simmered steaming hot in the pot on the back of the stove. She would drink her coffee with her girls gathered around her, talking to her, comforting her.

She crossed the street and ran up the steps to her porch, flung open the front door, calling the girls' names over and over, one by one, like beads on a rosary. But the house was cold and dark and she knew she was alone. It was too early for them to be home. Early dark had fooled her. It could not yet be five o'clock, way too early for Jo Anna's picture show to be over, way too early for Lee Rose and Maribeth to be home from the big library downtown. They were studying this afternoon, using the *Book of Knowledge* at the big library.

The porch light was on because she had forgotten to turn it

off last night and Lee Rose and Maribeth had gone off and left the door unlocked. She would tear into them about that when they got home, leaving the door open for any Tom, Dick, or Harry to just walk in and have a good look around the house. She was furious with herself, too, for leaving the light on. She dreaded to see her electric bill this month. What a terrible, foolish spending of money that could have been saved. Still, she left it on now for the girls. She would not have them coming up the steps in the dark, unwelcomed.

Tired and heavy, she went through the house turning on lights. Might as well be hung for a goat as a sheep. Tonight she wanted light, needed light, no matter what the cost. The fires were nearly out in the bedroom grates, so before she pulled off her coat she built them up, pouring on more coal, poking them, coaxing them into a cheerful blaze. Then she went into the kitchen and turned the damper in the flue of the stove and opened the draft, putting in kindling until the front eyes of the stove glowed red. She put the coffee on to percolate; only then did she pull off her coat and sit down at the kitchen table to wait for her girls to come home.

2

AFTER CHRISTMAS, Callie made Maribeth and Lee Rose move into the back room. There was not enough coal left to keep fireplaces going in both bedrooms, the heater in the living room, and the stove in the kitchen. After supper every night they all sat around the fireplace in the back bedroom and listened to the radio. Maribeth could not sleep with the radio on, so Callie had to give up leaving it on until the "Star-Spangled Banner" was played at midnight. The radio helped to keep her from thinking and she was sorry she had to turn it off.

In January Callie made the rounds of all the department stores once again, but there was no job for her. On the way back home she got off the streetcar at the neighborhood stores and went to Kress's and asked for a job. She would do anything, she told them, there was nothing she was too proud to do. But the personnel manager smiled and shook her head; she was kind but said there just wasn't anything for a woman her age.

"You have to stand on your feet all day long, and it just

takes a young girl for that, hon'," she told Callie. "There's a job open but we can get a dozen *young* girls for it. Is your husband out of work?"

"No, my husband has work, I just need a little something to do to pass the time." Then Callie left the store.

She went to the Piggy-Wiggly scared to ask for more credit, but she had it to do. They had been carrying her on credit for two months, and each time she went in and asked the girl at the counter to put her groceries on the ticket she was afraid they would refuse. She bought a nickel bag of butter beans and a sack of cornmeal. The girl wrote out the ticket and Callie was so relieved she was not turned down that she went to the manager's office and asked if there was any work she could do, if there was a job open. She went home and cried with happiness because he had told her to come back on Saturday and work the swing shift because the regular girl was home with the flu. She would sack and check groceries until eleven o'clock Saturday night.

Callie worked from three o'clock in the afternoon until midnight and earned three dollars and seventy-five cents. She was also allowed to take home all the spoiling fruits and vegetables she could carry. She ran down the middle of the dark streets all the way home, the bags bouncing in her arms. The streetcar had stopped running at midnight and she was afraid someone would rob her. The manager of the store had offered to drive her home but Callie thought that wouldn't look right, him a married man and her separated from her husband; people would talk if they found out.

People were sleeping in the dark houses and she longed to wake them, ached to call them from their dreams onto the street, to shout at them, "Look, I've got groceries and money in my purse, isn't it wonderful!"

On Monday she went to the bank and offered the president two dollars on her back house payments but he wouldn't take it. He shook his head at her.

"Mrs. Berryhill, take that money and buy food for those children, then call your husband and tell him to come home, or else you go to him."

"No, I won't," she said, "I won't call him or go to Georgia. Not even if you take my house like you say you're going to do. I'll go up and down the street begging but I won't go to Georgia."

She leaned on the white marble counter, trembling, thinking she would fall on the floor, her legs were so weak. The people in the bank would gather around to gaze down on her as she had gazed at the Negro woman who had a fit in the grocery store last month. The woman had fallen over almost at Callie's feet, her eyes rolling in her head, foam drooling from the corners of her mouth.

It seemed to her that she had spent most of her life leaning on that white marble counter begging for more time. But every time she had come away from there she still had her house.

She left the bank and went to the coal yard down by the railroad tracks. She ordered a quarter ton of coal delivered to her.

"No slag," she warned the man who owned the coal yard. "If there's any slag in there I won't pay for it. I can't burn slag."

Then she went to the grocery store and bought a pound of stew meat. It had been weeks since they'd had any meat. She also bought a can of corn and a can of tomatoes and went home and made a pot of soup. She cut up three of the potatoes they had given her at the store on Saturday, added the carrots and celery they had given her, too. There was nothing like a pot of soup to bring cheer to a bleak winter day. And the smell of coffee percolating. The soup bubbled and the eyes of the iron stove glowed red. She had poured it full of coal against all thoughts of frugalness and caution. She smiled. *I'm still a grasshopper at heart.* By the time the girls came home from school she was gay, with the color high in her cheeks.

After supper they sat around the kitchen table, the soup warm in their stomachs. They played a game they sometimes played, taking turns telling one another what was the worst thing about the other and then what was the best. While the best was being told everyone was happy, the complimented person smiling and pleased, but when it came time to tell faults there was hardly a time somebody didn't stalk off to bed angry. But tonight no one broke the happy mood, not even Jo Anna when Lee Rose told her that her feet were the ugliest thing about her, too big and too bony. Jo Anna smiled and shrugged and they all laughed, soothed and drowsy with food, happy to be together in the warm kitchen.

After a while they walked through the cold, dark rooms to the back bedroom and Callie turned on the radio and sat in her rocker, dozing, waking now and then to watch her daughters studying. Outside it was cold and raining. The First National Bank was closed, its big plate-glass windows blind with darkness, the president gone home. Callie wondered what he was doing tonight in his big house on the hill, wondered what it was rich people did on winter nights. But she would not think about him or the bank tonight. This room, this time was all there was, and she was content, certain that the worst was over. The job at the grocery store was a good sign; there would be other jobs, of that she was sure. Callie slept in her rocker until it was time to go to bed.

The worst was not over. Callie went back to the Piggy-Wiggly, confident that there was sure to be another sick checker, another three dollars and seventy-five cents waiting for her after she worked the swing shift. But there was no sick checker and there was no job. She went back to the dime store and instead of talking to the woman assistant she went straight to the manager and asked for a job. When he told her she was too old she lost her temper.

"I am barely past forty," she told him. "I am a strong woman perfectly capable of doing the job. Your trouble is that you lust after young girls."

The manager's face turned fiery red, as red as his wavy hair, his freckles disappearing under his blush. He turned his back on her, walked away and left her standing in the aisle of the store. Callie walked on home then, but on the way she made a decision: Lee Rose would have to quit school and take the job at the dime store. She was sixteen and had only begun her second year of high school, whereas Maribeth would graduate next year. Maribeth was taking shorthand and typing and could get a job as a secretary if she finished school and Jo Anna was too young to work. It would have to be Lee Rose.

When Callie got home she pulled off her coat and sat at the kitchen table waiting for school to be out. She listened as the streetcars passed and when finally Lee Rose got home she called her to the kitchen and told her what she had decided.

"Lee Rose, one day this house is going to belong to you children. When I'm gone it'll be a haven for you—no matter where you are, you can always come back here. Let me tell you it's good for a woman to have a place to come to, to have property. If you have a place to live you can always scrape up a little something to eat, get along some way."

Lee Rose didn't say anything. Like Snow she had a discomfiting way of looking a person straight in the eye.

"Lee Rose, there's just no other way, you've got to quit school and take that job at the dime store. It's going to take all of us to hold on to the house. When Maribeth graduates she's going to work to help, and then Jo Anna, too, when she gets old enough. Lee Rose, do you mind? You never have seemed to like school much, anyway."

Lee Rose never said a word, but when she got up the next morning, instead of dressing for school as usual, wearing a skirt and sweater and bobby socks and Maribeth's old passed-down saddle shoes, she dressed in her church clothes. She wouldn't eat the oatmeal Callie cooked for her, but she did pour herself a cup of coffee. She didn't ask her mother if it was all right and Callie didn't say anything. If she was big enough to go to work she was big enough to have a cup of coffee to brace herself.

She sat at the table with the rest of them, not answering when Jo Anna talked to her, not looking at Maribeth as she chattered away about the pretty clothes the Silk Stocking Road girls wore to school.

"Mama," she said, "there's one girl that has every color sloppy-joe sweater you can imagine, pink and aqua and blue and yellow. It just makes me sick I can't have even one. Do you think we could charge one at Fershea's? I saw one in there that was only ninety-nine cents; it seems to me I could have just one sweater for only ninety-nine cents."

"Maribeth," Callie said, "if I *had* ninety-nine cents do you think I'd spend it on sloppy-joe sweaters? Here your sister has to quit school and go to work and you sit there talking about sloppy-joe sweaters."

Lee Rose left the table without saying good-by to any of

them and Callie followed her to the front door and watched her walk away down the sidewalk. She wore Callie's pink coat and Callie's hat with the quivering peacock plume. She wore her Sunday black patent leather pumps and stockings. Callie smiled because she looked so much like a little girl playing lady in her mother's clothes.

But she was not playing lady, she was her sixteen-year-old girl going to look for a job and not complaining. But then she never had complained about anything, had hardly ever cried when she was a baby; even now when she was sick, she lay in bed asking for nothing, taking what was offered her. Maribeth and Jo Anna moaned and carried on when they were sick, running Callie back and forth bringing them cold cloths for their heads and broth for their upset stomachs.

Lee Rose was not affectionate, either. Jo Anna often was kissing and hugging and telling everybody how much she loved them. She was quick to anger and quick to make up. Even Maribeth still kissed Callie good night. Sometimes when Jo Anna flung herself on Callie, hugging and kissing her, Callie would catch Lee Rose watching, smiling. Callie would reach to draw her in, would try to hug her, too, but Lee Rose stood stiff and straight, allowing Callie to hug her, but she never hugged back.

After Maribeth and Joe Anna left for school, Callie sat down at the kitchen table to wait for Lee Rose to come back home. Her thoughts ran in circles, full of doubts and what-ifs: what if Lee Rose didn't get the job and what if she couldn't do *any*thing but pack up and move them all over to Georgia? She couldn't let her children starve. But she knew she would rather stand on the street corner with a tin cup than go crawling to Snow, and she dropped to her knees beside her chair and prayed, asked God to let Lee Rose come home with that job.

141

She could sit still no longer, so she washed the breakfast dishes and straightened the house, hurrying through the cold rooms to the warm ones. It was one of the few bright, sunshiny days they'd had in January, but still she could see the vapor of her breath in the rooms where there was no fire. It was nearly noon before she heard Lee Rose's step on the porch. She went to open the door for her. Lee Rose smiled. *You are a beautiful girl, my daughter, even the funny clothes can't hide how pretty you are.*

"Well, look who's here," Callie said, "imagine seeing you here this time of day." She kissed Lee Rose's cold cheek.

Lee Rose took off her hat and coat and they went to the kitchen, and Callie poured them a cup of coffee. At first Lee Rose did not mention the job, whether she had been hired or not, and Callie was afraid to ask her, terrified that she might have been turned down.

"Would you like something to eat, Lee Rose? You didn't have a bite before you left."

"It's all right, they hired me, Mama. I'm going to work behind the sock counter. I work every day until six and on Saturdays until nine. I'll make seven dollars a week."

"Seven dollars a week," Callie breathed, suffused with happiness. "Imagine that, seven dollars a week. You mean you just walked in there and got a job, just like that? It's not fair, you know, Lee Rose, I've been looking for a job for months and they just tell me I'm too old. I don't *feel* old." Bitterness was in her voice. "Make the most of it while you're young because it won't last long. I didn't know *I* was old until somebody told me."

Callie went to the pantry and got the cheese and bread and mayonnaise and made Lee Rose a sandwich. Then she poured each of them another cup of coffee.

"That's twenty-eight dollars a month you'll make, Lee Rose.

You'll have to give it all to me, you know; it's going to take every penny of it to make the house payment. When Maribeth graduates I want you to go back to school, go to summer school even, and catch up and graduate. I want every one of you girls to graduate. I didn't graduate; your daddy came along and I went with him, fool that I was. Not that I regret it. I couldn't regret it, having got you girls out of it. You all have been the blessing of my life, you know that, don't you?"

She set the empty coffee pot in the sink and ran cold water in it.

"I've got to get back down there, Mama. They want me back this afternoon to scrub out candy bins. I only came home to eat lunch and to tell you I got the job."

"They hired you for the sock counter, Lee Rose. No girl of mine is going to scrub out candy bins. You just tell them when you get back down there that you weren't hired to scrub out candy bins."

"Mama, you're not the boss down there. If they tell me to scrub out candy bins, then I'll scrub out candy bins."

After Lee Rose had eaten the cheese sandwich, drunk her second cup of coffee of the day, and had gone back to the dime store, Callie sat down at the kitchen table to figure expenses. She got a pencil and paper and soon the white sheets were covered with numbers added and subtracted and divided.

It would take most of Lee Rose's salary for the house payment, and there was still food to buy and coal to heat the house. Two of the worst winter months were ahead and she would have to buy coal at least once more. She could save the house, but they would starve or freeze to death, one or the other. It looked as if she was going to have to take Maribeth out of school, too, and that was a shame with her having such

143

a short time left before she graduated.

Callie sat for a long time, thinking. They needed more money than Lee Rose would bring in. Finally, she decided to do what she had been thinking of for a long time. The thought she had before let creep only to the edges of her mind she allowed now to come in full blown. She would find a boarder, someone to rent the front room that was going unused. They were living in only two rooms of the house, the kitchen and the back bedroom; the rest of it was just sitting there, unused. That front bedroom could be making money for them, and with Lee Rose working they could make it. She hated the idea of a stranger in her house, cringed from the thought that someone she didn't know, who was not in the family, would be sitting on her toilet, sleeping in Lee Rose's and Maribeth's bed, eating from her dishes. But she would do what she had to do, and once the decision was firm in her mind she felt excited and spent the rest of the day cleaning and airing the front room.

The next morning she walked all the way downtown to the newspaper office. She was scared when she went through nigger town but no one bothered her; the people scarcely looked at the white woman in her spring coat and no hat on her head half running down the rutted, gravel street. No life stirred so early in the morning except the maids who were going to their jobs on the hill. Most of them were dressed better and more warmly than Callie. They wore scarves around their heads and heavy wool coats passed down to them by the white ladies they worked for.

When Callie reached the newspaper office, she leaned on the white marble counter waiting for someone to take her ad. It seemed that most of her life was spent leaning on white marble counters trying to save her house.

Two weeks passed and she had heard nothing from the ad. It was near the end of January, almost the deadline the president of the bank had set for her to make up three of her back house payments. Again, she would have to go and lean on that counter and beg for more time and this time she did not think he would give it to her. Lee Rose had brought home two paychecks that came to nearly twelve dollars after tax, but Callie would not spend a penny of it except for a few groceries. She was saving every dime so that when she faced the president she would have at least one back payment in hand.

One morning, before she had gotten up, there was a knock on the front door. Callie got out of bed and put on the old blue bathrobe Snow had left behind. She quickly brushed her hair, then went to the living room and peeped around the window shade on the front door to see who was knocking so early in the morning.

A man was standing on the porch wearing a brown derby hat and a brown suit. In the thin, pink light of dawn his shoes shone with brown polish and a gold watch chain gleamed on his huge stomach. He stood straight, unmoving, his arms slack at his sides, as if he knew he was being watched. Callie opened the door only an inch or two.

"Yes, what do you want?" she asked.

At once, the man took off his hat and half bowed to her.

"Good morning," he said.

"Good morning."

"There was an ad in the evening paper," he said, and he unfolded a half-torn sheet of newspaper as if to prove it to her. "See, right here, a room with board."

"You're here about the *ad*?" she asked.

"Yes, indeedy, I surely am. I only hope the room's not been rented."

"I'd given up on the ad, that was two weeks ago—"

"I've been away on vacation, visiting my sister. I saved the ad, hoping the room wouldn't be rented—"

"No, it's not been rented." Callie opened the door wider. Her hand moved automatically to make sure the screen was latched. "But I can't rent to a man. I suppose the ad should have said so," and she was annoyed with herself for having left out that bit of information. "There's only women here, me and my daughters, and it wouldn't be proper to have a man in the house that's not related."

"You're a widow then."

"Yes," Callie lied, "I'm a widow. My husband's been gone over a year now."

"Well, then, that makes it all right, doesn't it—a widow woman properly chaperoned by her three daughters. And I have good character references to show you. If you'll allow me to come in?"

"I hoped to rent to a schoolteacher or a working girl—" and her voice slowed, considering.

"I'm a railroad man, madam." And he took a white envelope from his inside coat pocket. "If you'd care to see my references?"

When she heard the words "railroad man" she relaxed. Railroad men were honest and trustworthy—hadn't her own uncle been a railroad man?

"Come in," Callie said at once, and unlatched the screen and stepped back to allow him in. "There are no finer people on earth than railroad men. My maiden name was Braden. Maybe you know my uncle, Henry Braden? He was with the Southern Railroad for years."

"I'm with L&N," the man said, stepping just inside the

146

door, "but I believe I've heard the name." He thrust out his hand to Callie. "My name's Arthur Foote."

"I'm happy to know you, Mr. Foote," and when she shook hands with him was pleased that his palm was not hard and calloused like Snow's.

Arthur Foote's smile wrinkled his face and his stomach shook with good humor. Callie thought he looked like Santa Claus and she was happy he wanted to live at her house. Suddenly, she was embarrassed for this handsomely dressed man in his suit and white shirt to see her in a man's old bathrobe, her bare feet sticking from beneath her gown.

"I'm Callie Berryhill," she said, and hurriedly sat down, hiding her feet beneath the folds of the gown.

He sat on the sofa and Callie sat in the chair opposite him.

"I'm asking five dollars a week for the room and that includes board. I hope that's not too much."

She was worried, ready to back down on the price if he frowned or shook his head when he heard the large amount she was asking.

"No, no, Mrs. Berryhill, the price is more than reasonable. The lady that runs the rooming house on Thirty-third Street asks seven and a half a week. I inquired there more than a month ago but it's full up now. I was about to give up finding a place close to the depot when I saw your ad in the paper. I think I'm very lucky."

Callie wished she had asked seven and a half, too, but it was too late now to go up on the price.

"Your letter says you're a conductor, isn't that nice." She nodded her head knowingly as she read the letter of introduction. She did not want him to think she had no business sense about her so she read every word, though it wasn't necessary, him being a railroad man.

"Everything's in order," she said, handing back his letter.

"I'm a bachelor, Mrs. Berryhill," he said, folding the letter and putting it back in his pocket. "I'm set in my ways, you might say; I'm rigid, my sister says. I'm in town four nights a week, the other nights I'll be out on a run, but when I'm here I want my meals strictly on time and when I'm sleeping I want the house quiet."

"I think the girls and I can make you comfortable, Mr. Foote." Reluctantly, she added, "It'll be nice to have a man in the house again." She looked down at her hands clasped in her lap, ashamed because That was the second time she had told a lie within the short space of fifteen minutes. "I suppose I'd better show you the room before you decide for sure, it could be you won't even like it." And she laughed to show him what an absurd idea it was that he might not like the room she had worked so hard to make attractive.

She led him into the cold bedroom. The room was spotless, the bed freshly made and covered with a white bedspread. She had furniture-polished the wardrobe and washed all the woodwork; she had mopped and waxed the floor. Maribeth and Lee Rose had taken their clothes out of the wardrobe and hung them in the back bedroom closet with hers and Jo Anna's.

"The room's cold, Mr. Foote," she said, "because I haven't been making a fire in here," and she indicated the empty grate. "I have to be frugal, and if a room isn't used I don't heat it. Of course, there'll be a fire in here if you rent the room."

Arthur Foote walked all around the room, opened the wardrobe doors and looked inside, sniffing. "Cedar," he said, nodding approval. He pushed on the mattress, then sat on it, the side sagging low with his weight. Then he went to the window and pulled aside the sheer, white curtains and looked onto the street.

"It's a fine room, Mrs. Berryhill," he said, turning back to her. "I'm glad to rent it and I'll pay a month in advance."

He pulled his billfold from his back pocket and riffling through some bills selected a twenty. "If it's all right with you I'll pay you on the first of each month. This being the end of January, this twenty will take care of February."

Callie did not argue, though she knew he was getting the best of the bargain. Paying every week would have meant more money for her, but she did not say anything. She had not seen a twenty-dollar bill in so long she had forgotten what it looked like. Her knees went limp with pleasure, her hand trembled as she reached to take the money. She smoothed it in her hand and thought that she would cry because with this twenty, and the ten that she had managed to save from what Lee Rose gave her, she could make two house payments. She could face the president with two payments instead of one. When Lee Rose got paid again on Saturday she would buy food.

Callie turned from Arthur Foote as the tears came. She did not want him to see her cry, so she knelt in front of the fireplace as if she were blowing away soot from the hearth, pretending the soot had gone in her eyes. She wiped her eyes on the hem of the wool bathrobe and wished Lee Rose would give her all the money she earned at the dime store but Lee Rose would not. She kept a dollar for herself to eat lunch at Puro's every day and sometimes she even bought things for herself, some rayon stockings and a pair of red-glass earrings. Callie fussed at her and told her to come home and eat, but Lee Rose wouldn't, and neither did she buy presents for anyone else.

Callie and Arthur Foote went back to the living room and she told him to have a seat while she went to wake the girls. She wanted him to meet her girls before he left. She went to the bedroom and turned on the light. Lee Rose lay vulnerable

149

in sleep, her jaw slack, her eyes twitching with some dream she would never tell anyone. Maribeth slept with her arm across Lee Rose, her silky, brown hair set in tight pin curls all over her head.

Callie leaned over them, shaking them gently, calling to them. They stretched and she went to yank the cover off Jo Anna. You had to make Jo Anna mad to wake her up, she slept so heavily.

"Wake up, wake up, Maribeth, Lee Rose, and Jo Anna," she singsonged to them. "Christmas came late this year, but it finally came and guess who's in the living room. It's Santa Claus."

Maribeth woke up immediately, tense, alert as she always was, ready to face the day, but Lee Rose groaned and pushed further under the covers. Callie shook her again and thought how much she loved her, how much she depended on her. Once she started to tell her, started to tell her how much she appreciated her going to work to help save the house, wanted to tell her how much she loved her, as she always told Maribeth and Jo Anna. But Lee Rose had looked her so straight in the eyes, waiting, unsmiling, that Callie had fussed at her instead for wearing too much purple lipstick and spending her money on cheap earrings. Callie knew that when she lay dying her last regret would be for the things she had never told Lee Rose.

"Wake up, my darling daughters," she said, and pulled the cover once again from Jo Anna. Jo Anna screamed with rage and Callie went to the grate and started to shake down the ashes, poking at the coal still softly glowing from last night's fire. She stuck bits of kindling among the embers, and when it looked as if it had caught and would burn, she went to sit on the side of Maribeth's and Lee Rose's bed.

"Get up, all you chillun'," she said, clapping her hands like a child on her birthday, "because Santa Claus came last night. He's in there in the living room, sitting on the couch. The reason we didn't have any Christmas was because he lost his way. And *look* what he brought us." She unfolded the twenty-dollar bill she pulled from the pocket of her robe.

Callie was not disappointed at their response: their jaws dropped, their eyes were six satisfying round "O's."

"*Ma*ma," Jo Anna whispered, grabbing for the money, but Callie laughed and jerked it away.

"*You* all thought that Santa Claus comes in December but *I* know he comes in January. If I'd had this money in December we'd have had something for Christmas dinner besides beans."

"Mama, *what* are you talking about?" Jo Anna begged. "Quit acting silly and tell us where you got that money and what you're talking about."

Maribeth groaned and fell back on the bed.

"*I* know what she's talking about. She's rented my room, that's what she's done. Some constipated old maid school-teacher is going to be sleeping in my bed, that's what."

"It's Lee Rose's room and Lee Rose's bed, too, Maribeth," Callie said, "and I don't hear her complaining. Those that do the least, yell the loudest, seems to me. And it's not a schoolteacher, it's a railroad man, and he didn't look the least bit constipated to me."

"Don't be crude," Maribeth said.

"You were the one said it first, or can only mothers be crude?" Callie said. "Anyway, he's in the living room and he wants to meet all of you before he leaves."

Maribeth rolled her eyes heavenward.

"I *hate* being poor. One of these days I'll leave here and I'll live in a nice house with rugs on the floor and have a gas stove like the Coxes. I think it's *common* to have some strange person living in our house, sleeping in my bed and using our bathroom. Besides, Mama, you can't have a man living here with Daddy gone. What will the neighbors say?"

"I told that man I'm a widow—now don't say anything, just hush," Callie said when they protested. "He's an old bachelor and I know he wouldn't stay a minute if he knew I have a husband. I also know that if he doesn't rent the room nobody will, so just keep quiet and he'll never know the difference; he's gone most of the time, anyway. None of the neighbors even ask about Snow any more."

Lee Rose pulled the pillow over her head to shut out the sound of their voices, so that she could not hear them talking about her father as if he were dead. She'd dreamed many times since he'd been gone that he *was* dead, and in her dreams she cried, but when she awoke her eyes were dry, there were no tears. But her head hurt.

Her head hurt most of the time, a light, tiptoeing throb behind her eyes that she noticed hardly at all, and then again the headache became so fierce that she saw flashes of light and was sick at her stomach. It was during those times that she had to go to bed and stay home from work and then her pay was docked for the lost time. The next time she had a headache and went to bed, Callie grieved so over the lost money that Lee Rose had gotten up and walked to the dime store, her head pounding each time her foot jarred against the sidewalk. She stood behind the counter the rest of the day, automatically waiting on customers, the row after row of pink and blue and yellow socks blurring into a prism of rainbow colors.

She pressed the pillow tighter over her ears and wished her father was back home again; she did not want a strange man in the house. A long time ago, she got Jo Anna to write a letter to Snow and ask him to come home, but they never got an answer. He was gone for good; Lee Rose knew that now, but still she missed him, especially the sound of his snoring, his cough in the night that she had always been aware of even as she slept, but that never waked her. It was like the story the library teacher at school had read to them, about how the Chinese kept crickets in tiny cages to warn of thieves. The crickets sang all night unless a stranger entered the house and then they stopped singing, and in the silence the sleepers woke and were warned of danger.

Lee Rose had not slept well since her father left. Sometimes she dreamed he had come back, and on the edge of sleep struggled to hold the dream, wanted unreality to be truth; when finally she woke she knew that even though she slept in his bed, it was Maribeth beside her.

"Lee Rose," Callie said, pulling the pillow from off her head, "get up, you'll be late for work. Maribeth, Jo Anna, *all* of you hurry up and get dressed because I want you to meet Mr. Foote, he can't wait around all day."

Callie went back to the living room to talk to him while they dressed. They shivered around the fire that flamed and burned bright but that had not yet warmed the room.

"Quit hiding behind your nightgown, Maribeth," Lee Rose said. "I know exactly what you've got, I've seen you bathing lots of times when Jo Anna and I look through the transom at you."

"*Mama,*" Maribeth yelled, "come in here."

Callie appeared in the doorway making motions toward the living room, hissing at them to be quiet.

"Mama, you make Lee Rose and Jo Anna quit spying on me. It is im*pos*sible to have one bit of privacy around this house—" and Maribeth yanked Lee Rose's hair, then shoved her.

Lee Rose stumbled over the coal scuttle that sat next to the grate and grabbed the poker; just as she was about to smash it over Maribeth's head a voice spoke to them just outside the bedroom door.

"*Stop* it girls," the voice said.

From the shadows appeared a man with hair so white it glistened even in the half light. The poker stopped in midair and Maribeth and Jo Anna scrambled to cover themselves with their nightgowns, but Lee Rose stood there wearing only her slip.

"Girls," the man said, his jolly face pulled into tight lines of disapproval, "my name is Arthur Foote. I'm moving into your front bedroom and I must have absolute quiet every morning because it will be late when I get to bed. I'll need my meals on time, strictly on time, and for twenty dollars each month and four women in the house I don't expect I'll have much trouble with that?" and he smiled, waiting for an answer.

All of them stood watching him. The wind blew down the chimney, sending soot swirling into the room; the tank factory blew its seven A.M. whistle.

"I know with your Daddy gone it's been hard," he said, "but I've come to help now and I know we'll all get along fine." He smiled again, his merry eyes twinkling at them.

Slowly Lee Rose lowered the poker. Already she despised this soft, pudgy man who thought that for twenty dollars a month he could take her father's place.

"Up yours," she said to him.

3

Arthur Foote moved into the front bedroom, bringing with him his conductor's uniforms packed in a green canvas zipper bag with "L&N Railroad" stamped on the side in gold letters. Callie hung his two uniforms in the wardrobe for him, touched her hand lightly to the gold stripe down the side of the trouser legs.

For a while they were all polite with him, subdued. They played the radio low or not at all when he was there, and Callie put a lock on the door between the two bedrooms; that meant Mr. Foote had to go all the way around through the rest of the house to get to the bathroom, but he didn't seem to mind; at least he didn't complain.

When he'd been there a few weeks everybody relaxed, and Mr. Foote even joked with Jo Anna, seemed to like her best. He had nothing to do with Lee Rose; he ignored her as if she weren't there. On the nights he wasn't out on a run he ate supper with them and when they were through eating told them stories of the places he'd been, the things he'd seen. He brought back the old longing Callie had as a girl to travel someplace far away, as far away even as Washington, D.C. She'd always wanted to see the President, had pictured herself watching him as he walked across the green lawn of the White House. The farthest she'd ever been in her life was over to Georgia to meet Snow's people.

Arthur Foote had only one flaw that Callie could see: he liked to eat every bit as much as Snow did, and was more particular about what he ate. Snow liked plain food, one never mixed with another, but Arthur Foote liked fancy food, casseroles and rich desserts. He let Callie know right away that he did not like boiled beans, so she got out her old cookbooks and borrowed Maribeth's magazines borrowed from the library. She read all the food ads and gradually she learned to cook the kind of food he liked without having to spend much money. She intended to keep Arthur Foote full without having to dip into the money she put away each month for her house payment. But Callie did not mind cooking for him because she got paid for it, and that, she found, made it worth all the trouble.

Winter passed, and when spring came Callie would not allow herself to think of the nightmare of the past months. All that was over now—Lee Rose had a good job, and on the first of each month Arthur Foote handed her a twenty-dollar bill. There was nothing about her life she would change; the days slid by, one much like the other. She worked in the yard and cooked and after supper at night sat on the porch, relaxed and content.

It was one night at supper that Callie found out that things were not so peaceful, so uneventful, as they had seemed to her. Mr. Foote did not like conversation at a meal, he said it distracted him, kept him from full concentration on the food. The only comments made were by him. Sometimes he discussed the rough texture of the cornbread or the superb smoothness of the chocolate pudding.

Jo Anna was chattering away about some happening at school and did not appear to notice that Mr. Foote had stopped eating and was waiting for her to stop talking. After a while Callie left the table and in a moment called to Jo Anna from their bedroom.

"Jo Anna," her voice sang sweetly, "come here a moment, I *need* you."

When Jo Anna went to the bedroom, Callie grabbed her and shoved her into the closet so that Mr. Foote could not hear her fussing.

"So long as Arthur Foote is paying twenty dollars a month, we'll have supper without a word, or dance in the middle of the table if that's the way he wants it. "But Jo Anna pushed past Callie and stood in the middle of the room glaring at her.

"Lee Rose gives you just as much money as he does and you don't let *her* boss everybody around and tell us we can't talk at the table. He's come in and taken over and people are talking about us behind our backs. Sammy says he hears talk at the store and people say it's disgraceful him living here when you still have a husband."

"Nobody trades at that store but colored and Italians. And brick-yard trash. Nobody that counts for anything talks that way—besides that boy made all that up anyway."

"He did not make it up. Sammy says people talk about Lee Rose, too, that Morgan Greer was in there the other day and he called Lee Rose an awful name."

"What did he call her?"

"A whore, he called Lee Rose a whore."

"You stop talking like that, Jo Anna. I don't care what that big-eyed brick-yard boy said, you ought to be ashamed to

157

repeat such things about your sister. He's a common boy and she had no business dating him in the first place."

The next day Callie went to the bank and made her house payment and the president smiled at her as she handed him the money. After he had given her a receipt and she was headed back home, suddenly she made a left turn instead of a right and went across the park, taking the path that led around by the brick yard. After a while she was on the sidewalk that led into the white-trash neighborhood.

It was only just past noon but children played on the hot sidewalk. Some of the yards were decorated with old wagon wheels propped against a tree or against the house. The houses were small, they had only front stoops, there were no screened-in porches as in Callie's neighborhood. All the houses were built from the same plan, they were all alike. Some of the yards had old tires that were made into flower beds; white and lavender petunias sprouted from their centers.

Callie walked slowly down the sidewalk looking at the houses, but there were no names on the mailboxes to identify the people who lived there. The children stopped playing as she passed, were utterly still as they watched the strange woman in the pale lavender voile dress walking down their street. They did not recognize her so she did not belong there.

A group of boys was shooting marbles, shirtless and barefoot, in the early summer heat. Their hair had been cut so short, the bumps on their heads showed the pale, unhealthy gray of their scalps; they knelt around the circle, the sun glinting on their shooters and agates and cat's-eyes. Callie stopped to ask them where the Greers' house was, and there was the strong odor of their sweating heads.

"Who wants to know?" one of the boys asked. He was a skinny boy of ten or eleven, dark-skinned and knotty-headed.

"Callie Berryhill wants to know," she answered. "Do *you* know where the Greers live, son?"

"Hell, I ought to, my name's Freddy Greer."

"Well, Freddy, would you show me which house it is?"

He pointed to a cream-colored house next door. The paint on the house had almost all peeled away, the front yard was patched like a crazy quilt with crabgrass and clover and some kind of pink flower that Callie could not identify. The flowers grew at random, with no pattern, as if someone had thrown the seeds out the window, not caring what they were or where they landed.

"Is your brother Morgan at home?"

"He's down to work at the brick yard."

"Is your mama home?"

"She's home, but Daddy's home to lunch and Daddy don't want nobody bothering him when he's home to lunch with Mama."

Callie looked at the house and saw that the shades were down, there were no signs of life. She thanked the boy and walked across the yard to the Greers' front door. She knocked and waited but there was no answer. She knocked again. And again.

"Ain't no use, lady," the boy called to her, "Daddy don't *never* come to the door when he's home to lunch."

Callie knocked again, harder and louder. This time the door opened and a young woman was standing there dressed only in a slip that was dirty gray from too many washings. Coarse black hair fell around her shoulders, her skin was dark like her son's. She had large brown eyes and Callie thought that she was pretty, as common young women sometimes were; but she had no breeding, no culture in her bone structure. It didn't matter how pretty she was, bones would always tell. When she got older her flesh would flatten like putty, there would be no strength or shape to her face.

"My name's Callie Berryhill," Callie said. "I came here to talk to your son but since he's at work I'll talk to you instead."

"What d'you want to talk to Morgan for?" the woman asked, her eyes narrow with suspicion.

"Morgan insulted my girl. He called my sixteen-year-old girl a name that I doubt she even knows the meaning of."

A man's voice called from back in the house.

"What in the *hell*, Grace, are you doin' standin' there talkin' when you *know* I got to be back at the yard in ten minutes. I'm fast, but I ain't *that* fast."

The woman sighed and shrugged and rolled her eyes.

"Burt, he comes home ever' day to get some. Christ, I get tired of it, ever' day right at noon, rain or shine, but Burt says he cain't make it through the day unless he gets a little."

"*Grace*," Burt yelled.

A baby, not more than a year old, toddled from the shadows back of the woman and held up his arms to his mother. She picked him up.

"Balls," the baby said, fingering his diaper.

"I got to get on back to Burt," the woman said. "What did you say Morgan did? He called somebody a name?"

"He called my girl a whore," Callie whispered, loath to say the word. She did not want the boys shooting marbles to hear.

"Now why'd he do that?"

"I don't know why he did, but you tell your son Morgan that if he ever even looks sideways at my girl again or if he ever speaks to her or comes in our neighborhood I'll call the police. He has no business in my neighborhood."

"Say, *I* know who you are now. You're the woman got the

old geezer living with her." She smiled as if she shared a secret with Callie. "Yeah, Morgan told me about you. My God, Burt'd kill me if I did somethin' like that, I don't care if we was separated. He says what's his is his. But he's got lots of money, huh?"

"Grace, goddamn it, I said *come in here*," Burt bellowed. "Now I got *five* minutes before I got to be back."

Callie thought she would die of shame before she got off their front porch. She ran down the steps away from the low, common woman who had talked to her as if she were her equal, had even discussed her with her common son. A battered old pickup truck came down the street, creaking and wobbling, the back end filled with a bunch of children. They yelled at Grace still standing in her front door.

"Hey, you're a nigger, ain'cha?"

"You little bastards, you come back here and say that, I'll skin all of you," Grace yelled, setting the baby down with a plop on the front steps. She chased the truck down the street until it turned the corner and was out of sight. Burt stood in his undershorts in the front door waiting for her.

In the changeable weather of early summer, Maribeth got sick. She caught a chest cold and ran a fever and Callie doctored her for a week. Just as she was getting better, Lee Rose and Jo Anna came down with it. Lee Rose missed a whole paycheck because she was not allowed any paid sick leave. They were sick another week, and Callie was tired and depressed. She had not worked in the yard at all and the grass was high, the bushes needed trimming. One afternoon, about dusk, when they were all just about well again, Arthur Foote asked Callie to go for a walk with him. He took long walks every night after supper.

"Come on, Mrs. Berryhill, it'll do you good to get out of the house for a while," he told her.

She put on a clean housedress and combed her hair and when she looked at herself in the mirror saw that there were gray hairs that were not there a year ago. She dabbed on a touch of pink lipstick, pinched her cheeks to make them rosy. She did not like to look so pale and tired.

She walked through the neighborhood with Arthur Foote, up and down the streets, until finally they climbed the long hill that led to Silk Stocking Road. She had not been here before. She had heard Maribeth talk of it. Maribeth had friends who lived here; Callie was uneasy and thought the people who lived in the big houses perched on the high terraces were peeping from behind their curtains at her, shaking their heads with disapproval because she walked down their streets with a man who was not her husband.

They strolled along the sidewalk, passing a dark red brick house with bay windows; the name on the mailbox was that of the president of the bank. She hurried along, she did not want him to see her on his street. The sounds of laughter and talk were coming from his front porch; it sounded as if there were many people, as if they were having a party. She walked faster and Mr. Foote puffed along behind her. If the president came out he would speak to her, might even ask her how Snow was doing over in Georgia.

They came to the street behind Callie's house and when they reached the top of the hill at the golf course, it was full dark. They stood on the soft, thick grass and the wind blew and the night was warm and sweet with the smell of flowering trees and bushes. A mockingbird still sang and, all at once, Callie took the notion to run down the hill as fast as she could go; the wind rushed past her ears, her heart pumped hard with the joy of being alive.

She was a young girl again, visiting over in Georgia right after she and Snow had married and she had made him take her at nine o'clock at night to climb Stone Mountain. When they had gone a long way up the mountain, she took Snow's hand and challenged him to a race back down, but he wouldn't run with her so she had run alone and stood waiting for him at the bottom.

Now she waited for the cumbersome form of Arthur Foote to catch up with her; she was elated, the years dropped away from her like old clothes she had discarded. She pulled off her shoes and through she stockings the cool wet grass pricked the soles of her feet; in a moment she would lie on her back and look at the stars. She had forgotten how it felt to be so happy.

Arthur Foote stood next to her.

"I believe you have your shoes off, Mrs. Berryhill." His voice was thick with disapproval.

Callie looked down at her feet sunk in the grass.

"Why, yes, I guess I do." Suddenly she was ashamed for being so foolish, her shoulders heavy, drooping with disappointment that he did not share her happiness.

She stooped to pull on her shoes and wondered why she was so disappointed. After all, she had not really expected a man nearly sixty-five years old to race down the hill after her, to pull off his shoes and dance with her in the summer night. But she *had* expected it, just as she had wished for Snow to share her joy, to run with her down Stone Mountain. *The voice of my beloved: behold, he cometh leaping upon the mountains, skipping upon the hills. My beloved is like a roe or a young hart . . .*

He talked to her as they walked slowly home, told her again of the places she had never been to, would never see: St. Louis, where Royce had died, Louisville, Chicago, Miami. When she was a little girl she had ridden the train. She had gone with her mother from Seddon to visit her grandfather, her mother's father, in the hospital at Birmingham. He was an old man and she didn't know him well, he'd only been to see them a few times. The doctor left a stitch in his stomach after removing his gallbladder and he'd died from gangrene.

She remembered him holding out his hand to her, and the skin was wrinkled, the fingers like birds' claws; she hid behind her mother's skirt, afraid of the shrunken old man who talked to her in whispers. After she was grown, she felt guilty when she realized how much she must have hurt him. She wished that her mother had never taken her to that hospital. Whenever she thought of her grandfather, she saw the long, dim-lit halls of the hospital, smelled the faint odor of his bedpan.

Arthur Foote did not invite Callie to walk with him again. But she did not mind, their living arrangement suited her; he was gone most of the time and when he was there he bought extra food for the whole family. He had a sweet tooth, and often brought home bakery cakes and pies and round steak that he asked her to country-fry.

She hacked at it with a butcher knife until it was tender, and when she had floured it and it was bubbling and steaming in the big iron skillet, she pulled back the curtains and made sure the windows were opened wide so the steam would float outside toward the Coxes' house. Might as well let Chester and Birdie know the Berryhills could have steak as well as anybody else.

As the summer passed, Maribeth and Jo Anna began to like Mr. Foote. Jo Anna even met him at the streetcar stop each afternoon and walked home with him; Maribeth brought home books from the library to read to him because his eyes were bad—a cataract smoked the pale blue of his left eye. He liked books like *Freckles* and *The Keeper of the Bees*. Sometimes Maribeth read to him late into the night, stopping only when he nodded, his head drooping against his chest.

But Lee Rose didn't like him. She was barely civil to him; she answered if he spoke to her and that was all. Once he told her to help her mother, to go and set the table for supper.

"You're not my father, you can't tell me what to do. Besides, I bring as much money into this house as you do." Then she went for a walk and didn't come home until bedtime.

When Mr. Foote was there, Callie sat with him on the porch and they were comfortable together, like an old married couple. She was happy because she had all the advantages of marriage without having to sleep with a man: there was plenty of food, her house payments were made on time every month, the president of the bank smiled on her. Sometimes Mr. Foote sent Jo Anna to the drugstore for ice cream; he bought each of them a whole pint. Before they finished eating, they were lisping because their tongues were nearly frozen. That was much the pattern of their whole summer. It was long and easy and predictable and that was what Callie liked most; she did not have to wonder what would happen to her and her children from day to day.

It was toward late September that Callie noticed many strangers in the neighborhood. People walked past the house whom she had never seen before.

"Mr. Foote," Callie said, "have you noticed the woman that just went by? She's been by here at least three times. Why do you suppose she keeps going by?"

"Curiosity, I suppose," he said. "That's what people do most things for, they're just curious. I'm new in the neighborhood and they want to get a good look, I suppose."

"Why, you've been here nearly a year, and, besides, those aren't people from around here. I've never seen those people, except for Mrs. McNabb, she's been passing by, but she's nosy, always nosing around trying to find out something."

She thought they might be people from the Baptist church, but they did not look like the refined white-gloved ladies who had visited her, who had come to her house and sat on her sofa and looked around her living room, their eyes darting here and there.

"My *good*ness, isn't everything nice," they'd drawl and invite her to church.

When she didn't go to church, the white-gloved ladies were followed by the black-suited deacons, and finally, after Snow had left, she'd been honored with a visit from the preacher. He'd read to her from the Bible and told her she would burn in hell if she did not accept Christ as her Saviour.

"My religion is my private affair," she told him. "There are many ways to worship the Lord. I do not have to sit each Sunday morning in a red brick building to worship the Lord."

He shook his head with pity for her.

"Your children have no father to guide them, they need the firm, strong hand of a man. The Bible commands wives to obey their husbands."

"My daughters go to church, I have always sent them to church. When they are grown, they may choose or not choose to continue. As for obeying my husband, never in this world will my girls ever see their mother minding some man, that is, unless I lose my mind and need a father again like some idiot child."

The preacher took off his glasses and blew his breath on

them, took out his white handkerchief and polished them. When the glasses sat once again on his nose he said, "Let us pray."

After that, no one from the church had visited her again. For that matter, no one at all visited her; Callie was polite to her neighbors around her, but she had no friends nor did she want any. Her children's companionship was all she needed, her work in the yard fulfilled her as no friendship ever could. She talked with Birdie Cox over the back fence when they were both in the yard, but they never went into each other's house. Birdie had come right out once and asked Callie if she and Snow were divorced; no doubt she had spread the word through the neighborhood that she and Snow were still husband and wife.

Arthur Foote went on a three-day run to Augusta and Callie stayed in the house with the front door closed because every afternoon those people began walking past the house. Jo Anna said they were brick-yard people, were Holy Redeemers.

When Mr. Foote came back he was angry and puzzled when they came along the sidewalk to stare at him.

"I don't understand it, I don't understand it at all. Haven't these people around here ever seen a boarder before? That widow over on Thirty-third Street takes in boarders; there're two men among them and nobody bothers her."

One afternoon some children were brazen enough to run right up on the porch.

"Mrs. Berryhill's a *har*lot," they yelled, and Mr. Foote jumped up from his chair and chased them away.

"Get off this porch and stop tormenting Mrs. Berryhill, she's a good woman, what's wrong with you people anyway?"

"Whoremonger," they called to him, "you're a whoremonger," and they ran back down the sidewalk.

Mr. Foote went in the house, slamming the front door. He

lit his cigar inside for the first time. He paced up and down the living room.

"I don't understand it," he said, "it just doesn't make any sense to me. How come those people are acting like that?"

Callie had it on the tip of her tongue then to tell him that she was married, that Snow wasn't dead at all. But even as the words formed in her mouth, she stopped. Without a doubt, when he found out her husband was living, he would leave and there would be no more twenty-dollar bills on the first of every month. If he left, Maribeth would have to quit school and go to work. And yet she knew that even if he didn't find out about Snow, sooner or later he would leave because he was a man who loved routine and comfort and now that was spoiled for him. Already, he was unable to indulge his favorite pastime, and that was to sit on the porch and watch the cars go by.

Callie knew he was only staying now because he hated change so much and because he had no place else to live.

4

LEE ROSE LAY on her back in the deep grass of the golf course; she stared up through the thick matted branches of the tree and listened to the roar of the twittering sparrows as they went to roost. The night was soft around her, the sound of the birds filled her head, blotted out somewhat the ache behind her eyes.

Norman lay beside her, the sweet, passionate, virginal Norman lay beside her, and then he raised himself above her to kiss her. She endured, tried even to enjoy, the softness of his lips, but finally he sighed and lay back in the grass.

"You don't like me to kiss you, do you?"

"No. It doesn't matter, I don't care."

"You know that I love you."

"That's what you told me."

"You're not dating Morgan Greer any more?"

"No," she lied.

She wished that he would be quiet; when he talked her head ached worse, she could not concentrate on the roosting birds.

"I want you to *promise* me, Lee Rose, that you are not dating Morgan Greer."

She was bored with his questions, sorry now that she'd

brought him with her to the golf course. It was the first time she'd brought anyone here with her. But Norman loved her, he said he had loved her since the day he hired her to work at the dime store. Norman was the manager and he saw to it that she didn't have to do the harder work that the other girls did, like scrubbing and polishing the glass on the counters. Neither did she wash candy bins any more.

"*Do* you promise, Lee Rose?"

"No, I don't promise, I do what I want to do. I'm seventeen and I don't expect to stay around this town much longer; one of these days I'm going away."

She knew that she worried him, that his lips trembled when she said that she was leaving. In the light of the full moon she saw the boyish curve of his cheek; when he was old he would still look young, his face would always have the fullness of youth. She brushed her hand lightly over the thick curly hairs of his arm.

"You're so young," she said. "You're the youngest thing in the whole world."

"I'm older than you, I'm old enough to be manager of the store." He pulled her to him, kissed her eyes and her cheeks, her throat. "You're so beautiful, there's nobody else as beautiful as you—"

She smiled at his eagerness, the way he trembled when he held her and she pressed close to him, strained to love him back. But there was nothing, he was just a boy, unreal, someone she never thought of unless she was with him. His hand touched her knee and she straightened her legs, brought them close together. She would not let him make love to her; Morgan was for making love.

"Let me love you, Lee Rose, only pretend you love me—"

She pushed him away from her. "You talk too much of love," she said, and she sat up and wound her dark hair to the top of her head, pinned it in place. "I'm not at all a lovable person, how can you talk of loving me so easily? Morgan says he loves me too, and when we're in the park I unbutton my blouse—"

"*Shut up*, I don't want to hear it, I don't want to hear it," and he clasped his hands over his ears like a child.

"—when I unbutton my blouse he touches my breasts—"

"*Shut up*," he shouted, and flattened his hand to slap her.

She was surprised that this mild boy could be so violent, yet pleased, as she always was, when she hurt him. Violence did not suit him; his slightly built body quivered under his anger like the fragile limbs of a willow tree trembling in the slightest breeze.

"Did you know my father?" she asked, and his hand fell limp to his side.

"No," he whispered, and he would not look at her. "You don't care that I love you, that all these months I've cared for no one but you. You're so rich in love you can just throw it away, Lee Rose?"

In profile, his shoulders slumped, his white shirt was luminous in the moonlight. She thought him no more than a shadow in the grass beside her; when the moon went behind the clouds he would disappear, blending into the dark around her.

"My head hurts most of the time," she said. "I lie in the dark and I'm in my father's bed, only it's my sister next to me. When I press my face into the mattress I can smell him, the way he used to smell, like dirt and sweat and sunshine. I can see him in my mind and he's realer than you are, and I hear him laugh the way he used to do when I ran to meet him."

He was still and waiting and then she pulled him down next to her. They lay on the grass together and she linked her arm through his, clasped his hand.

"My mother has a man that sleeps in her front room and she takes walks with him and she laughs with him, they sit on the porch and rock and my mother cooks for him like she never would for my father."

She turned on her side to stroke the back of his neck, ran her fingers across the silky waves of his hair.

"I dream about my father, that he's come back home. I dream that I wake up and he's standing there in the door of the bedroom and he says in a deep, gruff voice, 'Who's been sleeping in my bed?' and I sit up and laugh just like I did when I was little and he read to me, before Jo Anna was born. I jump out of the bed and run to him and he throws me in the air and I scream because I'm afraid, but he's so big he won't let me fall—"

"Why did he leave, Lee Rose?"

"Because Mama made him leave, she told him he couldn't live in her house and she told us lies about him the night he left, terrible, wicked lies, and then she brought that man to live with us, and Maribeth says the lies she told are true, but Maribeth lies too, she's Mama's pet—"

The boy lay close to her, it was too hot a night to lie so close together and she could not bear the touch of him. She moved away from him and she was exhausted, heavy; she felt as if she were sinking into the ground.

"Mama likes money, that's all she thinks about. She sits at the dining-room table figuring, all the time figuring and writing numbers on white pieces of paper that she wads up and throws away. She sits there night after night drinking coffee and figuring. If she lost the house then we'd have to move over to Georgia to be with Daddy—"

She wished she'd stop talking; she did not want to tell these things to Norman, but she was tired of loneliness. A long time ago she tried to love Jesus, to have Him for her friend. She went to church and sang His love songs, but in the end she grew bored with Him and the preaching and the good people of the church. And that's when she'd found Morgan.

One night after church he was there on the sidewalk waiting for her. He was a brick-yard boy, but he came to their church even though a lot of the people didn't want him there; they said he was common. But he was handsome, a big boy with his sleeves rolled above the muscles of his upper arm, his black hair glinting in the light that shone from the church windows.

He was walking up and down the sidewalk that night, smoking a cigarette. When she came down the steps he took her by the arm and walked away with her just as if that's what they'd been doing every Sunday night, just as if it were the natural thing to do.

He took her to the park and they sat on a bench under a tree; he told her he'd been watching her for a long time, that she was the prettiest girl he'd ever seen. He smoked another cigarette and then he kissed her. She let him touch all the cold parts of her; when he pulled her down to the grass she didn't resist, she let him make love to her. She was detached and unresponsive, but during the passion of his lovemaking he told her over and over that he loved her, so she went with him after church every Sunday night.

She was never afraid of becoming pregnant: there was no seed that would grow in her; her womb lay like a green love apple, hard and cold, in the pit of her stomach.

The moonlight filtered down through the leaves of the tree, dotted their faces and their arms, speckled the black grass with bursts of light. The birds were quiet, asleep now; she heard only the restless fluttering of their wings, the scrape of leaves, as they moved on the boughs. The world was splendid with

173

light, it lay on the ground like a blanket of snow, the leaves of the trees turned silver. Lee Rose disengaged herself from Norman and sat up.

Many times she came here and sat in the dark on a high hill and looked at the tiny lights of her mother's house far away. The part of herself that she used to be sat on that hill, the wind blowing on her face; always she liked the wind in her face. At those times she was happy, the ghostly triangle flags fluttering from the greens, the voices calling to her, speaking to her: *Come with us, lost girl, to gray fields and dark woods where summer never ends, where wild flowers bloom in endless summers—*

Norman stood up.

"It's time to go home," he said.

She stood beside him.

"If you married me you wouldn't have to work any more, there'd be children for you to take care of—"

"No, thanks. I don't want to get married and I don't want any children to take care of." She began to walk slowly down the hill.

Norman walked beside her. Softly she said, "On Saturday night they're coming to Mama's house to run that man away—"

"Who's coming, Lee Rose, what are you talking about?"

"The Holy Redeemers are coming. Morgan promised me that this year they'd come by Mama's house on the way to revival and they'd run that man away who sits in Daddy's rocking chair, who sits in his place at the table—"

"Lee Rose, you can't do that." He gripped her arm, turned her to face him. "You can't do a terrible thing like that to your mother, bring that trash to her house—"

She shook loose his hand and continued walking.

"How can you be so cruel," he said, "so casual, Lee Rose?

Why don't you talk to your mother, tell her how you feel—"

"No, I won't talk to her, she wouldn't listen. Besides, there's nothing to say." In a while they were at her front steps, their shadows long in the moonlight.

He stood on the sidewalk outside her house until she had gone inside and shut the door.

5

THE SUMMER PASSED away slowly, a dying old friend that Callie longed to see gone. He took way too much time about it, late September hotter than mid-July; in his death throes he rallied and the apple trees bloomed white again, and the roses too, their red blossoms drooping in the hot, dry heat. Summer was a corpse, painted and laid out, ready for the burial.

Callie stayed indoors most of the time hiding like a woman who knows she's guilty, yet not knowing what crime she has committed. In the smothering heat she wished for cold weather because then everyone would have to stay indoors close to their fireplaces and heaters, too occupied with chopping kindling and bringing in coal to be concerned with her affairs. In another week it would be October and she hoped that then the weather would turn cold. She remembered Octobers so cold there was ice on the animals' watering buckets every morning.

She despised cowering in the house, waiting and helpless, while those trashy people tormented her. She wanted them to go ahead and do whatever it was they planned to do—it was the suspense of waiting that was worst of all. She longed to run onto the porch and scream at them when they passed by, tell them to leave her alone, she'd done nothing wrong, but she would not give them the satisfaction of making her lose her temper. She was too high-minded to explain herself to them.

So every morning she worked early in the front yard before it was time for them to begin passing her house. She dug in her flowers, pulled weeds, and though outwardly calm, she was afraid and shaken, wondering what was their purpose.

Sometimes when there were no more weeds to pull or no more bushes to move, she sat on her front steps and drank a cup of coffee, pretending that everything was the same, that nobody at all cared that Arthur Foote lived in her front bedroom.

She thought it peculiar how everything got started so suddenly; Arthur Foote had lived there a long time before people started caring that he did.

It was the last day of September on a Friday afternoon that Callie sat in the living room listening to the afternoon news on the radio. A pot of beans was boiling on the stove; the smell of them filled the air, sickening her. She wished she could raise the windows and air out the room but she dared not; school was out for the day and then the children would come to run past her house and yell insults at her. So she would leave the windows closed and soon would pull down the shades and turn the radio up loud to drown out their voices.

Afterward, when they had left, she would sit alone in the kitchen and eat her beans and wait for Jo Anna and Maribeth

to come home from school. When they had eaten, she would fix
Mr. Foote's dinner for him, would mash his potatoes and fry
his steak. Mr. Foote was not happy, he did not eat supper with
them any more. Callie missed all of them sitting around the
table with him, missed the long evenings when they had sat together on the porch.

She heard the children coming along the sidewalk now, and
she squeezed her fingernails into the palms of her hands,
braced herself for the taunts that were sure to come; she sat
rigid in her chair, waiting. She waited for a long time, but
when there was nothing, no shouting, trampling children on
her front porch, no rapping on the glass at the door, she went
to look out the window. There was no one, the children had
gone on home. All was quiet except for the clatter of jays
fighting in the fig tree at the side of the house.

She looked as far up the street as she could; heat waves
shimmered, a white dog crossed the street, a sparrow was
taking a dust bath in a flower bed, but there was no child
anywhere. Disbelieving, she watched the hot, deserted street
and behind her the radio droned on.

There was some news about Hitler invading Russia, and in
the weather report the newscaster said the temperature had
reached 101 degrees that afternoon, that it was the hottest
September since 1905. Tomorrow was expected to be hotter.
No rain was in sight for Jones Valley or for Magnolia Hills.
Puzzled, Callie turned from the window and switched off the
radio. Why hadn't the children come to holler at her, why
weren't they even now throwing rocks at the house and
screaming insults? They had grown bored with it, as children
will, she thought, their attention directed somewhere else
now. Suddenly, she was suffused with happiness and felt like
dancing around the room because they were no longer interested in her; from now on they would leave her alone. Instead

of eating, she would go to sit on the porch, she would eat her supper with Maribeth and Jo Anna tonight.

She opened the front door and the fresh air was the sweetest balm; she breathed deeply over and over again, erasing the smell of beans. As she sat in her chair on the porch, a fan-shaped leaf fell off her sycamore tree and she thought that never before in her life had she longed for winter, never before been so glad to see fall.

It was too sad in fall with the fading trees, the dying flowers; it brought back too hard the memories of people gone, people lost to her forever: her mother, her father, Royce, all the cousins she had played with when she was growing up. All of them gone, the years stretching away behind her were filled with ghosts, their voices came to her in the dark when she lay in bed or sat late on the porch. They spoke to her, sometimes loud, sometimes so faint it was only whispers she heard over the creak of the rocking chair. She cried then, longing to see them again. *What's the matter, Mama? Oh, I'm just feeling blue tonight, Jo Anna.*

It was four-thirty before the streetcar stopped at the corner and Maribeth and Jo Anna got off and came up the sidewalk. Callie decided she would eat later with Mr. Foote, and when they came up on the porch she sent them on inside to fix their supper. She was happy, but still felt uneasy as she rocked and watched the empty street. By now, there ought to be children jumping rope, boys kicking a football back and forth or shooting marbles under the trees; still, it had been such a hot day, the children were probably being kept inside, waiting until the sun went down.

Whatever the reason, she was grateful for the quiet. It might be that she and Mr. Foote could sit on the porch tonight; maybe she would talk with him about the offer of marriage he had made her several weeks ago.

179

"I won't talk of love," he'd said; "I'm too old for that, but I do think we could take care of each other, there'd be companionship in our old age."

Callie was surprised he would even consider marrying at his age, and she didn't fool herself that it was anything more than he said. His eyesight was failing and he was terrified that one day he'd be blind. All the family he had was one older sister. Callie had thought the proposition through, and what it meant to her was that Lee Rose could go back to school, and she would not have to worry about her house payments each month. The idea was tempting, but if she decided to marry him, she would first have to think of a way to divorce Snow without Mr. Foote finding out.

At dusk, the streetcar stopped and Arthur Foote got off. He came walking up the sidewalk with a white bakery box, the string hooked over his finger. Callie stood up from her chair and waited for him by the steps. A gay mood suddenly struck her.

"Mr. Foote," she said, "don't go in the house just yet, wait until later to eat. Do you know that nobody's passed by this house all afternoon? I do believe that everybody's finally gotten tired of looking at my boarder, isn't that a shame? Let's sit on the porch and watch the moon rise." She took him by the arm and led him to his rocking chair.

Arthur Foote set the cake on the bannister, lowered himself into the chair and took off his hat, fanning with it. Then he took a cigar from his vest pocket. When he lit it, the match glowed in a streak of light as he tossed it away over the bannister. The smoke hung in the air and Callie decided she liked the smell of it as she never had Snow's Bull Durham tobacco.

They sat quietly rocking, not talking; the faint night breeze brought with it the smell of the night-blooming primroses that grew bright yellow around the front steps.

Inside, Maribeth was listening to Sammy Kaye on the radio and Jo Anna was in the bathroom washing her hair. She washed her hair all the time, every night or two, using up Lee Rose's shampoo that she brought home from the dime store. Jo Anna was going steady with the Tancretti boy, though Callie didn't know why they only now started calling it "going steady." Jo Anna had never dated another boy and Callie didn't like it. There was no reason not to like the Tancretti boy, he seemed nice enough, and she admitted to herself that the reason for her dislike was that the Fersheas had refused her a job when she needed it so badly. She thought his kind of people were all alike: they were clannish and stuck together.

Callie and Arthur Foote rocked and the motion of their chairs moved them closer together until the arms of the chairs scraped; they laughed and pushed themselves apart again. The streetlights came on and a streetcar turned the corner heading back for town; Callie thought it was full of people on their way to the picture shows. Once she went to the picture show with Jo Anna on a Friday night and the movie theater was full. But now she never went anywhere with Jo Anna any more, Jo Anna went everywhere with the Tancretti boy. Soon he'd come down the sidewalk to pick her up, and they'd walk away together in the night, going wherever it was that they went.

She sighed and knew it was time to go in the house and cook Mr. Foote's supper, wondering if she would ever be able to call him Arthur, as he'd asked her to. Sammy Kaye was going off the air, so it must be seven o'clock; she stood up to go in the house and when she looked up the street she saw a faint light flickering over the hill toward the steel mill. At first, she thought it was the flame from the smokestacks pouring into the sky; then it streaked and disappeared and she thought it must have been a falling star. She watched, and after a minute it appeared again, weaving and glowing, a shapeless mass of light that seemed to move closer.

"Look, Mr. Foote, on the hill toward the steel mill," she said. "What's that light?"

He stood up and leaned on the bannister next to her, looking up the sidewalk. The light flared brightly in the next block, and as it came closer they saw a crowd of people behind the light, at least fifty or more. They were singing:

"Onward Christian soldiers, marching as to war, with the cross of Jesus going on before . . ."

"Why, I do believe that's the Holy Redeemers on their way to revival," Callie said. "They start their tent meetings this time of year. You ought to hear them when you pass the park, they sing and talk in languages you can't understand. It's enough to make your hair stand straight up. They're common as dirt, all of them, it's them that's been passing the house to stare at you—"

Silently, people up and down the street came onto their porches when they heard the singing. The weaving, bobbing crowd of people came closer, and when they were about three houses away Callie saw that it *was* the Holy Redeemers and that they were led by their preacher, a tall, gaunt-faced man carrying a lantern.

"—Onward then ye people, Satan's host doth flee . . ."

Callie was furious. Imagine them having the nerve, the gall, to march through *her* neighborhood. They marched to tent every year at revival, but never through her neighborhood. Her face burned with anger as she watched them, the beam of light from the lantern swaying back and forth with the preacher's steps. She did despise those people, forever going around witnessing, trying to save souls, minding other people's business. Not long ago in the Piggly-Wiggly, one of those Holy

Redeemer women came up to her and took her by the arm.

"Are you saved, sister?" she asked Callie.

Callie had jerked away from her, turned her back on her.

"Jesus holds you, sister," the woman said.

The crowd marched forward soundlessly now and when they came to Callie's house they stopped; they swayed back and forth, they seemed as one person, their shadows long and eerie in the light. They were filled with God's spirit; they were, in fact, dangerously close to their heavenly climax when they would fall to the sidewalk, writhing and chanting.

"Go on, *shoo*, get *out* of here," Callie yelled at them, waving her hands at them. "This is Callie Berryhill's house, you people move away from in front of my house—"

Maribeth and Jo Anna came onto the porch to stand with her.

The preacher left the sidewalk and climbed the steps, dared to come all the way onto the porch.

"Get *out* of here!" Mr. Foote bellowed, shaking his fist at him. "This is private property you've come on, sir, we'll have the police on you if you don't get off this porch—"

"Leave my house," Callie said, "you're scaring my girls—" and she pushed them behind her, Maribeth and Jo Anna, out of the light. The smoke from the kerosene lamp choked her, bringing tears to her eyes.

"Let's go inside, Mama, please." Maribeth was pulling at her arm.

"Sister," the preacher said, "I am a messenger of the Lord. Your children have nothing to fear from me. You're living in sin, sister, with a man not your husband."

"Mrs. Berryhill is a good woman, sir," Mr. Foote said, stepping forward out of the shadows. "She is a widow who has done her best to raise these girls properly. She sends them to church and she is living in sin with no one."

The preacher held the light high to shine on Arthur Foote's face.

"Brother, this woman has a *living* husband," he said. "I have read that it is better for a man to spill his seed on the ground than to put it in a whore's belly, and I am here to tell you that your immortal soul is in danger of hell fire. 'Vengeance is mine, saith the Lord.' "

Nothing moved; it was suddenly deathly quiet. There was only the white and startled face of Arthur Foote in the flickering lantern light.

All at once, the preacher dropped to his knees, and the Holy Redeemers began to sing again; their swaying grew faster, more frenzied.

"Heavenly father," he prayed, "cleanse this woman, though her sins be as scarlet, You can make them whiter than snow—"

Numb with fear, Callie pressed close to Maribeth and Jo Anna. She clasped their hands and wished she were not so ashamed, so afraid, wished she knew something brave she could do to show her girls and the neighbors that she was an innocent, wronged person. But she only stood there watching the tableau unfold; it seemed she watched from far away, that she was no longer a part of what was happening.

A man left the crowd and came onto the porch, leaning to whisper in the preacher's ear.

"You better come on now, brother Sid," he said, "some of them out there are just before passing out. We better get them on down to the park and into the tent. You remember last year the police said if we didn't keep them in the tent when they got like that they'd arrest us—"

The preacher rose hurriedly from his prayer.

"It wasn't such a hot idea coming here anyway, Harold," he said. "Whose idea was this anyway?" and he ran down the steps and led his flock away down the sidewalk.

184

When they were out of sight, when all that could be seen was their light flickering away into the distance, Callie went to sit back down in her rocking chair. Her legs would hold her up no longer.

"Just go back inside," she said to Maribeth and Jo Anna, "go on inside and don't let grownups' business worry you. Go do the things that children are supposed to do."

They went inside and, for once, Jo Anna did not argue with her. Arthur Foote still stood by the bannister, his back to her. For a long time he stood there; they said nothing to each other.

"The moon came up full tonight," Callie finally said. "I haven't seen the moon this big and round in I don't know when."

Arthur Foote turned to her then.

"Is it true what the preacher said?" he asked. "*Do* you have a living husband?"

"I don't know, he may be living and he may not, I haven't heard from him in nearly two years."

"Why did you lie to me? Would you have married me and never have told me that you already had a husband?"

"I don't know what I was going to do, I hadn't decided yet."

He cleared his throat to speak again, changed his mind and went into the house. The light came on in the front bedroom, shone through the window onto the porch. The stars came out, shiny and glittery as the pieces of glass Lee Rose used to save. Callie sat rocking in her chair; her eyes burned from the kerosene smoke and her throat ached with rage. In the morning she would go to the police station and have all those people arrested; she would laugh as she watched them all loaded into the police wagon and hauled away to jail. She would have her revenge on them; if she had a gun she would go to the park now and shoot them all, could see the round holes in their heads just like in the pigs Snow used to shoot—

Mr. Foote came onto the porch. He carried his suitcase and he walked past her without looking at her. He went down the steps holding onto the post to steady himself.

"Good-by, Arthur," she called to him, but he didn't answer her.

Callie went to the bannister then and watched him cross the street, watched until he was out of sight. It was then, for the first time, that she thought she would cry; apart from the money he gave her each month, she would miss him; already she was lonesome for him. It was the first time in her life she'd known companionship with a man. She was deeply grieved that she had lost his approval, that he no longer thought well of her.

She sat back down in her chair and brushed Arthur Foote's burned-out cigar off the bannister onto the grass; his white bakery box with the cake inside was still there. She thought it must be a rum cake, they always were because that was his favorite. The screen door creaked and Maribeth and Jo Anna crept out.

"I'll go to work like Lee Rose, Mama," Maribeth said. "Don't let those common people worry you, everybody in the neighborhood looks down on them, knows they're common—"

Jo Anna put her arms around her mother.

"It'll be all right," Callie said. "As long as we stick together we'll be all right. Just hold your heads up and go on about your business, act like nothing at all happened—"

After they had gone back inside, she sat staring at the empty sidewalk where only minutes before the Holy Redeemers had gathered; she felt no anger now, only languor and sadness and disappointment. And anticipation. She was waiting for something else to happen, only she did not know what it was. The tank factory had just blown its eight-o'clock whistle when she saw Lee Rose appear out of the shadows across the street.

She leaned forward, watching her, her heart beating hard. It was Lee Rose she was waiting for; she knew without a doubt when she saw her that it was Lee Rose who had sent the preacher to her house that night. She hated Arthur Foote, had never wanted him there. Callie felt the sweat come out on her forehead, her chest so tight it was hard to breathe; she trembled, though the night swam with heat.

"You're home late tonight," Callie said, as Lee Rose came onto the porch.

"Yes, I know I'm late. I had to get my counter ready for Monday."

"Would it be news to you to hear that the Holy Redeemers came here tonight and accused Mr. Foote and me of living in sin?"

There was no answer from Lee Rose, only a taut waiting.

"Those trashy people ran Mr. Foote away, Lee Rose; he wouldn't stay here any longer when he found out Snow was living—"

"He's really gone then?"

"Yes, he's really gone. I hope it makes you happy—"

Lee Rose went inside, but Callie didn't follow her. What use?—the damage was done, the good times over. Maribeth would have to quit school and get a job; she could not wait to graduate next June, to be a secretary as Callie had dreamed for her to be. Trouble, always trouble lurking in the shadows, waiting its chance to jump out and pounce on her. But behind her was the comfort of the familiar rooms of her house, there was always that.

The Tancretti boy came and she sat and watched him and Jo Anna walk away down the sidewalk headed for the picture show. Still she did not go inside, she sat rocking and watching the lights go out up and down the street as people went to bed. Finally, there were no lights at all except for the street-lights.

She wished that she could sit forever in the dark, that day would never come. But after a while she took the rum cake and went inside and threw it in the garbage. Then she locked up and went to bed.

6

ON A SUNDAY AFTERNOON in December, Jo Anna and Sammy sat huddled close together on the last row of the Delmar Theater. They were huddled partly for warmth, for the theater was cold and drafty, but mainly to embrace each other, to push their hands between the buttons of their heavy coats and feel the warmth of the other. The theater on Sunday afternoons was filled mostly with teenagers who had come to neck.

Jo Anna and Sammy still went to the movies on Saturday, but they came now on Sundays as well, because it was a part of growing up. Jo Anna knew they were old enough for the Sunday movies before Sammy did. She told him she was tired of nothing but cowboy movies and silly things like Abbott and Costello. She said she wanted to see the grown-up pictures on Sunday afternoon and Sammy agreed, as he always did to anything Jo Anna wanted him to do.

All week Jo Anna looked forward to those afternoons on the last row of the theater necking with Sammy. As Sammy grew older he grew handsome too, though he didn't seem to realize it. The girls at school looked boldly at him, tossing their long hair, flirting with him, but he didn't seem to notice that either.

He was tall, his hair was thick and curly, and he wasn't puny any more; Jo Anna was jealous of the girls who bumped into him deliberately in the halls at school.

Sammy kissed her now and she sank against him. His lips were cool; he unbuttoned her blouse and there was the clasp of his hand on her breast. She'd had to show him how to do that; at first he thought it was wrong of him, but she made him understand that it was all right since they loved each other. Bright thrills of pleasure ran through her stomach, but then the usher came down the aisle playing the bright spot of his flashlight up and down the rows of seats. They sat up straight again, they did not want the usher leering and grinning at them. Sammy coughed and took out his handkerchief to cover his mouth, and Jo Anna was scared, she hoped that the cold and dust of the theater would not bring on an attack. He hardly ever had attacks any more, but last summer she'd tried to cure him for good. Lee Rose had seen an ad in the paper about a faith healer who was coming to the fairgrounds and she told Jo Anna that's where she ought to take Sammy. Lee Rose said the faith healer could probably cure Sammy and, just as when they were little girls together, Jo Anna believed what Lee Rose told her. She had made Sammy get on the streetcar and go all the way across town with her. . . .

The faith healer preached in a huge tent, bigger than the one the circus was in when Callie had taken them in the spring after Snow had left. Jo Anna thought there must be at least five hundred people in the tent; they had heard the singing as soon as they stepped off the streetcar. All they had to do was follow the wheelchairs and the people on crutches to find their way.

Inside the tent, they found two chairs nearly at the back

and sat down, embarrassed when people stared at them, and afraid too of all the sick and deformed people gathered there. It was a horror convention—people shaking with palsy, faces cut away; there were the blind and the crippled, the deformed with their backs twisted, their heads swollen, misshapen. Sickened, Jo Anna half rose to leave. Sammy was not grotesque like these people; she looked at him sitting there, his face grim, unsmiling.

"Maybe Reverend Porter can cure you, Sammy," she whispered, taking his hand. "It's worth a try, isn't it, to be well? Just don't pay any attention to the others." She had come this far, and they would stay to see if the preacher could help Sammy.

There was no piano, no musical instrument of any kind. In the front a man stood on a raised wooden platform leading the singing. He tried without success to keep the shuffling, milling crowd of sick people on key. They sang the same songs Jo Anna sang at the Baptist church, "Let Him In" and "Let the Lower Lights Be Burning." There were no songbooks, but Jo Anna knew the words, as did most of the people there; those who didn't, moved their lips anyway and muttered along with the singing. Jo Anna nudged Sammy to sing and then remembered that he had never been in a Protestant church before; he could not join in the singing even if he wanted to, which it was plain from the scowl on his face he did not.

The tent was close and sweltering hot, and the man leading the singing, his pop eyes shining, told them:

"If you think this is hot, folks, just think what it's going to be like in Hell," and the crowd shouted, "Amen."

In the stagnant air of the tent was the strong odor of fever and old bandages crusty with sweat and pus, bandages that should have been changed days ago. Many children were there lying in their mothers' arms, their legs in braces, some of them with swollen heads that seemed too big for their bodies.

The song leader shouted, "Let's sing 'There is a Balm in Gilead,' " but no one seemed to know the words to that one, so the crowd hummed along, sounding much like a huge swarm of bees, while the leader sang a solo:

Sometimes you feel discouraged and think your work's in vain,

And then the holy spirit revives your soul again.

There is a balm in Gilead to make the wounded whole,

There is a balm in Gilead to heal the sin sick soul.

Jo Anna thought he needn't look so smug for knowing the words; after all, he was the only one there with a songbook.

A wrinkled old woman in a green crepe dress with a dimestore cameo fastened at the neck was walking up and down the aisles, wandering around among the crowd. Her stockings bagged around her ankles; her yellowed, gray hair was wispy, sticking out around her head like a halo. She smiled and talked to people as she moved along, patting them, touching them. She came to where Sammy sat on the aisle.

"Are you saved, boy?" she asked.

He would not look at her but stared at his hands clasped in his lap.

"Go away," Jo Anna hissed at her, "go away. He didn't come here to see you, there's nothing you can do for him."

The old woman leaned close to Jo Anna and a few inches from her face stuck out her tongue, pink and pointed, through her toothless old gums. Jo Anna was so startled she laughed, and the people around her glared at her, muttered at her, and she was afraid of them; she looked down at her lap, linking her arm through Sammy's. The old woman crossed over to the other side of the tent.

After the congregation sang "Throw Out the Life Line

Someone is Sinking Today," the faith healer came through a flap door in the side of the tent. He climbed onto the wooden platform, and the song leader wiped his neck and forehead with a white handkerchief and sat down on a chair in the front row. A stillness settled over the people gathered there, and from where she sat, Jo Anna thought the faith healer didn't look like much, thought he looked too much like an ordinary man to do such miraculous things as healing people. She had thought he would wear flowing white robes, looking much like Jesus with a light shining all around him. But he was short and skinny, with a big Adam's apple showing through the open neck of his sport shirt. He wore a black suit and carried a big, black Bible.

He stood there on the platform waiting, and when there was complete silence, except for the fretful cries of babies and children, and the rush of traffic on the highway only a few yards from the tent, he raised his arms to heaven and shouted so suddenly that Jo Anna jumped, startled at the huge voice coming out of the small man.

"Be *healed*, be *healed*," he shouted, and then he lowered his arms and told them all to bow their heads and to join hands with one another.

Jo Anna knew how Sammy hated to touch strange people, but she saw that he obediently placed his hand in the hand of the man's hand who sat next to him. A young woman held Jo Anna's hand; her face was red splotched, her bottom lip swollen and bloody from biting it. Jo Anna was uneasy, wondered if the woman was diseased and if so if it was catching. She must remember to wash her hands as soon as she got home.

"Peace," the faith healer said, "is floating like stardust over our city. Close your eyes and feel the peace of God as it filters through the fabric of this tent. If you will let God come in, *I will cast out devils in His name.*"

193

The people shifted and murmured, turning their faces toward heaven, willing the Spirit to heal their wounded, diseased flesh.

"Oh, yes God," the crippled man behind Jo Anna cried, "I can feel your healing hand," and the faith healer, his face blood red with the fire of God, raised his clenched fists to heaven.

"Be *healed*, be *healed*," he cried, his eyes squeezed shut.

He lowered his arms and waited. When they were all quiet again, he spoke to them in a voice so low Jo Anna had to strain to hear what he said.

"There are those here," he said, "who resist me, who resist the will of God. I command you,"—and his voice rose once more to a shout—"to open your vile and wicked hearts and let Him come in, to lie prostrate at His feet, kiss the hem of His garment and *then* you will be healed."

About halfway up the aisle a woman stood up and threw down her crutches, and when she did, fell onto her hands and knees. She crawled up the sawdust aisle to Reverend Porter's outstretched hands, and when she reached the platform the faith healer held down his hand to her and raised her up. She kissed the cuff of his trouser leg and then he lay a white square of cloth over her hair; his fingers squeezed into her head and he called on God to heal her of her paralysis, as God raised Lazarus from the dead.

"Some of you here might as well *be* dead, hadn't you, the shape some of you're in; isn't that right, you might as well be dead? But God can change all of that, can take away the curse He's put on you."

He opened his Bible and read:

"Take away the stone from the place where the dead was laid, and Jesus said, Father I thank Thee that Thou hast heard me. And when He thus had spoken, He cried with a loud voice, Lazarus, come forth. And he that was dead came forth, bound hand and foot with graveclothes: and his face was bound about with a napkin. Jesus said unto them, Loose him, and let him go."

He closed his Bible and shouted to the woman who clutched his arm, trembling before him.

"Be *healed*, woman, I command you to be healed."

He pulled her hand loose from where she clutched his arm. She stumbled back down the aisle, staggering, but on her feet, and she was crying and shouting, "Praise God, praise God." The congregation shouted "Hallelujah, sister, hallelujah."

The woman who sat next to Jo Anna, the woman whose hand Jo Anna had held, moaned and half fainted in her chair, jabbering words Jo Anna could not understand; her head rolled onto Jo Anna's shoulder and, frightened, Jo Anna pushed her away. People shouted and went down the aisle to kneel at the preacher's feet. A boy went, about ten or eleven years old, and the preacher gently lay his hand on the boy's dark hair.

"What's the matter with you, son?" he asked.

The boy reached in his pocket and brought out a hypodermic needle and a bottle of insulin and showed it to the preacher. The preacher clasped the boy's shoulder and closed his eyes.

"In His name I cast the devil from this boy, in His name I command this child to be well again."

The faith healer stooped to look into the boy's eyes.

"Do you believe me, boy? Is the devil gone from your body? Did Reverend Bob get rid of that old devil or did he not? Answer me, boy."

The boy looked uncertain, and he turned to search in the crowd for the face of his mother. The faith healer snatched

195

the hypodermic and the bottle of insulin from the child's hand. He broke off the needle and flung away the bottle.

"We don't need things like that, do we, boy? We don't need the devil's medicine because we're filled with God's healing love, isn't that right, boy?"

The boy ran back down the aisle crying and calling to his mother.

"I don't have to take them old shots no more, Mama." He fell into his sobbing mother's arms.

The people gathered around the boy and his mother reached out to touch him, to feel the miracle of his healing.

"Praise God," they cried, "praise God."

The crippled rolled in their wheelchairs down that aisle, and the blind too, faltering and groping their way to the sound of the rich, deep voice that could make them see again.

"Sammy," Jo Anna said, "go on up there now and let him heal you. You see what he's been doing for those other people. If he can heal that crippled woman and that boy, I *know* he can heal you. Go ahead, *please*," she begged him, urging him from his seat.

Pale and terrified, Sammy walked down the aisle because Jo Anna had asked him to. There was no one else on earth he would do that for but Jo Anna. He walked between the rows of people who reached out to pluck at his sleeves, to pat him as he passed by.

"God will heal you, brother," they said.

Sammy felt unreal, as if he were pushing slowly through pale green water, that, icy cold, carried him closer and closer to the bulbous-nosed man on the wooden platform. A thin humming was in his ears, he could hear nothing, but he saw mouths opening and closing, bodies thrashing. When he reached the platform the preacher spoke to him, and when he didn't answer, shook his shoulder.

"I said, you have to kneel down, brother," the preacher said.

Sammy stared into his face and was horrified to see that his savior had close-set eyes and pitted skin, that his nose spurted from his face like the core of a ripe boil that has just been squeezed.

Sammy knelt.

"What's your ailment, boy?"

Sammy tried to speak, made only a croaking sound and cleared his throat.

"I have asthma."

"Exactly what is that, son? I've heard of it, but I've never had one before. I'm a lot better with cripples than anything else, to tell you the truth."

"I can't breathe sometimes, sometimes it's hard to catch my breath."

"Where does it get you?"

"In the chest."

The preacher took his square of cloth that looked like a white handkerchief, but that he called a prayer cloth, and spread it over Sammy's chest. He raised his arms and shouted, "Be *healed*, be *healed*," and then he took away the prayer cloth.

"Move along now, son," he said to Sammy. "There's lots more behind you. The collection plate is there to the left of the platform. If you thank God for what I've done for you tonight, put a little something in the plate."

Sammy passed by the collection plate but he didn't put anything in it for that old faker. The bits of sawdust swirling through the air were choking him, he could hardly breathe. He held his handkerchief to his nose as he hurried back to his seat to tell Jo Anna that he was ready to leave; he hoped the fresh air would make him feel better, would keep him from having an attack. He did not want to disappoint Jo Anna by not being healed. If he were lucky he would be home and in his room before he had to spray his nose and throat with the yellow liquid that even now bumped in its glass bottle against his leg.

The preacher's voice reading from the Bible followed them as they left the tent:

"And in that same hour He cured many of their infirmities and plagues, and of evil spirits; and unto many that were blind He gave sight. Go your way and tell what things you have seen and heard, how the blind see, the lame walk, the lepers are cleansed, the deaf hear, the dead are raised, and blessed is he whosoever shall not be offended in Me."

The Previews of Coming Attractions were over, the Sunday afternoon show was done. The lights came on and they sat for a moment, heavy, still slightly hypnotized from the long afternoon of make-believe.

Jo Anna sighed, remembering the movie. It was her favorite kind, a musical with lots of singing and dancing, Betty Grable wearing chiffon and jewels, Betty Grable dancing and loving, gorgeous in Technicolor. Jo Anna especially liked movies about rich people, people who had servants to wait on them, who owned big cars and went to the theater. Sometimes she lay in bed after Callie had called her to breakfast, lay there still half asleep and dreaming—when she got up, instead of the cold floor beneath her feet there would be a warm, soft rug, and in the kitchen, waiting to serve her breakfast of pancakes and maple syrup, a fat, smiling Negro mammy like the one on the pancake box.

She and Sammy moved away from each other, sat watching the other couples stretching and unwinding their arms from around each other like sea creatures disengaging their tentacles, swimming in the yellow glow of theater light. Jo Anna yawned, reluctant to leave the warm popcorn smell of the theater for the raw cold of early December. She pulled Lee Rose's coat closer around her and they went up the aisle and pushed through the door into the cold wind that whipped along the sidewalk. Sometimes Jo Anna borrowed Lee Rose's coat to go to the movies because her coat was warmer, and because Lee Rose hardly ever went to the movies with them any more.

Jo Anna was glad when she didn't come because it was more fun to neck with Sammy when Lee Rose wasn't there. It wasn't that Jo Anna was embarrassed, it was just that she didn't want anyone hugging and kissing her if Lee Rose didn't have somebody, too.

It was barely four o'clock but already the neon lights were on over the stores; by four-thirty the streetlights would come on. The sky was gloomy and heavy with gray clouds, the sidewalk shiny with drizzle. They crossed the street and turned left to walk home through the business district. They did not take the short cut home because then they would miss looking in the shop windows. One time they had ridden the bus home, but had been sorry that they had, for they missed the shops and got home so quickly when they wanted to be together as long as possible.

They passed the dime store and stopped to look in the window at the rings.

"When we get married, Jo," Sammy said, "I'm going to buy you a real diamond ring, one as big as that one in the corner," and he pointed to a ring with a big square-cut piece of glass sparkling in the electric light of the window.

Jo Anna linked her arm with his, squeezed him close to her and thought how much she loved him. If it were summer they would wait until it was dark and then, cutting around through the park and behind her mother's house, they would go to the golf course. They had been there three times, but there was no place warm to go in the wintertime.

"One of these days I'll have some money, Jo Anna. You wait and see. One of these days I'll run Papa's store and it'll be as big as the Piggly-Wiggly. Just wait. Papa thinks he's still in Italy, still runs the store the way they ran stores fifty years ago in Italy. He's too stubborn to get modern. You know how he still thinks you have to dress up on Sunday, wear a suit and a vest and a white shirt. He walks up and down the sidewalk in front of the store smoking his cigar and makes fun of my uncles and cousins because they come to visit us wearing sport shirts. He won't change what he sells in the store, either, all that fancy cheese that nobody but Italians will buy."

She squeezed his arm with sympathy, though talk of the store bored her; he talked a lot about what he was going to do to the store and when he did she let her mind wander, thought of other things.

They passed the furniture store that was Jo Anna's favorite place on the way home. She moved up close to the window, let her eyes go out of focus and imagined that she and Sammy lived in there, lay together in the mahogany spool bed with the fluffy pink bedspread. It was the most beautiful room she'd ever seen, with thick white throw rugs on the floor, brass lamps on the bedside tables. She wished the owners of the store would keep the window the way it was forever, would never change the furniture in the window. She imagined herself there with Sammy, the record player playing the music Sammy had taught her to like. Sometimes on Sunday afternoons, instead of going to the picture show, she went to his house and they listened to the opera on the phonograph, Sammy's father striding back and forth singing along. He knew every word of *La Traviata*.

They walked on down the street, strolling along in spite of the cold weather, hating that the afternoon must end. They would not date again until the next weekend, but they would see each other at school, they would pass in the halls and at lunchtime they would sit on the steps outside to eat their Dixie cups of vanilla ice cream sprinkled with salted peanuts. They would laugh as they shivered, the ice cream making them break out in goose pimples, but they would not touch; always the teachers were watching to make sure the boys and girls did not touch one another.

In the spring she and Sammy had played hookey. They passed in the hall and when they looked at each other, without a word they turned and went out the front door. They took their lunch money and went to the picture show, then went to sit on a bench in the park, holding hands. After a while, they picked a daffodil and played tag on the new green grass, jumping over the flower beds as they ran.

They were suspended the next day and Callie and Sammy's mother had to come to the school. Callie was furious when the girls' advisor asked her if she ever gave Jo Anna money for the picture show. She was so mad she couldn't speak, all she did was sputter and try to explain that Jo Anna lived at the movies, sometimes she thought she ought to take her bed to the Delmar Theater and live there.

Mrs. Tancretti was furious with Jo Anna; she thought it was Jo Anna's influence that had made Sammy do such a bad thing as play hookey from school. She told Sammy he couldn't go with Jo Anna any more, but he had the worst attack of asthma he'd ever had so she promised Sammy then that she'd never even mention that he couldn't see Jo Anna.

They were almost to the drug store when they heard the shouting. When they crossed the street and were catercornered from the park, they saw a boy about thirteen years old standing on the corner. Jammed under his arm was a bundle of newspapers.

"Extra, extra, get your extra newspaper," he called. "Read all about it, Japanese bomb Pearl Harbor."

He waved a newspaper at them.

"Japanese bomb Hawaii," he said pleasantly, walking up and down the sidewalk. He shifted his newspapers and pulled his cap down further over his ears against the drizzling rain.

Jo Anna and Sammy were the only people on the street. Neither of them knew what Pearl Harbor was, though they were familiar enough with Hawaii; they'd seen many picture shows about Hawaii, girls in grass skirts lived there dancing under the swaying palm trees. Why would the Japanese want to bomb a place like that?

"What is it, what's happened, Sammy?"

"I don't know, it's something about war, I guess. Mama and Papa talk a lot about it, about Hitler and Mussolini. We'll find out when we get home."

Jo Anna shivered and thought that it must be something terrible; it was always something terrible when an extra newspaper was on the street. The last time there was an extra was when the bakery workers struck and broke into the manager's office and killed him.

"Don't be scared, Jo Anna," Sammy said. He put his arm around her shoulder. "It can't mean very much; it doesn't have anything to do with us. Whatever could a war have to do with us?"

When Jo Anna got home, all of them, her mother and sisters, were gathered around the radio. Still in her coat, she went to sit on the floor and listen to the newscast. H. V. Kaltenborn was reporting.

"At 7:55 A.M. December 7, Hawaii time, the Japanese bombed Pearl Harbor. It is unknown at this time the extent of the damage—"

"What is it, Mama," Jo Anna asked, "what's happened?"

"I don't know what it means," Callie answered, snapping off the radio. It's something to do with war, but I can't worry about that now. In the morning I've got to go to the bank and tell the president I can't make my December payment. All the money I saved is gone and nobody's answered the ad to rent Mr. Foote's room. It looks like, close as she is to graduating, Maribeth's going to have to quit school and get a job."

Maribeth didn't say anything, she just sat staring at the floor. Callie thought that as bad as war was, it couldn't be half as bad as having to go to the bank tomorrow to face the president and tell him she couldn't make her house payment.

7

On December eighth, 1941, President Roosevelt asked Congress for a declaration of war against Japan. He said that December seventh was a day that would "live in infamy."

In Tokyo, the Japanese declared war on the United States and Great Britain. On December 11, Germany and Italy also declared war on the United States; Congress then declared war on Germany and Italy.

In Russia, General Zhukov was pushing back the German army in their drive toward Moscow, and by mid-December China was at war with Germany, Italy, and Japan.

Men were flocking to induction centers in the United States in response to the posters of an old man with a white beard whose finger pointed at them and said, "Uncle Sam Wants You." Those who didn't enlist were drafted. *What's good is in the army, what's left will never harm me,* sang the Andrews sisters.

Peacetime factories were converting to wartime. All the way across town from Callie's house, close to the airport, a civilian airplane factory was making plans to convert to war planes. This would be fully accomplished by late spring. Also by then there would not be enough men left in all of Jones Valley to fill all the jobs that were open.

When Callie went to the airplane factory in May to apply for a job, the personnel director did not shake his head at her and tell her she was too old. He commended her for her patriotism and hired her on the spot. He took her into the plant to show her where she would work on the assembly line fitting Plexiglass rear gunners' bubbles onto the tail of the airplanes.

Proudly, she wore coveralls to work, carried her black lunch pail and bought war bonds. She paid strict attention to the posters on the walls of the factory that said, "The slip of a lip can sink a ship." In the summer, she planted a victory garden and put blackout curtains over all the windows. One night a week she was a civil defense worker. She put on her helmet and went with her flashlight up and down the street on practice blackout nights to make sure her neighbors had pulled their curtains, that not the slightest bit of light shone on the outside.

In the fall, she made Maribeth quit her typist's job at the steel mill and go back to high school to finish her secretarial course, to complete her study of shorthand and commercial arithmetic. Maribeth graduated only a semester late. Callie wanted Lee Rose to go back to school too, only Lee Rose wouldn't. She said she couldn't stand being with that bunch of kids again and having to wear bobby socks. Besides, when Norman went to the army, Lee Rose was promoted to floorwalker and she wasn't about to give up the extra money that meant. But she did go to Maribeth's graduation with Callie and Jo Anna, watched Maribeth in her black cap and gown march down the school auditorium aisle while the band played "Pomp and Circumstance." She even gave Maribeth a big blue bottle of

Evening in Paris perfume from the dime store for a graduation present.

Callie had enough money to buy a burial plot in the big cemetery across town and didn't mind at all the two-hour bus ride to and from work (she had to transfer twice) morning and night. The president of the bank smiled on her when she came in, beamed when she handed him extra money for her savings account. The war did not worry her because she knew without doubt her country would win, and because she did not have anyone fighting who was kin to her.

The whole world, kings and prime ministers, presidents and dictators, generals and admirals, had joined to help her save her house, to make a job available to Callie Berryhill.

Part Three

1

MARIBETH STRUGGLED, calm and with stoic determination. The soldier who tried to hold her still to make love to her finally pushed her away from him and, disgusted, stared through the breath-frosted car window at the lights of the city spread out below.

Maribeth sat up straight and smoothed her hair and pulled at her dress until it covered her knees. Shivering, she settled deeper into her brown camel's-hair coat; she wished she had not left the USO dance hall to take a ride with this boy. It was against the rules for hostesses to leave with servicemen, so they had left separately to meet again a block away.

The boys Maribeth dated at the Baptist church thought her prudish and prim, she never let them do more than kiss her good night; but they did not know the dreams she had, that she had promised herself that when she married she would be pure and virginal. In her mind she had lived it all, hundreds of times—the tenderness, the respect her husband would have for her when he knew she had saved herself for him.

For the last two years of the war, Maribeth and Lee Rose had been going to the USO. There were no neighborhood boys to date; all of them had gone to war except for the 4-F's, boys like Sammy Tancretti and James Owens with the oversized aquamarine eyes and bad heart who had a crush on Lee Rose. But then lots of boys had crushes on Lee Rose. It wasn't long after Snow went over to Georgia that she stopped being a tomboy, stopped running and turning cartwheels, and when she did, all the sharp, bony angles of her body began to round out. She could have all the dates she wanted but she turned most of them down.

Maribeth, though not as popular as Lee Rose, found that most boys liked her, reached to touch the long hair she shook away from her face; they laughed and grabbed playfully for her, but she pushed them away, these boys with their faces warm with passion, their voices whispering to her that she was beautiful in the moonlight. The soldiers in their rough, wool khaki uniforms embraced her and told her how patriotic it would be for her to make love to them. But they didn't seem to mind that she refused them, and in the light of her front porch wrote down her address in their small black books, called good night to her as they walked away, their hands shoved deep in their pockets. The letters came to her, signed Chuck and Rob and Dennis, but she never saw any of them again.

The soldier sitting next to her now ran his fingers through the black forelock of his hair and reached for her with the same gesture. Maribeth put her knees sideways on the seat and braced her back tightly against the door. Boys called girls who used that trick a d.d.p., a damn door pusher. She thought if she talked she could distract him, could talk her way off this mountaintop and get him to take her home.

"I'll bet you didn't know it got so cold in Alabama, did you? I'll bet you wish you were home right now in California, I know I wish *I* could be where it's warm all the time."

But the soldier only shrugged and pulled her away from the door, forcing her close to him. She struggled, squeezing her lips shut against his kiss, pulled his hand from its roving under her dress. His searching fingers were dangerously close to the prize she was saving for the man who married her.

Sometimes when she lay in bed at night her temples throbbed with thinking of how it would be, how on her wedding night her husband would carry her tenderly to the marriage bed. This soldier, passing in the night, would not take her husband's prize, and her anger gave her strength to push him from her. Lying shivering in a parked car, her underpants around her ankles, doing it with this soldier, would not be her marriage bed; he would not appreciate the gift she had given him.

Breathing hard, the soldier turned her loose.

"There's a name for girls like you, Maribeth."

"What?" she asked, curious, really wanting to know.

"Prick tease. A girl like you is called a prick tease."

She looked through the window at the Christmas lights of the city; over the charity hospital a white electric Star of Bethlehem marked the place of the sick and dying poor people of the county. This was the first Christmas in four years that there was no war. The department stores were playing happy Christmas carols like "Deck the Halls" instead of only the sad ones like "Silent Night" that made her want to cry for all the boys who were lying in the mud and couldn't be home to eat turkey and sweet-potato pie.

Maribeth loved walking the streets at Christmastime; she dropped money into the Salvation Army pot and the cold wind caught at her and the gay carols chimed from the belfry of the downtown Baptist church. She was glad the town was filled with soldiers coming home from the war. Somewhere among those faces might be the man she was going to marry and she looked closely at them at they passed by; some of them smiled at her and sometimes they whistled, and then she shook her hair around her face and looked down at the sidewalk, walking quickly away from them.

She was glad the war was over, that at last there would be some talk other than war talk and the boys would come home; now she could get on with the plans she had for her life. She was twenty-two, past the time she had planned to be married; already she should have had her first baby.

One of the boys she had dated in the neighborhood would not be coming back home. His name was Tom and it was sad to pass his house and see the gold star woven into blue satin hanging in his living-room window. A list of the boys gone to war hung in the vestibule of the Baptist church. Sometimes a boy's mother cried to see the gold star pasted alongside her boy's name, and people spoke in whispers as they tiptoed into church as if they had come to his funeral. The preacher patted the gold-star mother and led her to her pew and told her that her boy was in a place where there was no more trouble or sorrow. He spoke as if the grave was exactly where the strong young boy had yearned to be.

The soldier was on Maribeth again. She struggled against his weight that was slowly pushing her onto her back. The lights of the city disappeared and over his shoulder she saw the black, crooked finger of a low-hanging tree limb scratching at the window. Then it was dark as he covered her, the sweet, moist smell of his breath in her nostrils as he pinned her arms over her head. She struggled until she was exhausted; she could not push him off her.

In the warm closeness of the car, she heard the winter rain falling softly on the roof, heard the metallic scratch of his pants ziper. Here on this mountain, less than a week before Christmas, all her plans would be cancelled, the plans of her whole life ruined, as if they were of no consequence. Now she would have nothing to give the man who married her; she was not rich, she was not beautiful like Lee Rose, and now she would not have her virginal maidenhead.

The soldier's knee held her pinned so that she could not move while one hand roamed over her body. She went limp, closed her eyes and responded not at all to his whispered vows of love, his kisses on her throat and face. She lay as if dead, and it was true, soon she would *be* dead. When finally he was finished, she would jump from the car and throw herself down the rocky abyss that lay a few feet to the side of the car. They were parked at the place on the mountain called Lover's Leap, and in the last second before she jumped, she would beg forgiveness from the shadowy, nebulous man who would have been her husband, and from her children who would spend eternity waiting to be born.

The soldier's teeth scraped hers as he pressed his lips against her slack mouth.

"Damn," he swore and sat up.

She lay with her eyes closed waiting for his lovemaking to start again.

"You can sit up, Maribeth, I'm not going to rape you," he said. "I've never raped a girl and I won't start with you."

Slowly, she sat up, giddy and dizzy, flirting with the edge of hysteria. Her babies were saved, they would not spend eternity in limbo. In the dim light from the dashboard a long, round protuberance rose from the open fly of the soldier's pants.

"Maribeth," he said, "I want you to look, look at what you've done to me with your teasing. It's wrong to tease like that, didn't you know it?"

Maribeth stared, fascinated, terrified, yet with a throbbing in her temples. It was the first man's Thing she had ever seen. She had no idea, never imagined it could be of such size. She looked away, her face and throat hot in the cold air. Where did it come from? Surely, nothing of such size could be concealed.

She looked out the window toward town, and far away a miniature Buffalo Rock sign flashed off and on, the brown bottle pouring neon foam into a waiting glass, over and over again. *Rhodoro, if the sages ask thee why this charm is wasted on earth and sky, tell them, dear, if eyes were made for seeing . . .*

"Maribeth, I want you to hold it in your hand," he said, and she jumped, startled, her mouth forming the round, silent "no" of her answer. But she knew that holding it in her hand was her reprieve and her children's; it was the soldier's compromise for going all the way.

"You are a crude person," she said; "you say crude things, ask me to do vulgar things . . ."

"I said *hold* it, Maribeth."

Her hand clasped around it loosely and she was surprised at its warmth, unbelieving that she sat on this winter's night holding this soldier's Thing in her hand. She turned away from him and the tears of fury came at the war that had ruined her plans; Adolph Hitler's plans could not have been made longer or with more care than hers had been. Nothing less than war could have thwarted her. She leaned her forehead against the cold windowpane and cried for months of no dates at all and for the months of dates with boys she knew she would never see again, did not want to see again. She cried for all the fun she'd missed.

The soldier's arm was around her and she shrugged him away from her. He pulled her close to him, gently, not rough and urgent as he had before. From the corner of her eye, she saw that the ghostly appendage, the unbelievable growth that had appeared like some magician's trick, was no longer in sight but was caged once again inside his trousers, locked behind the talon zipper. She sighed and shuddered, trembling with relief.

"Ah, Maribeth, I'm sorry to make you cry," he said, caressing her, stroking the slick cleanness of her hair.

She slumped against him, surrendering to the polite touch of his hands, the fluttering of his lips across her cheek.

"You're not *really* a virgin," he murmured, and his hands burrowed beneath her hair, stroked the tendons of her neck.

"I never have," she whispered, and he held her tighter.

"You're a funny girl. I could have sworn when you left with me tonight that you'd make love with me."

After a while he lit a cigarette and opened the window to let out the sulphur smell of the match. His breath steamed in the cold air and they laughed because he could not tell when he had blown all the smoke from his lungs.

Maribeth looked out over the city toward home. Home was past the Buffalo Rock sign, past the tank factory. Home was Callie lying in the dark listening for her step on the porch, waiting for the front door to open. If Maribeth was not home by midnight, she would get out of bed and turn on all the lights and sit in the living room waiting for her. Callie didn't like them to be out in cars; as long as they rode the bus she didn't say anything because the last bus ran past their house at twelve o'clock; she knew they had to be home by twelve.

"I have to go home now," Maribeth said. "My mother worries when I'm out late."

The soldier flipped his cigarette into the weeds at the side of the road and raised the window. In the dim light, Maribeth thought he was handsome, with his long face and high, intelligent forehead. While they danced, he had taked to her about things like philosophy and mathematics. He was going to college when he got home to California, he was even going to graduate, he said. Maribeth thought that was wonderful. There was nothing she liked better than college graduates, though few of the boys in her neighborhood even went to college let alone graduated. Most of them went straight to work in the steel mills after high school. What Maribeth wanted most in the world was to fall in love and get married, to keep working at her secretarial job until the babies started coming. That was what all her friends were doing.

He reached for her again, pulling her close to him. Maribeth closed her eyes as he kissed her, tasted his cigarette and pulled away. He held her so tight she could hardly move and the throbbing began in her temples and this time she kissed him back. His fingers pushed between the buttons of her coat, rubbed her breasts through the slippery material of the jersey dress.

"Why, you're not cold at all," he said, surprised, and pulled her hand to the rough khaki of his crotch.

"*No*," she said, pushing him away. She thought Callie's face was staring at her through the car window, thought it was Callie's finger tapping against the glass. Callie had told her what it was men wanted and when they got it they were through with you, laughed about you to other men.

"Leave me alone," she said, and the soldier sank back against the seat, combed his hair with his fingers.

"You're teasing again, Maribeth." His voice was flat.

She stared across the black tops of the trees that grew in the valley below.

"Take me home. My mother is worried about me, I have to go home now."

"You talk only of your mother. Were you hatched? Don't you have a father?"

"Yes. Yes, I have a father but my father is away."

"They're divorced?"

"No. It's none of your business, I don't like you. Take me home."

"You ought not to act like you will and then you won't, Maribeth. One of these days you'll get yourself in a lot of trouble. How often do you come up on this mountain anyway? You directed me here like a homing pigeon."

"My Sunday school class comes here lots of times on wiener roasts. I can't help it if you get wrong ideas."

He began to stroke her hair, his fingers rising and falling over the ridges of its waves. Idly he said, "We could get married," and Maribeth thought he was teasing her.

"I wouldn't marry a boy like you even if you meant it. I have to go home now."

"Ah, sweet Maribeth." He pulled her close to him, rubbed his cheek against hers.

Cold chills ran up and down her arms, and when she shivered he pulled her coat close around her.

"You're a good girl," and he hugged her without passion. "I guess I really do want to marry you."

She believed him then, thought he really did want to marry her, and she let him kiss her, did not stop his hand from burrowing beneath her coat to fondle her breasts and the insides of her legs; she saw that his eyelashes lay curved against his cheeks. In the shimmering half-light of the car his skin was pale and she pulled his head to her chest and held it there for him to listen to the blood rushing through the valves of her heart. They sat that way for a long time and she thought that never had she been so happy, holding the soldier who had come home to her from the war. She only wished they had known each other before, had written letters she saved in a candy box, that the paper of the letters smelled faintly of long-ago chocolates.

The soldier wanted to marry her; she had not known when she left home that she was going to meet her husband. *Raise me a dais of silk and down, hang it with vair and purple dyes,*

carve it with doves and pomegranates and peacocks with a
hundred eyes, work it in gold and silver grapes, in leaves and
silver fleurs-de-lis, my love has come to me—

Her babies hovered close to her, she heard the sighing of
their angel wings, felt their hard, greedy mouths at her breasts.
When Jo Anna was a baby, Maribeth had sat on a stool at her
mother's feet watching her nurse. She remembered reaching up
to touch the taut, white breast, blue-streaked with veins. Her
mother sat rocking the baby and at Maribeth's touch had
taken the nipple from Jo Anna's mouth and sprayed the thin
blue-john fluid onto Maribeth's face; she had wiped her face
on her mother's lap.

The soldier turned his head so that his mouth was on her
jersey-covered breast and she held him there. Her groin ached
to get her baby started; she did not object when he pushed her
onto her back on the car seat. Then cool air touched her face
like the fanning of wings and she opened her eyes to see her
babies floating away, fading into the dark December night.

"*No,*" she said, struggling to sit up, "I told you I won't and
I *won't.*"

When she was sitting up again, she smoothed her hair and
opened the car window to let the damp air cool her face. It
was raining, as it did almost every year near Christmas, a slow
drizzle that lasted two or three weeks into the new year. There
had been years when the sun didn't shine all of January, winter seeing how mean it could be before February came and the
warm weather made it turn loose for spring.

She stared into the darkness and despaired, knowledge like a
devil sitting on her shoulder: she would never marry, never
have children. She was going to die an old maid in spite of the
hundreds of beauty articles she had read on how to wear your
hair, what shampoo to use, and how to dress well on a small
budget. She had followed all their advice, done all the exer-

cises, used the vinegar rinses. She had done all the things she
was supposed to do, and she had never let a boy go all the way.

"I'll take you home now and we can tell your mother," the
soldier said.

"Tell my mother what?"

"That we're going to be married."

"I haven't said I'd marry you."

"Will you marry me, Maribeth?"

"If you love me."

"I do love you, I want to marry you."

He kissed her without passion, then lapsed into silence.
They sat for a while longer, not talking, and then he started
the car and they drove back down the mountain to tell Callie
that they would marry.

Lee Rose saw Maribeth leave the USO. Over the shoulder of a
tall marine she saw Maribeth slip away out the side door looking guilty, though she was trying to look unconcerned and
casual. Lee Rose thought that Maribeth would not make a
good criminal, she never knew how to hide her feelings. She
was going to meet the soldier she'd been dancing with all evening even though it was against the rules, and that was a brave
thing for Maribeth to do; Maribeth always went by the rules.
At the door, she smiled and waved good-by to the hostess, and
Lee Rose thought surely the hostess knew what Maribeth was
up to.

Later tonight, Maribeth would come home and crawl into
bed with her, would wake her up and whisper in the dark, *I'm
in love, Lee Rose, this time I'm really in love.* Then for days
she would grieve over the letter she must write to the last boy
whom she had told she loved; she would sit at the dining-room
table biting the end of her pen, wondering how to tell the poor

boy gone off to war that she loved someone else. Sometimes she cried as she wrote her Dear John letter, sad to tell some apple-cheeked boy the terrible news that now she could never be his.

Maribeth was sincere; she really thought she loved the soldier or sailor or marine who loved her. Even Callie was disgusted with Maribeth and told her she was just like Miss Liza Owens, an old maid back in Seddon. Put pants on a forked stick, everybody said, and Miss Liza would fall in love with it.

Lee Rose was dancing with a marine who looked grand in his dress uniform; he was so tall she had to look up at him when they talked, and that was an unusual experience for her. Nearly always, she was as tall as the boy she danced with. Even Morgan Greer, big as he was, was not taller than she. Morgan. Sadness clutched her. Morgan was dead, killed in Germany in the Battle of the Bulge. She found out about it when she ran into his brother on the sidewalk down in the Magnolia Hills business district.

"I don't know if you've heard," he said, "but Morgan got killed. We heard over a week ago. Mama's proud, though, that we've got a gold star to hang in our window."

Lee Rose was stunned, and angry, too, at the boy for telling her in such a casual way. When they shipped the body home, she went to the funeral at the small white Holy Redeemer Church across the park; Mrs. Greer cried and threw herself across the flag-draped coffin, but it was like Morgan's brother said, she looked to Lee Rose as if she were enjoying herself, was proud to be the center of attention. The women gathered around her, holding her up, and Lee Rose left the church then and went to the park and sat on the bench that was under the tree where Morgan had made love to her.

Before he went away, Morgan told her he loved her and he didn't care whether she loved him or not, he still wanted to marry her when he came back home. She wouldn't tell him yes or no and they hadn't written to each other; she'd sat there in the warm afternoon and wanted to cry, for the first time in years tried to cry, but she couldn't. She never cried except when she dreamed.

The music changed from a slow "Apple Blossom Time" to a fast "Don't Get Around Much Any More," and she changed rhythm with ease. Dancing was easy for her; no one had taught her how, just as no one had ever shown her how to turn cartwheels. Before Callie made her leave high school to go to work in the dime store, the gym teacher had started her working on the parallel bars. She told Lee Rose that if she worked hard she could be a fine gymnast, might even be state champion before she graduated. But she'd had to quit school; Callie thought she didn't care about it the way Maribeth did.

The marine was a good dancer, he whirled her away from him and back again to the fast beat of the music. When she danced, any time she used her body in a strenuous physical way, she forgot herself and felt light and free as she never did any other time. It was obvious to the circle of people who had gathered to watch the tall girl and the tall marine dance that she was enjoying herself; he flung her away and pulled her back again and she laughed, the soft chiffon of her blue dress swirling around her legs; the marine laughed too, happy because the girl he danced with was beautiful, her face warm and flushed, her dark hair flying around her shoulders.

The beat of the music grew faster, but Lee Rose never missed a step; there was no trick of his dancing that was too hard for her, too fancy. The faces of the crowd spun past, the lights blurred, and she was only aware of the music and the marine who, like the parallel bars, was only an instrument she used to do tricks with her body. He swung her back and forth, across his knees and under his arm. Then it was over, the fast music ended, and the crowd cheered for them, clapped their hands for them, then drifted away to begin their own slow dancing again.

The marine pulled Lee Rose close to him and gradually her elation faded away, her body settled itself once more into the slow rhythm of the music. The room was dark except for the dots of light that moved over them from the revolving mirrored chandelier on the ceiling.

"You're the cutest thing," he whispered in her ear, "you're just the cutest thing I ever saw."

"No, I'm not, I'm not cute," she said, and she pushed farther away from him. She felt as if she were smothering from the musty, dark smell of his uniform.

At twelve o'clock, the gray-haired hostess punched the button on the juke box that played "Good Night Ladies." It was the last dance of the evening and because the war was over, Lee Rose knew she wouldn't be coming here much longer, was sad that the Saturday night dances would end. She danced, and the marine's face was spotted with the leprosy of light, a Cyclops eye shone in the middle of his forehead and was gone. She had met many men here, they paraded facelessly through her mind: some she had only danced with; some she had walked with through the streets of the town and listened to them talk, tell of wives and girl friends they were going home to; a few she had slept with; but never would she let them take her home or write to her, there was none she had wanted to know longer than for an evening. She felt restless, at loose ends, wondering what she would do when the Saturday dances ended.

There was still Norman. Soon he would come home. All through the war he wrote her letters that she never answered, that had written across the top of the page in his small and pinched handwriting, "Somewhere in the South Pacific." He wrote messages to her that had whole lines inked out by the censor's stamp and she had smiled, wondering what the pure and innocent Norman could possibly have told that required censoring. Norman had confided to her that he was a virgin and that he would remain a virgin until he married; he would never make love to her unless they were husband and wife. But, of course, he had not written such intimate confessions in a letter.

When the music ended, Lee Rose got her coat and went into the cold and rainy night, and though he had said nothing, she knew the marine would be waiting for her. She walked down the sidewalk that reflected back the lights of the city, and when she reached the corner he took her arm; they walked along slowly, the thin sharp mist of rain stinging their faces. They did not talk, but now and then they paused to look in the shops; they stopped to admire the diamond rings and the ruby and emerald necklaces and bracelets that glittered under the hard light in a jewelry-store window.

Lee Rose stared at the jewels and she was fourteen again and sitting in the back yard in the grass with those boxes of glass she had collected with Jo Anna and Sammy Tancretti; they'd take a piece of glass and place it on their fingers like a ring, hold their hands stiff and straight, turning the glass until it caught the light and in a burst of color glowed red or green or gold.

But there was a day—she could not now remember the exact day or even the year—when she had taken the boxes from their hiding place under the house. She was alone, and when she held the bits of glass up to the sun they weren't jewels; they were just boxes of broken Seven Up bottles and old taillights and amber-colored bottles that once held somebody's creomulsion cough syrup.

She quit playing in the alley after that and walked on the sidewalk like everybody else because the alley was just a place to dump trash; it wasn't magic any more. That had happened not long after her father went back over to Georgia. Callie was glad she'd quit being a tomboy, but Jo Anna and Sammy pestered her to play with them, tried to get her to go to the picture show, but she wouldn't because now she didn't care about those things. Jo Anna and Sammy roamed the alley for a while after that, but it wasn't long before they quit too and the cigar boxes stayed in their hiding place under the house; the cardboard rotted in the dampness and the emeralds and rubies spilled onto the ground and sank into the mud when it rained.

They left the jewelry store and crossed the street and then they were at the marine's hotel. They crossed the bright lobby and rode the elevator up to his room. Without a word, both of them undressed, and the marine turned off the light and when they were in bed he made love to her. As always, she tried to love back, hoped that tonight the stiff whiteness of her face would crumple, that the ecstasy she had only heard about would flood through her and she would cry out in joyful celebration. But there was nothing, and she lay rigid in the dark, despairing, while the tall marine performed the act of love, alone.

In the corner of the room, her other self stood watching, despising, scornful of the woman who lay sprawled amid the twisted sheets, so passively allowing the strange man to love her. When he was done, she was so cold her teeth chattered and he pulled her close to him; when she looked back over her shoulder she was wild with terror because her real self was melting, fading away into the shadows.

"Ah, honey, what's the matter?" he said. "You're not afraid of me, are you, honey?" and she was glad he held her close to him; for the moment she was not afraid.

When she got home that night she went straight to the bath-room, as she always did, and stripped off her clothes, climbed into the tub and soaked herself, scrubbed her cold, white skin over and over again; she gazed, detached and lethargic, at her long legs stretched straight, at her round thighs shimmering under the water.

2

On the first Sunday night after Christmas, shortly after the preaching service at the red brick Baptist church, Maribeth married the soldier. Lee Rose was maid of honor and Maribeth followed her slowly down the long aisle to the sanctuary where the black-robed preacher waited for her; the white-haired woman who was church pianist thumped out the notes of the "Wedding March."

Maribeth wore a pale gray crepe suit with a large white orchid pinned to her shoulder, and a small gray pillbox hat sat on the back of her head. Lee Rose wore a yellow wool suit with a yellow velvet band holding back her dark hair. She carried a small bouquet of gardenias. Callie and Jo Anna sat on the second pew back, Callie's best georgette handkerchief pressed tightly to her lips.

For days before the wedding, Callie and Maribeth had run around shopping and cleaning house and cooking for the quiet and solemn boy who came every night to eat supper. Lee Rose agreed with Maribeth, when she asked her, that the soldier was handsome, but privately she though him ugly, with his too-white skin and delicate frame. He did not look strong enough to go to war; she could not imagine him crawling into a foxhole; but he said that not only had he slept for many nights in the cold ground in Germany, he had read a book of calculus as well while he was there.

Lee Rose thought she would drown in the tide of gaiety that flowed through the house during those days of preparations for the wedding. Though Callie was sad that Maribeth was going all the way to California to live, she was proud, too, that she was marrying so well; Lee Rose heard her bragging to Birdie Cox over the back fence how the boy had paid cash for a new car, and from the pictures of his mother's big house that he showed her, she said the mother must have money too.

Maribeth blossomed under her mother's praise, and from her pinnacle of happiness she was the soul of good humor. Nothing made her mad; she was forgiving and generous when she found out Jo Anna had worn her best cashmere sweater and dribbled chocolate ice cream down the front; she even made her a gift of it.

Now the wedding was over, the last kiss given, the last goodby said. Callie, Lee Rose, and Jo Anna stood at the top of the church steps and waved to Maribeth as she drove away with her brand-new husband in his brand-new Chevrolet. They were the last to leave the church; behind them the preacher was turning off the lights and locking the door.

Lee Rose was too restless, too keyed up to go home. It was not late, not more than ten o'clock. She felt like walking; she could not go home now and go to bed to lie staring sleepless into the dark. She needed to move, so when Jo Anna and Callie turned in the direction of home at the bottom of the steps, she would not go with them; she watched until they were out of sight and safely past the alley behind the grocery store that Callie was afraid to pass in the dark. Then Lee Rose threw the wilting gardenias, already brown around the edges, into the gutter in front of the church.

She walked along the quiet streets, her hands jammed into the pockets of her suit. Most of the houses were dark, though some of them were still decorated for Christmas; some people would leave the colored lights strung across their porches until the new year. She walked along, the tension gathering in her instead of easing as she had hoped; she thought she heard a voice call to her from one of the dark houses and she stopped and held her breath, waiting.

Lee Rose! Lee Rose!

She stiffened and listened, but there was nothing; it was her imagination, no one had called to her; only a dog barking in the alley. Still she waited and looked upward at the black December sky looming over her. She was afraid and did not know why; she thought she had forgotten her own name and she whispered it to herself, and her address—again and again she whispered them as if she had amnesia and this was all she could remember. She felt blank, as if she had no identity, and yet at the same time was acutely aware of herself, each strand of hair, each cell of her body; she felt the beating of her heart, the blood tingling in her fingertips.

Slowly, she began to walk again, the breath from her lungs billowing in the air about her face, and she remembered the wedding, the joy on Maribeth's face. Maribeth had walked back down the aisle, a new woman with a new name, holding proudly onto the arm of the soldier she could love enough to marry in only a week's time. How could she love so easily, from what inexhaustible well did her love spring so freely? Always it was there, waiting only for someone willing to accept it.

Lee Rose had walked all the way to the business district without realizing the direction she was going; there was no purpose to her walking. Straight ahead, across the railroad tracks, were the lights of the tank factory that never closed. All the shops were dark except for their neon signs and their

windows lined inside with yellow cellophane paper and lit
with a dim bulb. All the stores had done this during the war
to conserve electricity. The somber yellow light was depressing,
but nevertheless she stood staring at the boots and galoshes
and rubber raincoats displayed in the window.

Sounds were going around in her head, mixed up, discon-
nected: the short, flat notes of the wedding march, the sonorous
voice of the preacher—

—entreat me not to leave thee nor yet to return from
following—and the twain shall be one flesh—leave father and
mother and cleave to thy husband, *cleave* to thy husband.
Whither thou goest I will go—meet Mr. and Mrs. Glenn
Martin, beautiful bride, Lee Rose you'll be the next—

"Hey, lady," a man's voice called to her.

Frightened, she turned and saw a man leaning from the
window of a car parked next to the curb.

"How about a ride, lady, it's a cold night—"

She shook her head at him and hurried along the sidewalk
to show him she had some destination in mind, and for a
while he drove along slowly beside her, then sped up, the red
taillights of his car disappearing around the corner.

When she reached the park, she walked under the stark,
bare trees and thought she was losing her mind, thought the
tightness inside her was driving her crazy. She took the path
that led to the bathhouses behind the swimming pool, and
no light shone there, only hard, black shadows. She leaned
against the cold brick of the building and remembered pale
twilights when she'd come here with Morgan. Finally, toward
the last, shortly before he went to the army, their relationship
had gone beyond sex and they were friends.

Morgan talked to her and she thought he was not like the
rest of his family; he was ambitious, had plans and dreams to
be something in the world. She couldn't remember now all

229

the things he'd said, only the sound of his voice as she lay in the grass with him, her head on his shoulder; and there was the smell of his hair tonic and of the lilacs blooming. She wondered if the spicy smell of the tonic still lingered there among the blades of grass.

She was shaking with cold, the light wool suit was not enough protection against the raw December air. She left the park and knew that she would never go there again; it was done, nothing was left of him; but of all the men she'd known, she'd had the most affection for him.

She was nearly home when the thought struck her. When Norman came home from the army, she would marry him. He would be joyous, gleeful, when he learned she had finally decided to marry him after all his begging. She did not love him, but that would not matter; sweet, patient Norman would understand. When the preacher said the magic, mysterious words to her that he had said to Maribeth, she too would change into a new woman; she would go forth into the world with a new identity. Then the tension would go away, her head would stop hurting, and her mother would praise her. It was exactly the right thing to do; she was surprised that she had not thought of it sooner.

After she was home and in bed, she lay in the dark and was glad that Maribeth was gone, that when she stretched her legs she touched no one. For the first time in her life she slept alone and was pleased that Maribeth's arm or leg was not lying heavy across her.

She thought that soon it would be she who would be walking down the aisle, her face shining and happy, leaning on the arm of her husband, her body light and airy as it used to be when she ran.

3

On a morning in June, nearly six months after her wedding, Maribeth sat at the table in her mother-in-law's kitchen and watched her break eggs into the skillet. The yolks stared back at her, huge yellow eyes that bulged from their sockets; she nearly overturned her chair as she ran to the bathroom. She knew that Glenn's mother watched with disapproval; Mrs. Martin had never, she said, ever had morning sickness.

Maribeth closed the bathroom door, leaned over the toilet and vomited; she turned on the water in the sink to cover somewhat the sound of her retching. When she was through and had flushed the toilet, she raised the bathroom window. The hot July air fanned her face, the slender, swaying fronds of the palm trees brought back the feeling of nausea. She was nearly four months' pregnant and the doctor Mrs. Martin had taken her to said the nausea should be leaving any day now.

"One morning you'll wake up and it'll be gone, just like that," and he snapped his fingers and patted her and told her this was just one of the things women had to go through to be mothers.

She could not remember when she had not felt sick. In some long-ago life she had waked in the mornings happy, eager to start the day; but that was only a faint memory. Now there was this constant feeling of sickness in her throat that threatened at any moment to boil over into vomiting she could not control no matter how hard she tried. Glenn was impatient, he did not sympathize with her; his mother told him Maribeth was only trying to get attention, there was no reason for her to be sick for so long. Finally, Maribeth had humiliated him in public and now he would not go anywhere with her.

In May, he had taken her to a spring banquet at the university given by the students of the math department for their professors. Maribeth had been so happy to be going out; it was the first place they'd gone except twice to the picture show since she'd come to California. The banquet gave her a chance to wear the black crepe dress from her trousseau (she had never worn it before) and the string of pearls Callie had given her last Christmas. She thought she looked the perfect wife of a math student, dignified and elegant, her stomach still flat; no telltale bulge told that a baby was growing there.

The banquet room at the school was lit with candlelight and looked to Maribeth like a fairyland, the flickering light like fireflies on a summer evening. The tables were covered with pale green cloths and in the center of each was a bud vase with one red rose.

Seated on one side of Maribeth was a boy with wavy blond hair; he wore a tweed suit and he talked to her all during dinner as if he liked her. He listened to what she said as if he thought it important and, even though she was pregnant and should not be doing such a thing, she could not help but flirt with him. For the first time in weeks she was gay, forgot her nausea, and ate the shrimp and crabmeat casserole and the wedge of lemon meringue pie.

Before she realized what was happening, with no noise and no fuss at all, the shrimp and the crab and the lemon pie came back up her throat and lay in a thick pool on the pale green tablecloth. Glenn, his face frozen with anger, rose from the table to take her home.

"I'm sorry, I'm sorry," she said to the people seated at the table, "I'm sorry. I'm pregnant, you see, and shouldn't have eaten the pie; it's the pie that did it, I'm sure," and the tears came rolling down her cheeks.

Nobody at the table looked at her, not the young wives in their bright spring dresses, nor the wavy-haired boy who had talked to her. They all looked away from her and away from the mess of undigested food that lay on their tablecloth.

"I'm sorry, I'm sorry, I shouldn't have gone," she said over and over on the way home, but Glenn didn't answer or even look at her.

She cried all the way home because she had embarrassed her husband and she cried because she was so disappointed that they had not been able to stay the whole evening, to stay for the dance and meet the other young couples. She had hoped to make friends that evening, perhaps with one of the wives. Then she would have someone to talk to, to meet for lunch and call on the telephone. She would tell her about how scared she was to be pregnant when she thought she would be so happy.

When they got home, Glenn would not speak to her but went straight to their bedroom and pulled off his new brown suit that his mother had bought for him. He got into bed and turned his face to the wall. He would not let her touch him when she eased into bed beside him, shivering.

"I'm cold, Glenn," she said, but he didn't answer.

Maribeth turned down the lid of the toilet and sat down. She stared out the window at Glenn's sister, Melinda, hanging out

233

the wash. Glenn had not told her he had a sister and a brother and she did not blame him for that. They were the strangest-acting people she had ever met.

Melinda was tall and skinny, and even though she was in her thirties, she wore oxfords and bobby socks like a high-school girl. Her light blond hair was so thin that with the sun shining behind her, as it was now, Maribeth could see the curved dome of her head. She was neurotic and scary, afraid to walk down the sidewalk, afraid she would faint. Glenn said she'd always been like that, even when she was little, but that's all he'd tell. He wouldn't answer any of her questions about Melinda, or Evan either.

Evan was Glenn's brother. He was the oldest and looked like a nearly bald copy of Glenn except his eyes were round and blue and too big for his thin face. They all talked about how smart Evan was, about how nobody had ever beaten him at a game of chess. Glenn said their mother let Evan advise her in all her financial affairs. But, like Melinda, he never went out of the house, never went any farther than the front or the back yard. Maribeth didn't like him because he had never said a word to her. Not once since she had been living in that house had he ever spoken a word to her, not even the first day when Glenn introduced her to his family.

She wouldn't swear that he could talk at all except sometimes when he sat in the back yard under the avocado tree with his mother, she heard the low rise and fall of his voice. She was intrigued that he was having a conversation and wondered what it was he talked about and what he could possibly be saying. One evening she went to join them. She sat down in the redwood lounge chair and before she had even settled herself Evan left, without saying "Excuse me" or "My, isn't the moon full tonight." He just went straight in the house and Mrs. Martin stayed only another minute before she excused herself and went inside, too.

Maribeth was insulted and went inside to the bedroom where Glenn was studying and told him what had happened.

"*Why* don't they like me, Glenn? What have I done to them that they don't like me? And why doesn't Evan work? *Nobody* in this house *works*. I don't understand people that don't ever do anything."

"We are what we are," Glenn said. "Just take us as we are and quit deviling and pestering me all the time. Why can't you learn to leave people alone, Maribeth? You're always trying to change somebody; you might try changing yourself and that would be an improvement. Who do you think you are, anyway?"

"I think I'm your wife, that's who, and you brought me here and just didn't happen to mention your crazy sister and brother. I never in my life saw anybody that acts like them; one can't talk and the other can't walk down the street."

"Just don't talk about my family, Maribeth. We got along fine for a lot of years before you took it on yourself to point out our faults to us."

After she'd been there a few weeks she didn't care any more that they didn't like her; she played a game to see how long it took Evan and his mother to leave their chairs under the avocado tree when she came to sit with them. After a while, they stopped sitting under the tree at all and she was sorry —it had been something for her to do.

She sighed and leaned on the window sill, resting her chin on her arm. Idly, she watched the cars that passed now and then along La Brea Avenue. Mrs. Martin's house was on the corner and in a neighborhood of Spanish-style houses all painted in pastel colors. The lawns were wide and lush with thick coverings of grass; palm trees were in every yard. Lord, how she hated palm trees; she would pay money for just one plain ordinary oak tree.

She thought that when the baby was born things would be better; surely Glenn would leave his mother's house and find a job. The responsibility of the baby would help him to grow up and she would have plenty to do taking care of the baby and the house. She would not be bored and lonesome when the baby came. Sometimes she wished that in her eagerness to marry she had not forgotten to bring something along with her that would remind her of home: some pressed flowers from her mother's garden or the Bible Jo Anna had given her one year for Christmas.

She often took out the snapshots Callie had sent her of herself and Lee Rose and Jo Anna. Over and over she studied the pictures and thought that Lee Rose looked thinner, her face whiter, her eyes wide and dark. Callie wrote that Norman had brought home a bride when he came home from the service, a girl from Australia named Joyce. She said she thought Lee Rose was disappointed that he'd gotten married, but she couldn't tell for sure because Lee Rose never told her anything. She said Lee Rose was dating the brick-yard boys again, even Morgan's little brother Eddie, who was two years younger than she.

The pictures were unreal, strange, to Maribeth. She could not believe that their lives were going on without her, that they slept and breathed, were happy and sad without her. For her, their lives had stopped after her wedding when she saw them briefly, fleetingly, from the window of Glenn's car as they drove away. They must still be standing at the top of those steps, frozen, their arms raised in an eternal wave of good-by. *These our actors, as I foretold you, were all spirits and are melted . . . into thin air—*

There was a tap on the bathroom door. Glenn's mother called her because breakfast was ready and she was expected to eat whether she was hungry or not. It did not matter if later she threw it all up again, the important thing was that the ritual of mealtime be observed. No one spoke at meals; it was just as it was when Mr. Foote boarded with them so many years ago; mealtime was for eating and not speaking. The whole family was greedy and especially loved meat. Mrs. Martin always served a huge platter of meat—legs of lamb, roasts, whole turkeys. Maribeth was surprised that none of them were fat.

In the early weeks of her pregnancy, she'd had to leave the table one night, sick from watching Evan eat the drumstick of a turkey. He tore the meat away with his teeth, pulled at the tendons until she'd gagged. Glenn fussed at her for being so rude as to leave the table without asking to be excused.

They were all waiting for her at the table, they would not eat a bite until she took her place; still, she did not hurry; in a perverse way it pleased her to keep them waiting. She lingered, drowsy with the warm air blowing on her face, the tile cool under her bare feet.

When she was first pregnant she thought they would change, that they would like her and be happy that she and Glenn were having a baby. But when she had told Mrs. Martin, she had only been appalled.

"Oh, my goodness, Maribeth, wherever in the world will we put a baby?" And the gray-haired, plump-cheeked Mrs. Martin had clicked her tongue with disapproval. She was not thrilled that she was to be a grandmother.

"But we'll leave your house now," Maribeth said, "and Glenn will get a job. We'll have our own house—"

Mrs. Martin shook her head all the time Maribeth was speaking.

"No, my dear, Glenn will not leave here; he will never leave me, nor will Melinda or Evan. We're a close family, Maribeth, no one can separate us."

Even Glenn was not happy that she was pregnant.

"My God, Maribeth, why did you get pregnant? Don't you know I'll never get any studying done with a baby crying around the house?"

She was furious with him and screamed at him.

"What in the world did you *think* would happen, pushing me into bed all the time, Glenn? You're smart in math, but you're so dumb you don't even know what causes babies. You people around here are not to be believed."

She lay on the bed and cried then, her tears of disappointment soaking into the yellow daisies of the bedspread that Melinda had emboidered for the guest room. She cried for a long time, and when she had finished she ordered Glenn to quit school and find a job. She knew she sounded like Callie when Callie used to fuss at Snow, and she was ashamed but could not help herself. She did not want to live with her baby in the guest room of Glenn's mother's house. Glenn did not speak to her for two days after that.

She left the bathroom and went to eat breakfast, and when Glenn left for school she rode with him as far as the library, as she did every morning. She sat in the corner at a table, memorizing poems, and when she lay in bed at night, the words flowed across the closed lids of her eyes.

The weeks passed and Maribeth's stomach grew huge. No one in Glenn's family seemed to notice; all of them passed like ghosts in the hallways, and always there were the endless voices from the radio as Melinda listened all day to the soap operas.

All day long, the baby slept inside her, but at night it kicked and turned, keeping her awake. Sometimes she slept toward morning, but when she couldn't sleep at all, she went to the kitchen and in the early morning light wrote letters to her mother. She wrote how happy she was, how good Glenn's mother was to her and she told her how beautiful were the palm trees and the bonbon-colored houses. She told her mother the baby was going to be born in the same hospital where all the movie stars' babies were born; she thought that would give her mother something to brag about to the neighbors.

Sometimes, when she could sleep, she dreamed of her father, though she hadn't thought of him in years. She dreamed she was a child again and went with him to the fields, and when she awoke, reality was a dream and the dream reality—the sun was hot on her head and from between the stalks of cotton a corn snake lay coiled, hissing at them.

This city where she lived, this place of lacy-leafed palm trees and gingerbread houses, was not real; it was nothing but chalk pictures drawn by a child on the sidewalk that would melt and wash away in the rain. She was living between the garish pages of a child's storybook. When she went for her checkup she told the doctor that she felt hollow, of no substance, that buildings were seen through a mist. The doctor smiled and patted her and told her she had those feelings because she was pregnant.

"Pregnant women have funny feelings. After the baby is born you'll be too busy to have feelings like that," he said, and he gave her a prescription for a green nerve medicine that made her sleep but took away her dreams, so she wouldn't take it any more; her dreams were the realest part of her life.

There was nothing for her to do but wait. She envied Melinda because she had the house to clean, the clothes to wash. Every morning, she watched Mrs. Martin push through the

239

back gate and walk down the sidewalk to the streetcar stop on her way to the Farmer's Market or to whatever shop she was going to that day. Evan had things to do too. Each day he tried to beat himself at a game of chess; he read the racing sheet and listened to the races from Santa Anita on the radio. But she had nothing to do but walk or go to the library. She had tried going to the radio shows a few times, but after a while she was bored—movie stars had never fascinated her as they had Jo Anna.

Because Maribeth had no one to talk to, she talked to her baby. She was never lonesome now; already the baby was real to her. She lay on the bed with her hand on her stomach and recited poems, and when she talked, her stomach was still; the baby lay quietly to hear her. Every morning she told it her plans for the day, whether they were going to the library or whether they were simply sitting under the avocado tree.

One morning she was out walking, and she found herself standing directly across the street from a movie studio; as people went in and out she tried to catch a glimpse of a movie star so that she could tell Jo Anna. She thought she saw Mickey Rooney walking through the big gates and she ran across the street to ask for his autograph to send Jo Anna, but the guard waved his arms at her, threatening her.

"Get away from here," he yelled at her, "go on, get out of here." And she ran back up the street as fast as she could with her big stomach, terrified that the guard was chasing her to arrest her.

Fall came to Hollywood and it was just like summer except that the nights were cooler. There was no deepening blue of the sky, no changing colors of the leaves. Maribeth sat on the front steps every morning and every afternoon, waiting for the postman, hoping to hear from her mother. If a letter came, she skimmed quickly past the news of Callie's job and what the neighbors were doing, eager to hear of Lee Rose's dates, of the fun she must be having. Sometimes Maribeth yearned for the days when they had gone to the USO together, felt guilty because she wished to be carefree.

Maribeth developed a bladder infection and the doctor said it was just something pregnant women got, and she lay in bed for over a week swallowing huge tablets and apologizing to Mrs. Martin for being so much trouble. Because he had to have his sleep Glenn moved back into his old room where he'd slept before he married Maribeth—turning the light on during the night kept him awake. When she was well again he did not come back to sleep with her in the guest room. Then she slept with the light on all night; she was afraid in the sprawling, rambling house; there were too many shadowy alcoves, too many dark corners.

One Sunday Maribeth climbed on the streetcar and went by herself to Sunday school at the big Presbyterian church on Gower Street; she went to see if there might be somebody there she could make friends with. They sent her to a class of young marrieds and she was the only one in the class that day without a husband there. The people were nice to her, welcoming and polite, but none of them asked her back the next Sunday or invited her to stay for church, so she didn't go back any more.

"My God, Maribeth," Glenn said, "why did you ever go to that church anyway? Don't you know it's nothing but a country club with stained-glass windows?"

"I went because it was close by, and because I was lonesome," she said.

In late November, the doctor told Maribeth not to go far from home, that the baby could be born any time. So every

241

afternoon she sat in the yard under the avocado tree until it was time to go to bed, sometimes dozing, her chin drooped against her chest.

Maribeth sat in the easy chair in the living room, too weary to walk the few steps to the back yard and take up her station under the tree. It had been the longest, most miserable day of her life: her back ached, her fingers were so swollen she could not take off her wedding ring to wash her hands. There was no sign of where her ankles used to be, only puffy, blue-tinged flesh. The doctor told her not to eat any salt until after the baby was born.

She sat listlessly, idly flipping through one of Melinda's movie magazines. Suddenly, she felt a gush of warm liquid and she pushed herself from the chair.

"I'm hemorrhaging," she screamed, and Evan raised his eyebrows as he lowered his newspaper.

Melinda ran to the bathroom to splash cold water on her face to keep from fainting.

Glenn came from their bedroom and for the first time in months looked at her with sympathy and concern.

"It's time?" he asked.

She nodded, trembling. "I'm hemorrhaging, Glenn. I'm afraid."

"You're not hemorrhaging, Maribeth," Mrs. Martin said briskly, coming to stand next to her. "You're all right, it's just the water breaking."

Maribeth stared at her and was amazed that she knew what the water breaking was.

"Get my suitcase from the closet, Glenn, and let's hurry. I'm afraid."

"You're not afraid, Maribeth. It's why you got married, remember? It's what you said you wanted more than anything else in the world."

The cool fanning of angel wings brushed her arm and she was happy because soon her baby would be here and because her husband was looking kindly at her. *Raise me a dais of silk and down, hang it with vair and purple dyes, carve it with doves and pomegranates and peacocks with a hundred eyes . . .*

The first pain caught her, knotting her stomach, radiating through her pelvis and down into her legs. She held on to the door, straining with the pain, her eyes round with fear.

"Please, Glenn, let's go—" she said.

"I can't go with you," he said. "I have a calculus exam tomorrow and I have to take it. I *have* to study tonight, Maribeth, you know that. If I stay up tonight I'll miss my exam tomorrow. You'll be all right; women have babies all the time."

"Come with me," she begged, "you're my husband, Glenn."

Mrs. Martin went to the telephone and when she had called a taxi, she took Maribeth's suitcase from the closet.

"I'll go with you, Maribeth. Let Glenn study tonight; he needs to study and then to sleep."

Maribeth had another pain on the sidewalk waiting for the taxi and another in the wheelchair going to the labor room. The admitting nurse sent Mrs. Martin home because only husbands were allowed on the maternity floor.

Maribeth lay in the bed in the dim light of the labor room and a nurse came and shaved away her pubic hair and gave her an enema; she made her sit on a cold chamber pot until the water ran back out again. Then she lay huddled under the cover, trembling and ashamed, until a pain came and after that she didn't care any more. Another nurse came in the

243

room, bright and smiling as she listened with a stethoscope to Maribeth's stomach and drew a red heart over the spot where she heard the baby's heart beating.

In a while a doctor came, a young intern, and pushed his rubber-gloved finger into her anus and frowned at her when she protested. It was necessary, he said, to check the progress of the birth; he would come at intervals to put his finger in her anus and check the position of the baby. It's all routine, he said.

The nurse with the stethoscope came back and stuck a needle in Maribeth's hip and after a few minutes the light blurred and she was dizzy and floating, wondering where were the people who should be here with her. She went to sleep and when she woke thought Glenn was there, dressed in his soldier's uniform, and he leaned to kiss her with tenderness, happy she was having a baby; his long eyelashes lay curved against his cheeks.

She slept again, and the next time she opened her eyes Glenn was gone and Callie was there sitting in a chair by her bed; she told Maribeth that now she'd made her bed hard she'd have to lie in it and then she was gone, too, and Betty Grable sat there in her bathing suit and her upswept hairdo, telling Maribeth how her baby had been born in this very same hospital.

At dawn she screamed with a pain that twisted and arched her back. Faces were leaning over her—the nurses, and finally the smiling face of her doctor—telling her that soon it would be over, that the pain was just something pregnant women had to go through. A needle jabbed her hip and then she was rolling down a long hall, the lights on the ceiling blurred, whirling moons; she heard her own voice pleading for some-one to help her, for someone to give her some gas. The doctor

244

had told her that when the pains got bad he would give her gas.

The rolling stopped and they put her on a table and strapped down her arms so that she couldn't move and she panicked and struggled to free herself. But the nurse held her shoulders down.

"See here," she said, "you behave yourself, Mrs. Martin," and pressed a hard rubber cone over her nose and mouth.

Maribeth thought she was smothering, thought the earth, like a huge metal globe, was mashing down on her; she pushed it away from her, straining with all her might to hold it up, to keep it from slipping from her grasp and crushing her.

4

MARIBETH SAT in a rocking chair by the open window nursing her baby. With nearly orgasmic pleasure she felt the rosebud mouth, tight and greedy, pulling at her nipple, felt the baby's tiny fingers kneading her breast; blond hair, light and airy as thistle, covered her baby's head.

The kitchen door slammed and Melinda came down the steps carrying a laundry basket full of wet clothes; a canvas sack of clothespins hung from her shoulder.

"You shouldn't sit there in front of the window in your nightgown with your breasts hanging out, Maribeth," Glenn said from where he lay on the bed. "Don't you have any modesty at all? Melinda doesn't like that sort of thing, you know; it embarrasses her. After what happened at supper the other night I'd think you'd know better."

Maribeth watched the tall stiffness of her sister-in-law walk across the yard to the clothesline. She began to hang Laurel June's diapers, a large round clothespin sticking from between her clenched teeth.

That other night at supper Laurel June had cried and Maribeth brought her to the table to nurse her while she ate. She had not thought to be ashamed to open her dress and push the pink-pointed nipple of her breast into the baby's mouth, but Evan left the table and Melinda had covered her mouth with her napkin as if she were going to be sick.

At first, Maribeth didn't realize that all the fuss was because of her, and then she was disgusted at how stupid and ridiculous they were. She had watched Callie nurse both Lee Rose and Jo Anna. Jo Anna had nursed for so long that people at church laughed when, at three years, she would come and pat Callie on the breast, asking to nurse.

"Well, it's just that they don't like the baby, anyway, Glenn. Naming her June for your mother didn't make her love her granddaughter. How can she not love her own granddaughter? I wish now I'd named her for my own mother," Maribeth said bitterly. "Mama would love her, she's always sending her things, clothes and toys. Your mother didn't give her a thing for Christmas except the bottle sterilizer I don't need. That was just her sly way of telling me not to nurse the baby."

She looked with distaste at her husband lying sprawled on the bed dressed only in his undershorts. It was Saturday and he had come home at four o'clock that morning smelling of liquor and perfume. She knew he'd been with a girl named Peggy whom he'd said he loved a long time ago, before he went to the army. She pulled the light, cotton blanket closer around Laurel June, afraid the late spring breeze would chill her.

"I think it would be good for Melinda, and Evan, too, to see a baby nurse. They ought to get used to a lot of things that have to do with living, they don't do anything for entertainment but listen to the radio. I don't see how in the world Melinda can sit the whole afternoon listening to those soap operas, it would run me crazy," Maribeth said.

All day long, day after day, came the sound of the radio, the sound of the announcers' voices, rich and unctuous, telling

247

the story of what had gone before, setting the scene for today's episode. Maribeth could tell what story was coming on from the music alone. Melinda started the day with "Hilltop House" and ended it with "Portia Faces Life."

"Just be quiet about my family, Maribeth. I've told you before, don't talk about them."

"Are you going out again tonight?" she asked.

"I don't know, Maribeth, if I'm going out or not. Probably I am. What's to do around here anyway? Sit and watch you nurse the baby?"

Glenn went out every weekend, to the bars and the nightclubs. Maribeth went with him once, but she didn't have a good time, didn't enjoy the drinking; alcohol had never made her feel good as it did other people; it only made her sad and sleepy.

Besides, the men and women who came to the bar, Glenn's friends, had known each other all their lives and they talked of sororities and fraternities. When once Peggy asked her where she went to college, Maribeth was ashamed to say that she had never been, and felt compelled to brag to compensate.

"I had a *real* good job,' she said, "I worked in the office of the biggest steel mill in Birmingham and made real good money; why, having your own money is more fun than going to college, I'll bet."

After that, she wouldn't go with Glenn any more when he was meeting his friends.

"I'll bet if we had a home of our own," she said, "we wouldn't worry about who saw me nursing Laurel June. She's only seven months old so I'll be nursing her a long time yet, so I guess everybody around here just better get used to it."

She shifted the baby to the other breast, cooed to her and with my finger traced her baby softness from jaw to hairline.

"If you'd just quit school and get a job, Glenn," she com-

248

plained, "we could move. I don't think I can stand it around here much longer; you just tell me why you can't make us a living right now. Explain it to me, Glenn. I don't understand."

The baby lay sleeping against her breast, her mouth still holding loosely to the nipple; once she jumped, startled by some baby dream or thought, woke and began to suck again. Then she relaxed and slept, her head falling away from the great, blue-veined udder.

"When are you going to get a job, Glenn?" Maribeth repeated.

"Quit nagging, Maribeth. You knew the score when you married me; you just thought you could change things to suit yourself."

He turned on his side away from her, turned his back to her. She hated herself for nagging him; sometimes she heard her own voice as if it didn't belong to her. She did not believe the whiny, petulant sound came from her; she was not like that, not like her mother who constantly had nagged Snow to find a job. Even now, she could hear Callie's voice complaining in the night as they all lay in bed, and was surprised the next morning that sometime during the night she had fallen asleep listening to her, that in the early morning everything was peaceful and quiet.

Maribeth rose carefully from her chair to lay Laurel June in her crib, leaned over her for a minute to look at her, still marveling that this pink and white angel had come from her body. She was ready for the next one as soon as she and Glenn were settled somewhere permanent. There could not be too many babies; she hoped they'd come one behind the other. Their shadowy forms hovered around her in the night, begging to be born. Already, she loved them all.

She went to the closet and pulled out one of the cotton house-dresses Melinda kept washed and ironed for her. It did not matter which dress she chose; they were all alike except for their different colors; all of them unbuttoned to the waist, making it easy to nurse Laurel June.

Maribeth stood behind the closet door to dress so that Glenn wouldn't see her pull off her nightgown. It was not that she was modest, it was that her undressing excited Glenn. She was not interested in making love if there was no chance that there would be a baby; Glenn was making certain there would be no more babies. She pulled the smooth, starched dress over her head and wished she could stay in the dark closet, that she could lie on the cool floor and sleep. She wanted to sleep as she had when she was a child, that for the afternoon she could be sexless, flat-chested, with her skin smooth and hairless.

She closed the closet door and Glenn was lying on his back, waiting for her. The hump under his shorts told her he was ready to make love.

"Come here," he said, smiling at her.

Her mind raced, thinking of ways to distract him. She did not want to make love, she wanted to go with her book of poems and sit under the tree and read, to gaze into the branches and daydream. She did not want to waste the precious time that Laurel June slept, rolling around on the bed with Glenn.

"Let's play chess," she said brightly; "we haven't played chess in I don't know *how* long. I'll go get the set," and she started for the book case, but he pulled her next to him as she passed by.

He nibbled at her ear, but she pushed him away from her. He was sweating on her clean dress, had gotten germs on it and she would have to change again.

"Let's play *chess*," she said again, but she knew he would not. He had not played chess with her since she had beaten him on a Sunday afternoon several weeks after he taught her to play. He had not wanted to teach her, had only taught her after she begged him. He told her that she was not suited to the game, that she did not have a mathematical mind.

She lost every time, but that Sunday afternoon something happened. She was tired of losing, weary of his superior, condescending smile each time he won. She played him, aggressive and determined to win. She captured his queen, then checkmated his king with a knight.

"Look, Glenn," she squealed, "I do believe I've won."

Her face was warm, flushed with happiness, and she looked at him for approval, certain he would be happy that she was so smart. But he was not proud of her, he was furious. He tried in every way to free his king, even tried to make her believe her knight could not jump the way she knew it could; finally, he flung the chessboard to the floor, the way Jo Anna used to throw the checkerboard to the floor when Mr. Foote won at checkers. He had not played her since.

"We'd better not," she said now, moving away from him as he slid his hand under her dress, "it'll wake Laurel June."

She felt her breast contract at his touch, felt warm milk seeping through the cotton pads of her brassiere, darkening the red print of her dress.

"God," he said, lying back on the bed. "A man wants to make love and his wife starts spewing milk like a cow. I don't see how you can stand that, Maribeth."

She sat rigid next to him. If she did not allow him to make love to her, he would sulk; a refusal to make love was an even greater offense than winning at chess.

"I nurse the baby," she said, "because Dr. Spock says that gives babies the best start. You know you want the best for Laurel June."

He closed his eyes and lay her hand on the fly of his shorts.

"See what you did to him, Maribeth? You'll have to get him up again."

She lay stiffly beside him on the bed and his hand slid under her dress and she hated him; she let her thoughts slide away, willed herself not to be a part of her body.

When Laurel June wakes up, I will take her for a walk in her stroller to the Japanese market where cool water sprinkles the vegetables in the outdoor bins. I will talk to Mr. Ono, who will smile at Laurel June and bow to me, and on the way home I will talk to the people who live in the gingerbread houses and are planting flowers and watering their lawns.

She smiled to think how they would admire her baby, would stoop to talk to her and, looking up at her, would tell her that Laurel June looked just like her mother.

Laurel June stirred, then awoke and began to cry. Maribeth tried to sit up to go to her, but she could not free herself from the weight of her husband. Laurel June grew frantic, her whimpering turned to sobs and soon she began to hiccup for breath; still Glenn would not let Maribeth go.

"Let me *up*, Glenn, I have to see about Laurel June."

Furious, Glenn jumped from the bed and went to the crib. He slapped Laurel June in the face, then turned to push Maribeth back onto the bed when she stood up to follow him. For a moment, she was so shocked she didn't move, could not believe he had hit her baby. Then she started to scratch at him, to hit him.

"Let *go*," she yelled at him. "You hit my baby. Get *off* me." But he held onto her until he was finished, then he rolled onto his back.

Maribeth ran and took Laurel June from the crib and sat with her in the rocking chair, crooning to the baby until she lay quiet in her arms. Laurel June's head was wringing wet with sweat, her cheek red-striped from the imprint of Glenn's hand.

She sang to her baby and despised the man who was so unconcerned about what he had done that he lay sleeping, softly snoring, his breath puffing out his cheeks. A father who could slap his own child in the face was a mean person and she wondered now, as she stared at him, how she had ever convinced herself that she loved him.

After a while, he yawned and stretched and Maribeth knew that now he would shower and dress to go out and not come home until late that night. He was going to the fair and oval-faced Peggy, who had a mathematical mind and was working for a degree just like Glenn. Glenn admired her because most girls, he said, were not logical as was Peggy.

"Glenn," Maribeth said, trying to think of a way to get back at him for slapping Laurel June, "why won't any of you talk about your father? Every time I ask one of you a question you change the subject. Was he a criminal or something? Is that the reason you won't answer any questions?"

"What did you say?" he asked, looking at her incredulously. "Who do you think you are, to ask questions about my father?"

"I think I'm your wife and that your father is Laurel June's grandfather and if you don't think I have a right to know about him, she certainly does; she's his blood."

They stared at each other, their eyes unblinking, while Meribeth rocked and sang softly to her baby. Tears were puddled in the corners of Laurel June's eyes, moisture was beaded over her lips and on her forehead.

"Why don't you tell me about your father?" And she smiled at him, pleased she had made him angry.

Glenn got up from the bed and went to the dresser; he

opened the top drawer and took out the rhinestone bracelet he had given her for Christmas.

"See this, Maribeth? I'm taking it back. I'm sorry I gave it to you; a girl like you doesn't deserve nice presents."

"Take it back, what do I care? We never go anywhere. Where would I wear it, to take a walk with Laurel June or to sit under the avocado tree? Besides, you didn't buy it anyway; your mother did. You don't have a job; you can't buy anything."

"I guess it's useless to expect anything but stupid remarks from a girl who's never even been to college."

"If you're so smart, Glenn, how come I can beat you at chess?"

He dropped the bracelet on the dresser and came to her chair and slapped her across the face. Pain shot through her jaw and into her ear, but she did not flinch or take her eyes off him. The wind gently blew the white curtains and she saw Mrs. Martin go down the steps wearing a pink dress; she watched her until she went out the gate and walked away down the sidewalk.

"It's been a good day for you," Maribeth said, and when she spoke the tears began to flow. "First Laurel June and now me; I hope you've enjoyed yourself."

Glenn sat on the side of the bed.

"Stop with the tears, Maribeth, that's just one more act with you. We never should have married. You know that, don't you?"

She did not answer.

"You teased and dangled your virginity in front of me like it was the Holy Grail itself, and I'd been away for two years. I thought I loved you. It was a mistake, all of this was a mistake."

"What about Laurel June's grandfather," she said again.

254

She would not ask him about his father again, only about her baby's grandfather. She and Laurel June both had the right to know about him.

Looking down at the floor he told her about his father. He would not look at her.

"My father was a gambler. I mean by that, that he was a professional gambler, he made his living gambling. Sometimes he was gone for weeks at a time. I don't remember him at all, except flashes of him coming in late at night and waking me up to give me a toy or some candy. Mother says that Evan's the one that favors him, has blue eyes like him. Melinda and Evan, both of them remember him and what happened.

"When I was three, he came home late one night, it was about midnight. He put his car in the garage and somebody ambushed him in the driveway. He'd won a lot of money that night and somebody shot him in the head and took the money. Evan was eleven at the time and Melinda was seven. Evan was the one that got to the driveway first. He tried to keep the rest of us away but Melinda saw his head shot away and all the blood on the concrete."

"I don't want to hear any more," Maribeth said. "I'm sorry I asked; don't tell me any more," and she lowered her head, ashamed that she had made him tell her such an awful thing. The tears ran down her face dripping onto Laurel June, and she took the corner of the baby's shirt and dabbed away the tears that had fallen onto her cheeks.

"The police came, Maribeth, and reporters came too and took pictures of Laurel June's grandfather lying in the driveway and they printed it on the front page of the newspaper. Police came to guard the house because they thought the murderers might come back to kill us too, and people drove around the block and stared at our house and there were phone calls all the time from people threatening us because

255

Laurel June's grandfather was a gambler—"

"*Stop*," Maribeth shouted at him, "I said don't tell me any more, I'm sorry I asked—"

"Melinda and Evan got so they wouldn't go out of the house at all, but it didn't bother me because I wasn't old enough to know what was happening—"

"Why didn't you all just move away? Why did you stay here?"

"Because Laurel June's grandfather picked out this house. To live in California had always been his dream. We lived in Denver and he always hated the winters there. His dream was to live somewhere warm, Mother said, a place where flowers bloomed all year round—"

They were silent now. There was no sound but the creaking of the screen door as Melinda went inside after hanging out clothes. Maribeth rocked the baby and a dove cooed in the avocado tree outside the window.

"It's only an excuse, you know," Maribeth said.

"What?"

"I said, it's only an excuse. It's an excuse to keep you all here. Other people have terrible things happen to them and then go on to live normal lives. My father left my mother, but she's never used that as an excuse to keep us with her. She was sad when I moved away but she didn't try to stop me. Your mother's told me time and again since I've been here that none of you will ever leave her. If your father hadn't been killed she'd have thought of something else, she's that kind of person, neurotic—"

Glenn went to the bathroom and showered and dressed and when he had left the house Maribeth put Laurel June in her crib, then lay down on the unmade bed. It was not like her to leave the bed unmade or to sleep in the daytime. She had made the most of living in the guest room, trying to make it fill the need of a house to care for. She kept the floor around the edge of the green rug mopped and waxed, the dresser shined, with a picture of her mother and sisters on top.

She slept, and toward dusk heard the baby stirring in her crib; she was making soft, cooing noises and Maribeth smiled because she loved her so much; she had not been lonesome since she'd had Laurel June.

She lay on the bed until dark, and when the moon was shining straight overhead, she left the bedroom and ran across the back porch and through the yard to the driveway. For a long time she stood staring at the concrete, searching for some sign, some evidence of what had happened there those many years ago. But nothing was there; there were no terrible dark stains embedded in the rough cement. When the moon went behind a cloud she shivered and was afraid of what unknown danger might lurk in the bushes, and she ran back into the house.

Laurel June was crying, and hurriedly Maribeth pulled off her dress, put on her nightgown and took her baby to bed with her, pulled her close to nurse in the dark. Soon they both slept again.

When Maribeth awoke, the room was utterly dark. She did not know what time it was but it felt late, it must be after midnight. She got up, thinking to turn on the light, when she saw a figure, someone or something present, standing by the bathroom door.

"Who is it?" she whispered, the words barely audible through her frozen lips. She was limp with fright, she could hear its breathing there in the dark with her.

The dark shape started toward her, and when she screamed she felt Glenn's arm around her, his hand across her mouth.

"Hush," he said, "you'll wake up everybody."

He turned her loose and her breath rushed from her, her knees sagged so that she could hardly stand. He was drunk; the smell of liquor and perfume clung to him, and she was furious because she knew he'd been with the beautiful Peggy.

"Why didn't you just stay gone? Why didn't you stay with Peggy who you admire so much? Why aren't you out with her—"

"Because I came home to you," he said, and he dragged her to the floor and tore away the flimsy nightgown that she had worn on her wedding night. "You can't say no any more. We're married now. I can have you whenever I want you."

He pushed her back hard onto the stinging wool of the rug and she struggled, trying to get away from him.

"You're drunk; get away from me; you're scaring the baby—"

"I am drunk and I don't give a damn if I scare the baby," and he straddled her on his hands and knees, and afterward lay on the floor beside her in the square of light the moon cast as it came from behind the clouds.

"I want a divorce," he said.

"You're drunk; you don't know what you're saying—"

"I am drunk and I do know what I'm saying. We should never have married, but I'd been away to the army for such a long time and you wouldn't let me have any and I wanted some *so* bad—"

Maribeth got up and moved Laurel June from the bed back into her crib. Then she sat beside Glenn on the floor.

"I'm sorry for anything mean I've done to you, Glenn. I know it hasn't been easy for you trying to study and with the baby and all, but I know you love her. You don't mean it about wanting a divorce."

" I *do* mean it about wanting a divorce, Maribeth, I won't live with you any longer—"

258

"Don't you love Laurel June? Don't you love our little baby?"

"I don't know, she doesn't talk yet."

Glenn got up from the floor then and went to bed. Maribeth went to the dresser, and when she had taken out another nightgown, climbed into bed beside him. She talked to him in the dark, tried to reason with him.

"You don't want a divorce. I won't *give* you a divorce; you have no grounds. I've been a good wife and a good mother—"

"If I don't get a divorce I'll kill myself," Glenn said. "I'll run a knife through myself."

Then she hated him and she hated his family and the life she'd had with him, but still she did not want a divorce; she did not want to go home to face her friends at church.

"Please, Glenn, let's try to work it out for Laurel June's sake. A child needs both its parents. Neither of us had our fathers; don't let's do that to her—"

"It's too late; I knew it was a mistake the next day, when we started driving out here after we were married. I knew I'd made a mistake. We have nothing at all in common, Maribeth; we're not at all alike."

"And I guess I should thank God for that," she said bitterly. "You don't love me or Laurel June at all, do you?"

"All I want is to live in peace and not have to think about anything but math. There is a truth you may never have heard, Maribeth, never having been to college, and that is that a mathematician never really loves but one woman, and that is the goddess of math, Matissa."

He lay down and turned his back to her then, and Maribeth did not even try to sleep. She knew that tonight the poems would not come to flow behind her closed eyes to soothe her, so she lay staring into the dark until morning.

259

5

Maribeth sat under the avocado tree waiting for her taxi. Laurel June lay on a blanket on the ground next to the chair, wearing nothing but her diaper and rubber pants and chewing on her teething ring. Maribeth leaned to stroke the velvet skin and tickle her baby's stomach gently. Laurel June squealed with delight and Maribeth thought how much like a rubber toy she was, guaranteed to squeal with joy when her stomach was squeezed.

"And there's the hole in your stomach," and she tickled Laurel June's navel. The baby laughed and Maribeth smiled sadly at the happy picture she was sure she and her baby must make to passersby; they would think she was nothing more than a young wife playing with her baby before nap time, a young woman sitting in her back yard whiling away the time before her husband came home from work. But Glenn was gone—two weeks ago he had packed his bags and moved to the dormitory of the school. He would not live with her any longer and Mrs. Martin had taken her to a lawyer and arranged for the divorce proceedings. It was then she learned that Glenn would never have to work if he didn't want to, his father had left them all enough money to live on for the rest of their lives.

Laurel June gagged and coughed, and Maribeth, alarmed, reached to run her finger down the baby's throat to pull out the piece of grass she had swallowed. Laurel June bit Maribeth's finger with her new front teeth and angrily Maribeth bit her tiny baby finger to show her how it felt. Dr. Spock did not recommend biting back and she was amazed that she had dared defy Dr. Spock. Laurel June cried and Maribeth comforted her, rubbing at the red tooth prints.

"Did mean old mommy bite her sweet baby?" she crooned, but she would not pick her up because she did not want to muss her clothes. She was dressed in her gray wedding suit and a new white blouse that Callie had sent her for Christmas. It had lace at the throat and down the front and Maribeth thought it made her look the way she wanted to look: a wronged and innocent person. She was anxious to tell the judge the mean things Glenn had said to her. She flicked away a speck of dust from her white gloves and settled her gray straw sailor hat more firmly on the back of her clean and shining hair.

Maribeth leaned forward in her chair, pulled the cloth of her suit from her perspiring back; she was hot in the winter suit but it was the nicest thing she had to wear. She had had no new clothes since she married Glenn except for the clothes Callie sent her and the house dresses she wore when Laurel June was born. Wrinkling her nose, she sniffed at herself, at her underarms, afraid that in spite of her bath and the deodorant she used she had body odor. But there was nothing, only the faint smell of the damp crepe.

Melinda came out the back door, walking tall and straight down the steps; she carried her eternal basket of wet clothes.

She did not speak or look toward Maribeth. Neither Melinda nor Evan paid any attention to the baby, though Laurel June kicked and smiled at them when they came close to her. Maribeth did not care that they did not speak to her, but she hated them for being mean to her baby. After Glenn left, Maribeth would not eat at the table with them; every mealtime Mrs. Martin left a tray outside her door.

She watched Melinda hang the clothes—dresses and pink rayon underpants and Evan's undershorts. Maribeth stared at her and wondered how it felt to her and for a moment she *was* her and the summer wind blew her thin wisps of hair and the soap-scented smell of the clothes filled her nostrils. She must hurry and hang the clothes, it was nearly time for the afternoon soap operas; after supper tonight she would work on her card file, cataloguing the programs and writing a daily summary of each one.

When Melinda had finished hanging the wash, she stood with her hand on her hip and stared down the sidewalk; Maribeth thought she must be wondering how it would feel to be able to leave her back-yard prison and walk down the sidewalk in the sunshine to go to market or to one of the radio programs she listened to so faithfully every day.

The yellow taxi pulled up outside the gate and the driver blew his horn. Maribeth ran to the house to get Laurel June's freshly washed and ironed dress; as she came back out the door she stopped, startled that Melinda had stooped to stroke Laurel June's hair. When Melinda saw her watching, she took her empty wash basket and, brushing past Maribeth, hurried into the house.

Maribeth then went to pick up Laurel June, draping a diaper across her shoulder to keep the baby from drooling on her. As she passed the kitchen window, she saw Melinda peeping from behind the curtains, but when Maribeth waved to her, she pulled the shade.

When she was in the taxi, she told the driver to take her to the court house. He smiled at her and she thought him handsome in a common way; he was too big for her taste, but he had friendly blue eyes and black curly hair. His hands on the steering wheel were square-shaped, his fingernails clean, and she liked that.

They drove along, and when they turned on Gower Street and passed the Presbyterian church, Maribeth saw herself going up the walk, nearly nine months' pregnant; she stood under the high, arched doors, and the pale green, shimmering, light of the stained-glass windows gave her the feeling that she was under water, that she was home again and swimming in the pool at the park. She had been embarrassed at that church, had turned already to leave, when a woman in a hat covered with pink feathers took her by the arm and led her up the stairs to the Sunday school room. Those people there that day did not like her, they had not wanted her at their church.

The taxi passed the Japanese market and Mr. Ono was standing in front and she waved to him, but he did not see her, and she knew she would never see him again. She realized, suddenly, that though she had lived here for almost two years, she knew hardly anyone, had few happy memories.

Laurel June had fallen asleep on her lap; the swaying of the taxi had made Maribeth think she was home in the rocking chair. She was dismayed to see that there was a wet spot on her skirt that had seeped from around the edges of the baby's diaper. She took a Kleenex from her purse and rubbed at the dampness, but the paper handkerchief only added lint to the spot.

The taxi pulled up in front of a huge gray stone building that was the Los Angeles Court House. Maribeth's palms began to sweat inside the white gloves, and hurriedly she began to dress Laurel June, twisting and pulling her arms through the tiny sleeves, much as she had done her doll's arms when she was a child.

"There now, Rosa, it's all done," her piping voice came back to her. "Mommy has you dressed now," and she patted the flat, stuffed stomach and kissed the cool plaster forehead.

Laurel June began to cry, her chin crinkling, unhappy at being awakened; she was not smiling and happy as the dolls had been. Just as Maribeth buttoned the last tiny pearl button, a young man rushed up to the taxi from the court house, anxious to get in. She paid the driver with the five-dollar bill Mrs. Martin had given her, and as the young lawyer (from his buttoned-up vest and briefcase she could tell he was a young lawyer) opened the door for her, she smiled at him and wondered if he knew, as she did, that he was the kind of man she should have married. If she could have gone to college and worn sloppy-joe sweaters and ropes of pearls like the girls on Silk Stocking Road, no doubt, even now, she would be married to a man much like him. He took her arm and helped her onto the sidewalk, but she would not look at him; she turned away and ran to the top of the long flight of steps and the beating of her heart shook the ruffled lace of her blouse.

She pushed through the revolving doors, and in the foyer saw a long line of elevators stretching away in front of her; a clock on the wall over the elevators said that it was two o'clock. She was supposed to meet her lawyer in the divorce court at two o'clock and she walked quickly to join the crowd of people who stood gathered in front of one of the elevators.

Laurel June stirred and woke up and, when she saw the strange people, began to cry. Maribeth tried to quiet her, bounced her gently up and down, then tried to force her head onto her shoulder to sleep again. But the baby struggled, afraid of the people who didn't even glance her way, who only stared absorbed and attentive at the slow downward movement of the arrow over the elevator doors.

Maribeth crooned to her, talked softly to her, and wondered why no one smiled at the tender mother comforting her crying child. The elevator doors opened and she was carried forward with the flow of people, was pushed all the way to the back and mashed against the wall. When she tried to push forward to the operator to ask her which floor the divorce court was on, sharp elbows pushed her back again.

"Stand back in the car, *please*," the nasal voice of the operator said.

"Please," Maribeth said to a man in front of her, tapping him on the shoulder, "please, sir, could you ask the operator what floor the divorce court is on?" but he did not answer her or act as if he heard her.

The doors closed and the elevator began its upward climb, a moving womb that opened and closed, gave birth at each floor to men and women who scurried away, turned left or right purposefully, who knew where they were going. Laurel June screamed, terrified at being jammed into the dark corner of the elevator, but no one paid attention to her. Maribeth had the terrible feeling that she and Laurel June did not exist, that no one spoke to her or answered her because they were not there to make pictures on these people's retinas.

The doors opened and the last few people got off because the arrow pointed at ten. There were no more floors. Maribeth sagged in the corner no longer trying to quiet Laurel June. The operator turned to look at them. She was a middle-aged woman with bright orange lipstick and wiry black hair. Her cheeks were feverish with two bright spots of rouge on each high cheekbone. She wore a red cap that made her look like Johnny on the "Call for Philip Morris" cigarette ads. Maribeth giggled.

"It ain't so funny, lady," the operator said, "driving this damn thing up and down all day long, squeezed in with screaming kids and a bunch of mean people, half of them that don't know where they're going," and she looked pointedly at Maribeth. "Which floor you want off on? This is the last floor, you know."

Maribeth stood straight, pulling at her skirt, trying to smooth the wrinkles.

"I wanted off on the divorce-court floor," she said, trying to hold onto Laurel June and straighten her hat at the same time. "I got pushed to the back and I'm sorry my baby's crying, but she got scared with all those people shoving us and nobody would tell me where to get off. I got to thinking nobody even knew we were alive—"

"You're pretty hard to miss, you know, but you're right, nobody pays attention to you out here in this place. I been trying for fifteen years to break into pictures, been ridin' up and down in this thing waitin' to get discovered. Ya know what? I'm too damn normal, I ain't goin' to *get* discovered and that's too bad because I've got the cheekbones for it, see?" and she touched her fingertips to the rouged bones.

"I've got cheekbones just like Claudette Colbert and Myrna Loy, but, nah, you think anybody comes along and cares? I'm just too normal, that's my trouble. The divorce court's on the fifth floor." She clanged shut the doors and without stopping in between took Maribeth down to the fifth floor.

"Here's your floor, lady. Turn right down this hall, keep walkin' straight ahead and you'll walk right into the courtroom at the end of the hall. Gettin' divorced, huh? Well, it ain't so bad; course it's worse when there's kids. I been divorced myself. I've seen lots of movie stars walk through those doors. I got divorced the same day that Lana Turner did, makes you kind'uv proud, you know?" And as Maribeth stepped into the hall, the elevator doors closed and the Philip Morris lady sank from sight into the depths below.

Maribeth walked down the marble-floored hall stretching away in front of her to a tiny brown dot in the distance that was the door of the divorce court. Laurel June lay quiet and exhausted on her shoulder. The white dress she wore with the pink rosettes on the collar had been fresh and clean when Maribeth put it on her in the taxi; now it was twisted and wadded, limp as a handkerchief.

She felt nervous being the only person in that hall; she had thought there would be hordes, throngs of people rolling like ocean waves toward that door. She had hoped there would be a movie star with a photographer taking pictures, and that maybe, in the background, she would have been in the picture. It would have been something to show when she got back home.

The small rectangle of door was closer; she tried to tiptoe but her high-heel spectator pumps banged against the marble floor, the sound echoing off the walls and the domed ceiling. Behind that door that came closer with each step, people were waiting for her. There was a judge in black robes who would look down at her from his high perch and see how innocent she was with her guileless, pale blue eyes and little-girl sailor hat. He would smile to see how tenderly she held her baby in her arms.

The feeling came over her that she was in church, was walking down the aisle again to be married; she thought the people in the offices along the way would rise as she passed and in chorus sing the wedding march.

The oak door was directly in front of her; written on it in

267

gold letters was "Superior Court of the County of Los Angeles." The clock over the door said the time was two-fifteen. She was late and she hoped that there was no one there behind that door, that they had thought she was not coming and gone home. She would come back another day, her hair neat, her skirt dry and unwrinkled.

She pushed open the door and people turned to stare at her; the lawyer was there and he hurried to take her arm and urge her quickly into the courtroom.

"This is Maribeth Martin, Your Honor," he said. "I'm sorry she's late. She's here for a divorce on grounds of mental cruelty."

A man came and told Maribeth to put her right hand on the Bible; he asked her if she swore to tell the truth, the whole truth and nothing but the truth so help her God. Then she sat in the witness chair and Laurel June whimpered; judge and lawyer and mother all stared at her to see if she would cry and when she did not, Maribeth settled the baby on her lap and did not pull her away when she sucked on the shiny gray buttons of her jacket.

"Mrs. Martin," the judge said, "your petition for divorce says that your husband stayed away weekends, that he came home late at night and on many occasions had been drinking. It also says that he has left you, that you no longer occupy the same house. Is this statement true?"

"Yes, it's true, your honor, and what's worse than that—"

"And has he been seeing another woman?"

"Yes sir, he certainly has, and once he slapped me and he slapped this precious baby and he said he didn't know whether he loved her or not and—"

"And did this cause you grave mental anguish?" the judge asked.

"Yes sir, it certainly did," and Maribeth settled herself to tell her story to this sympathetic man. "One time my husband—"

"Divorce granted," the judge said. "Come back next year for your final decree, there will be a one-year waiting period. Custody of the minor child is given to the mother with visitation privileges granted to the father, who states that the child may be taken out of the state of California temporarily or permanently at the discretion of the mother. Mrs. Martin," he said, turning to her, "your lawyer will notify you of the exact date of the next appearance in court. If you do not wish to appear, you may be represented by your lawyer. Next case, please."

Her lawyer was stuffing papers into his briefcase and motioned for her to leave the stand. Already, they were swearing in another woman to sit in her place. Maribeth was bewildered and sat in the witness chair waiting for something more; she did not know what—perhaps for someone to say they were sorry. It was not possible for a marriage to end with only three questions—she was supposed to tell her story and be comforted.

"You can step down, Mrs. Martin," the judge said, waving his hand at her.

Maribeth left the stand and as if in a dream walked down the hall with the lawyer. She was divorced but still felt married and she rubbed at the hard smoothness of her wedding ring with the thumb of her left hand. The lawyer stopped at the elevator and, smoothing the crown of his bald head, said, "Sweet baby," and patted Laurel June. Then he left her and went back up the hall and through the door that said "Superior Court of the County of Los Angeles."

She took the elevator down again, and when she was in the foyer, saw that the clock said it was two-thirty. It had taken her thirty minutes to get divorced, counting the ride up and down on the elevator.

269

She left the foyer and went through the door into the hot day; Laurel June blinked and rubbed her eyes and pulled at Maribeth's hat. Maribeth pulled it off and gave it to her to play with. Laurel June was ready now to be her charming baby self when there was no longer any need for her to. Maribeth hugged her.

"I love you anyway," she told her.

She walked down the long flight of steps and wandered aimlessly along the sidewalk, people hurrying past bumping into her, glowering at her. She saw a streetcar coming and the sign on the front said Hill St.; she angled across the street to catch it. She would go back to the house and finish packing, and in the evening would sit under the avocado tree for the last time to think about all the things that had happened to her.

In the morning, she would take the ticket that Mrs. Martin had bought for her and fly home to her mother and sisters. She was anxious to see them, to show Laurel June to them; for two years she had seen them only in snapshots so now that was the way she thought of them.

When they met her at the airport they would be figures in a giant black and white glossy, blurred and one-dimensional, smiling and waving to her from behind the wire fence where they waited for her.

Part Four

1

THE EVENING that Lee Rose came, Snow was sitting on the
back porch with his two cousins watching the sun go down;
it sank behind the red hills back of the house, the winesap
apple grove shimmering in the light as if it were afire with the
flame that lit the sky.

The three men waited there, bathed in the rose-colored
glow, waited until the last pink light had faded from cousin
Cleveland's bald head and from the lens of cousin Charlie's
gold-rim glasses. Cleveland sat with his twisted arthritic back
curved almost to his knees, his neck and head curved upward
like a turtle. Charlie sat stiff and straight, his legs crossed,
waiting for dark.

They'd come from the fields at four—they always came from
the fields at four—to wash up and eat the supper the old
Negro woman, Macie, had cooked for them. Snow's heart
lightened when he heard the dinner bell ring. *Corn*bread,
*butt*ermilk, soup, soup, it called. When the mules heard the
bell they turned the plow right around and headed for the
house and they couldn't stop them because the mules knew, too,
that it was time for watering and hay.

It was the same every night. After they had finished eating

they sat on the back porch waiting for the time to do what each of them did. Each pretended he did not know what the other's secret was and that was the reason they got along so well. There were no women there to butt in, to try and change them, make them different from what they were.

When it was dark, when the last streaks of yellow and rose faded from the apple grove, Charlie would clear his throat, run his fingers through his thin gray hair and excuse himself for his evening walk. He went down the path past the barn and cut through the woods to his mistress's house, to his nigger woman.

Charlie had stayed nights with her for the past thirty years, since they were both young and she'd cooked for his mother. Her name was Lottie and her skin was creamy tan; she wore gold wire earrings looped through the tiny holes of her pierced ears.

On a Sunday afternoon, when Charlie was nineteen and Lottie was twenty-four, they were in the house alone, Lottie singing and cleaning up the kitchen, clearing away the dinner dishes. The rest of the family, Cleveland and his mother and father, had gone to the church for the afternoon sing-song. Charlie hung around the dining-room door, hung back in the shadows watching Lottie as she cleaned up and then he moved slowly into the kitchen and pushed her onto the slick oilcloth of the table.

He'd heard that a man didn't know what heaven was until he'd been with a black girl and he must have found that true, because he never did marry; no one ever knew of him going out with a white girl after that. When his mama and his daddy died, he started staying nights with her, and people around Clement snickered about how Charlie's nigger had better furniture than he and Cleveland had; but they were jealous because she had running water and an indoor toilet and a lot of them didn't even have that. Two times Lottie left her house and went over to Waycross to her sister's house and stayed for several months. People said she went to have Charlie's woods-colts but nobody ever knew for sure.

Charlie saw to it that her house was kept painted and repaired. Hers was the only nigger house in Clement that had grass growing in the front yard; all the rest kept theirs swept clean with a sage broom.

Cleveland waited until Charlie was out of sight down the path and then he would say good night, stretching as well as he could with his twisted back, go into the kitchen and gather the scraps of bread and meat left over from supper to feed his rats. He'd been going to the cellar after supper for years to feed the gophers that lived in the root cellar, that had burrowed dens deep into the red clay.

Once, Charlie had tried to make him stop feeding the rats, wanted to put poison in the cellar to kill them, but Cleveland had cried, tears dripping onto the floor.

"Don't kill my little friends. I don't want my little friends to die." He had wrung his hands and picked at the large brown mole that grew on his cheek.

Charlie never mentioned the rats again. Cleveland never had been exactly right in the head and Charlie took care of his younger brother when their mother and father died. Cleveland wasn't any trouble except he did things like feed the rats that didn't hurt anybody and sometimes, when he was nervous, he masturbated with his pants on, not even bothering to unzip the fly. He worked hard in the fields and when his arthritis got so bad he couldn't plow any more, couldn't see the furrow ahead of him because his back was parallel to the ground, Charlie let him chop the cotton and in the early fall help pick it.

When Cleveland went to the cellar to feed his rats, Snow

took the pint bottle of whiskey out of his sock where he hid it every night after supper and drank. He sat on the back porch and he drank and when the whiskey was finished, when his insides burned and his brain was on fire, he stumbled inside to bed or, if he wasn't too drunk, he went down to the quarter and slept with one of the Negro girls there. But he was always bright-eyed the next morning, ready to carry his load in the field. That is, he was ready until the first time he got the d.t.'s. He got them so bad one night that Charlie had to get rope from the barn and tie him to the bed, tying his hands and feet to the brass bars to keep him from running from the house. Snow screamed that Cleveland's rats were chewing his fingers off; he thought they sat on his chest and stared at him with their red eyes and he cursed Charlie for tying him there to let the rats kill him.

Then he thought he was back with Callie again and that she had poisoned him by putting Rinso washing powder in his breakfast syrup. The girls all stood around his bed sobbing. He lay there moaning and then the word of Jesus flowed in neon print across the wall.

"Read it to me, Callie," he begged, and the woman that was hidden in the shadows came to stand by his bed. She read, *Be afflicted and mourn and weep, let your laughter be turned to mourning and your joy to heaviness, Ye have lived in pleasure on the earth and been wanton;* the dagger that she held in her hand glowed red in the fading light, glowed red with setting sun or his own blood, he couldn't tell.

That had scared the hell out of him and he didn't touch a drop again until after Lee Rose left.

She came at sunset. She came swinging around the side of the house, tall and long-legged, her hair dark and shining around her shoulders. She wore high-heel, ankle-strap shoes and a blue and white pin-stripe suit with the soft, fluffy bow of her blouse tied at her neck.

Snow couldn't place her at first, couldn't quite figure who was the woman standing at the bottom of the back steps holding a red suitcase, looking up at him. Until she smiled. When she smiled at him, he saw it was Lee Rose and all the years between never had been: they were standing in the field, Lee Rose and him, and she was nine years old and wearing overalls. She had her hands on her hips swearing to him she could work hard as a boy any day, begging him not to send her to the house to be with the women. She jumped over the fresh plowed furrows when she left, looking back over her shoulder to smile at him; she would not let him make her cry.

"Lee Rose?"

She nodded, and it was Callie's blue eyes looking at him; now he could remember how Callie's eyes looked more than twenty-five years ago, dark blue and wide, and he'd had to marry her.

He rubbed his hands down the sides of his overalls and went down the steps to shake hands with her.

"Hello, Daddy," she said, shaking his hand, her fingers long and tapered, her fingernails bright with red enamel.

He walked beside her up the steps to meet Charlie and Cleveland. This was the first time one of his girls had met any of his people. None of them had ever been to Georgia and none of his people had been over to Alabama.

"This is my middle daughter, Lee Rose," he said, and Charlie stood up to shake hands with her and Cleveland grinned and bobbed his head.

Charlie left right away, disappearing down the path into the woods, and Cleveland, still grinning, went into the house. Lee Rose set her suitcase on the porch and sat down in a rocking chair. Snow sat in the chair next to her and they rocked and Snow tried to think of something to say to the tall, silent woman who sat next to him.

"I haven't had word from any of you since before the war. How's your mama?"

"She's all right," Lee Rose said. "She just quit working at the airplane plant. They gave her a pension and a watch she can pin on her dress. She's the only person that ever worked for them that never missed a day. She quit work when she got the house paid for."

"That house never stood a chance of not getting paid for, I knew she'd do it one way or another. What about you, Lee Rose? You look prosperous, looks like fine clothes you've got on."

She shrugged.

"I'm a floorwalker at the dime store down in Magnolia Hills. I've been working there for seven years now. Mama made me quit school to go to work there."

"That wasn't right," Snow said, shaking his head with disapproval. "You should have gotten your education."

They didn't say anything for a few minutes. Finally, Snow said: "Your cousin George got killed in the war flying a glider plane. We were all mighty sad about that, but I guess you didn't know George, did you? He was your uncle Otis's boy. Otis had five boys and all of them went to war but the youngest."

They sat talking even after the light had faded and it was dark. Lee Rose told him about Maribeth getting married, only now she was getting divorced.

"She's got a baby, though, a little girl, and she's coming home."

"What about Jo Anna? What's happened to her?"

"She's married to the Tancretti boy, you remember him?

Jo Anna never went with another boy, married him before she graduated."

"Well, I'm behind on all of you, it's been nearly ten years. I'm surprised your Mama would let you come over to see me."

"Mama doesn't tell me where I can go any more or what I can do. She didn't say anything when I told her I was coming."

Lee Rose went to the field each day with them, barefoot and wearing a pair of Snow's pants and one of his old blue work shirts. She chopped cotton from sunup until noon and then she went to the house and got lunch: sandwiches and cold milk. They sat under a tree by the fence and ate the sandwiches washed down by the milk, and Lee Rose dug her fuchsia-tinted toenails into the crumbling gray dirt. With her hair in braids and her lips pale without the purple lipstick, freckles popping out on her face and arms, Snow thought she looked like Lee Rose again, not the stranger who watched him from the yard the evening she came. He half expected her to turn cartwheels across the warm dirt and that Callie's voice, complaining, would call for her to stop before she burst her blood vessels from being upside down.

On the first Sunday afternoon she was there he took her in Charlie's Ford pickup all over the countryside to meet great-uncles and aunts and cousins whom she'd never even heard of or who hadn't heard of her. She wore her pin-stripe suit and her high-heel shoes and sat on a dozen different front porches talking to her relatives. Snow was proud of his beautiful daughter and introduced her as "your cousin, Lee Rose Berryhill" or "your great-niece, Lee Rose Berryhill."

She sat and talked to them and was friendly as she could be, as if she'd known them all her life. She bragged on

Aunt Helen's hand-pieced quilts and acted as if she never had eaten a pickled peach before. After she'd been there a couple of weeks Snow felt as if he was acquainted with her and wondered why he hadn't gotten to know his middle daughter before.

He couldn't say he loved her; he didn't know her well enough for that, and the truth was, he didn't think he'd ever really loved any woman. Not Callie, not even his mother, though he'd admired his mother for working so hard, and depended on her when he was a child. Women were for having babies and crawling into bed with when the need arose; sometimes he felt sorry for them for having to be women and having to stay in the house and raise the children, but that's the way things were, there was nothing to do about it.

Every day Lee Rose was in the field with the men and every evening they were four on the porch instead of three. When Charlie left to go to Lottie's house, and when Cleveland, drooling and smiling, went to the cellar, Snow and Lee Rose stayed on the porch, talking some, but mostly quiet. Snow appreciated that trait in her. He never could remember sitting on the porch with Callie that she didn't light into him, name over all the things wrong with him and finish by asking him why he didn't get a job. Lee Rose just mostly sat there in his old clothes and acted like she'd been there forever and was going to stay forever. He never did ask her why she came and she hadn't offered to tell him, but after a while the pattern was set: Macie cooked as she always had, but Lee Rose did the washing up and putting away of the dishes.

One evening when she'd been there about a month, when they sat on the porch watching the sun set, Lee Rose told him she was leaving the next day. Snow hadn't known he'd be so disappointed to hear she was leaving, hadn't felt the ache of somebody going away so much since his daddy died.

"I just didn't think about you going," he said. "I just got to thinking that you'd come to stay."

"I have to go back to work; it's time to go. I've got to get back to my job. I've been gone all the time the manager said I could have off. I couldn't have stayed this long except he's a real good friend of mine."

Snow didn't protest and he didn't ask her to stay longer, but he knew he would miss her; the feeling he had for her could be the beginning of love, but she was going and now he would never know. The soft roar of the katydids came from the woods back of the apple orchard and down in the cellar they heard Cleveland crooning in the dark, spreading his largesse for his rats, calling softly to the gophers that waited in their dens.

Lee Rose leaned back and stretched her arms backward in a long yawn. The faded blue workshirt, white in the moonlight, pulled taut over her breasts and Snow looked away, embarrassed that his daughter had breasts. Somehow it didn't seem right to him that his daughter had grown breasts; even Jo Anna the last time he had seen her had hard little crab-apple knots on her chest that pressed through his shirt when she hugged him good-by.

"Why didn't you ever write to any of us after you left?" Lee Rose asked. "Jo Anna wrote to you lots of times but you never answered."

"I wrote to your mama once after I got settled. Look at these hands," he said, holding up his big-knuckled, oversized hands. "Can't you see how hard it is for hands like these to hold a pencil? I never was a letter writer. Besides, what was there to say?"

"There was to say you loved us. That would have been enough, just to say you loved us."

"Lee Rose, you see right there back behind the barn? It's

281

hard to see in the dark, but there's a black gum tree; you can see by the moon that it's about twice as tall as the barn. One time my daddy was sawing wood out there back of the barn not far from that black gum tree and a lightning storm came up right quick, you know the way storms do sometimes in the summer. Well, I guess you know how hard it is to split a black gum tree; it's just next to impossible, the wood's like iron. That afternoon a storm came up and a bolt of lightning hit the pine tree my daddy was standing close to, split it right down the middle. It scared him *so* bad he said—and mind you he never was a cursing man—he said, shaking his fist at the sky, 'All right, you gray-headed old bastard, I know You can split a pine tree, now let's see You split that black gum over there.' "

Lee Rose didn't say anything and Snow rolled a cigarette and crossed his feet on the bannister. He was ready for her to go on back home now; she was just like all the rest, always nagging at you, wanting something from you that you couldn't give. What was it with women anyway, always talking about love? *Do you love me, Snow? How much do you love me, Snow? Why don't you love me, Snow?* He pulled on his cigarette and spit away the bits of tobacco that burned his tongue.

Love. He guessed if someone held a gun on him and he had to say he'd ever loved any woman, it was his mother, though he didn't think just being sorry when someone died was love. He remembered her cool hands on his cheeks when he was sick and the dry, musty smell of the herb bag she wore around her neck when she rocked him. Early one morning when he was sowing corn, they'd called him in from the field and his mother was dead in the bed where he was born. They said her rotten teeth had poisoned her. She was still a young woman, not yet out of her forties. He'd bent to kiss her, but his father's hand on his shoulder held him back.

"Berryhills don't kiss, son," he said.

The full moon had risen straight over the house, shining so bright they could see chicken tracks lettered in the dust like some ancient message from the past. Gnarled, choking vines of wisteria climbed from the lattice at the end of the porch, snaking across the roof and down the bannister of the back steps. The vines had been there almost as long as the house had; nobody had planted them, they had volunteered to come up in a place where they could climb, the tough fiber eating into the wood of the house until there was now no way to tell which was vine and which was wood.

They bloomed for the second time that summer, the smell of the drooping lavender blossoms heavy in the air. Snow smiled to remember the bar of wisteria soap in the purple wrapper that Callie had saved for some unknown visitor, the soap's fragrance, like its wrapper, fading over the years. He wondered if the guest had ever arrived, honored after all those years with the bar of scented soap.

Lee Rose left the porch and went to the yard, her shadow squat at her feet like it was noonday. She raised her arms over her head, curving them like a wheel. Whirling, head over heels, she turned cartwheels into the shadows of the trees and back again. She dusted her hands on her pants and climbed the steps to sit once again next to Snow.

"It's like riding a bicycle; you never forget how," she said.

They sat for a long time, silent. When the moon was behind the house and the yard and the porch were dark, Snow sighed and took his feet off the bannister.

"It's cool enough to sleep now, Lee Rose," he said. "We'd better hit the hay if you're going to get up early in the morning. You're sure now you really have to go tomorrow?"

"I'm sure. I have to get back to work."

Still they sat and then Lee Rose said, "Have you been

happy over here, Daddy? Are you glad you came?"

"Yes," he said, "I'm happy to be back with my people. We look out for each other; they're blood."

They went into the house then, the screen door slapping shut softly behind them. Lee Rose went through the house to the front bedroom that hadn't been slept in until she came; that room had belonged to his mama and daddy. Everything in there had smelled musty until Lee Rose opened all the windows and aired the room out, pulled open the heavy red draperies to let in the light and the sunshine. She had even made them drag the mattress to the yard to lie on the grass sunning all day; only then would she sleep in the bed.

Snow undressed and lay naked on his cot in the corner of Cleveland's room. He had not wanted to sleep in the room where his mother died, had chosen to share a room with Cleveland. A slender shaft of moonlight lay across Cleveland's twisted body like the finger of God's hand pointing out his handiwork. Snow pitied him as he pitied him every night when he went to bed. Cleveland was one of God's turds, it was the truth. God had breathed life into one of his turds for a joke. God was a funny man.

Snow lay with his arms and legs stretched out, willing a breeze to come through the window. Dizzy from the long day, he closed his eyes; green shoots of cotton with their tight, hard bolls flashed behind his eyelids. Cotton didn't talk, didn't ask him if he loved it; he tended it and it grew and so he loved it. It was there waiting for him every morning, and the softy, crusty dirt that sank beneath his feet. He slept and then he dreamed. He dreamed he had lost his clothes and couldn't find them and he was wandering naked up and down roads, through fields, walking until he was so tired he could scarcely lift his feet. Then he woke up.

He slept to dream again. Callie came to him and she was

young again, her hair long and silky around her shoulders. She pressed close to him, pushed her naked body against his and he was full of lust for her; he crawled on top of her and when it was over and he rolled onto his back, Lee Rose lay next to him.

"Lee Rose," he said, "oh, my God, Lee Rose . . ." and he covered his eyes with his arm.

"Do you love me, Daddy?" she whispered.

He pushed her away from him and when he opened his eyes, Cleveland, in his white nightshirt, stood bent and twisted over them.

"Oh, God," Cleveland prayed, his hands clasped, "I have seen Thy son Snow sinning with his daughter. Punish him, God, punish him," and he went back to lie on his bed with his face turned to the wall.

"Go on, Lee Rose, go on back to your bed," Snow said, his voice flat.

When she had gone, the horror of what he had done swept through him, over and over, until he felt paralyzed with loathing of himself. He lay without sleeping and heard Charlie come in toward daybreak and go to his room. He was awake when the din of the katydids faded away and the chirping of the tree frogs stopped; it was utterly quiet except for the flub-dub of his heart in his ears and the creak of the springs when Lee Rose turned on her bed.

When the bronze light of dawn lit the black square of his bedroom window, he heard Lee Rose moving about the house. He heard water running in the kitchen and after a while the front door opened and closed and he heard the hollow sound of her high-heel shoes going down the front steps. He got out of bed, went to the window, and watched her go out the front gate; she was walking down the road dressed in her blue pin-stripe suit, listing slightly with the weight of the red suitcase.

He watched her out of sight, all the way past the cotton field, and then he sat on the side of his bed and covered his face with his hands. He had ruined his daughter, had ruined an innocent young girl. He knew that everything that had happened to him before, happy and sad, was an interlude, unimportant occupations leading up to now. When he was a baby pulling at his mother's tit, God was watching him, chuckling over what awaited him.

When he was a boy, happy and running barefoot in the woods, it was only something for him to do, a diversion, waiting for this ultimate sin that he had committed. He had only been marking time; all the days of his life were leading him to this condition: he was the slimiest of all men, the filthiest of all God's creatures. Nothing on earth was lower than he, not the slippery, slimy creatures that lived under rocks nor the snakes that crawled on their bellies. He would kill himself, even started for the kitchen to get his hog-killing gun, but he sat again on the side of his bed because he was weak, his flesh shrinking from eternal nothingness.

He dressed and left the house, went out the front gate and down the road that Lee Rose had taken. He left the road when he had passed the corn field and took the path that led to the Negro quarters. It was barely day, the last stars had not yet faded from the sky; a light morning breeze blew, but he knew by midday it would be hot and dry, a good day for the fields, for chopping cotton. So strong was his wish that he could have things back the way they were before Lee Rose came, that he could erase his sins, cancel all that had happened, he stopped in his tracks. He was fifteen years old again and his mother was dead and he was crying. His father, tall, with a black beard that reached to his belt buckle, turned him away from his mother's bed. *Berryhills don't cry, son.*

He went along the path until he reached the cluster of

Negro houses; mist and thin blue wisps of smoke that came from the chimneys hung in the air. In the distance a low-hanging cloud sat like a crown on the top of the mountain. Snow was amazed that things looked so normal, that people still built fires in stoves, that clouds hung on mountains, that the sun rose. There was nothing to show that the end of the world had come last night.

A mustard-colored dog ran from under one of the tenant houses, wagging its tail and whining to be petted. Snow kicked it in the ribs and it ran, tail tucked between its legs, into the cotton field. He went up the steps of the second house and banged on the door. It opened a crack to show the round eyes of a small Negro boy. Snow shoved the door inward, sending the boy sprawling onto the kitchen floor.

Two men, dressed for the fields, one old and gray-haired, the other one not more than twenty-five, were sitting at the breakfast table. Their jaws stopped midway in their chewing and they half rose from their chairs, staring at Snow. Their faces were closed, without expression. The white man was in their house, the white man owned the land they worked and the house they lived in. They would wait to see why he had kicked open their door.

Black smoke rose from the skillet on the iron stove in the corner; a Negro girl stood with a fork poised over the skillet unaware of the burning salt pork. She wore a blue bandanna tied around her hair and a yellow dress. She was barefoot and light-skinned. All of them in the room were motionless, as if another Ice Age had caught them without warning and frozen them where they stood, with the meat still half chewed in their mouths.

"Ophelia," Snow said to the girl at the stove, "you come with me."

Once he spoke they came unfrozen; the boy on the floor

scrambled to his feet and ran to his mother at the stove to hide his face in the folds of her dress. The men at the table stood all the way up, their shoulders rounded, bowed slightly in respect to the white man. Lying on a cot in the far corner of the kitchen next to the fireplace, an old woman, her face black and shrunken with wrinkles, raised up on her elbows to peer through milky blue cateracts at Snow.

"What you all want with us old niggers, honey?" she asked in a high, shaking voice.

The young Negro man, his dark skin mottled with tan spots, left the table and sat on the side of her bed.

"Hush, now, Ahntie," he said, "you lie down. Ain't no cause for you to fret," and he gently pushed her head back onto the pillow.

"Buddy," Snow said to the gray-haired man, "you get me some whiskey, a whole jug of it. Ophelia's coming with me. She won't be helping in the cotton patch today because she's coming with me."

"Grandpa," the girl begged the old man, and her boy clung to her, whimpering.

"I don't know what's wrong, Cap'n," Buddy said, "but it be best if you leave 'phelia alone. She ain't strong; she weak ever since last winter when she be sick. You recollec' Mista Charlie sent the doctor over most every day to see about her. It would please me if you leave 'phelia here."

The young man stood slowly from the cot, facing Snow.

"Now I tell you, white man," he said, "this ain't slave days *no* more. Your folks own this house, but you can't come in here and take my sister just 'cause you say so. You leave my sister *alone*."

Snow, in two long strides, left where he had stood just inside the door and hit the boy across the side of his face. He stumbled backward and hit his head on the wall. The walls were papered from ceiling to floor with yellowing newspapers and pages torn from magazines; they kept the wind from blowing through the cracks in the boards in winter and kept out the insects in summer. A picture of Lana Turner smiled down at them, her platinum hair smeared with blood.

"Skewbald," Snow said to the young man, "don't you never talk back to me. It might not be slave days, but you niggers know who's boss in Georgia. I'll put that old woman out and your granddaddy, too. Now you and your sister might get along all right, but what are *they* going to do? Who's going to take in that old man and that old woman?"

"J.T.," Buddy said to the mottle-faced boy, "go get Mista Snow the whiskey he ask for; go on now, boy."

"Grandpa—"the boy protested.

"Go on now, son," the old man said, "go on."

The boy rubbed his hand over his head but he did not look at Snow again. When he left he pulled the door closed behind him and then he passed the window heading toward the barn.

"You'll have to 'scuse him, please, Cap'n. He still got lots to learn. I'm gon' send 'phelia with you, and maybe you don't know it but Mista Charlie sets a heap of store by J.T. and 'phelia. Looks after them like they was his. I'm gon' ask you to remember old times; remember we been down the road together and the Lord *knows* I owe you and your fam'ly. It was y'all took me in when I chopped off my finger at the syrup mill and couldn't work," and he held up his hand to show that his middle finger was a stump.

Ophelia's boy stopped crying and, sucking his thumb, went to lean against the old man's leg. Ophelia pushed the skillet to the back of the stove, the charred meat lying in black, smoking grease. Outside the window came the happy sound of laughter and the calling back and forth to one another of the hands as they headed for the cotton field. J.T. came through the door and, without a word and without meeting Snow's eyes, handed him a jug of corn liquor. Then he went to sit once again on the cot by the old woman.

"It's good whiskey, Cap'n," Buddy said. "It's good like you and me used to make when you wasn't as old as J.T. Remember how you and me and old Bear Cat made moonshine a *long* time ago? Remember that time how the sheriff come up on us in the woods and chased you and me and Bear Cat out of there shootin' that shotgun, blam, blam, right behind us all the time? Law' me," he laughed, remembering. "You and me, Cap'n, we go back a *long* way. We been down the road together, you and me."

Snow led Ophelia by the hand from the house, his hand nudging against her back, urging her down the path and down the long dusty red hill that led to the stables. She walked slowly, her head lowered, stumbling when he prodded her to move along faster; the colored they met along the way stepped off the path to let them pass, nodded their heads and said good morning, but their faces revealed not the least curiosity toward the white man and the Negro girl.

The sun was barely up but already it was hot; no breeze stirred now to rattle the curled, dry leaves of the black-jack oaks and the sycamores that grew across the road from the cotton field. A rabbit, lean and tan, jumped out of the grass in the ditch and ran across the road in front of them into the cotton, shaking the broad leaves as he jumped from furrow to furrow. There had been no rain for weeks; it was fine weather for cotton. And for killing.

Further down the road, in the Negro settlement outside Clement, there had been two killings within the past three weeks. Two brothers fought over a girl at the Negro honky-tonk called Green Gables out on the highway. They fought until one finally choked the other. A man stabbed his wife when he found her in bed with someone else. The sheriff came both times, but when he found out it didn't involve a white person he just grinned and said that's the way niggers were.

"Let 'em kill each other," he said. "There'll just be fewer of them."

When they got to the stables, Snow pushed Ophelia ahead of him up the ladder to the loft. Charlie came running down the hill, still dressed in his pajamas, and hollered for Snow to come on out of there, to let Ophelia go. But Snow told him he'd kill Ophelia with the pitchfork if he didn't leave him alone, so Charlie walked back up the hill toward Buddy's house. They sat in the hay then, and Snow drank for half the day or more and told Ophelia jokes. Right about sunset he tore her clothes off and whipped her with the mule whip.

"Why'd you come, Lee Rose? Why didn't you stay home with your mama and leave me alone. Your mama sent you, that's why you came, isn't that right, Lee Rose?" And he flung Ophelia into the hay and fell on her. The white clouds floated past the loft window; the sky was as blue as Charlie's eyes. He knew Charlie was Ophelia's and J.T.'s daddy.

Snow stayed with her all night and, early in the morning of the second day, sent a field hand who passed by the stable to get him another jug of whisky; he drank all day and in the afternoon fell asleep. Ophelia slipped away from him and ran naked back up the hard, dusty hill to the house.

Toward dusk all the Negroes in the quarter gathered at the top of the hill to listen to Snow Berryhill screaming from the window of the loft. He thought that Cleveland's gophers were eating him alive and that the end of the world had come.

"Save me, save me," he called to the dark cloud of people on the hill.

Just as the sun went down, sinking round and red behind the mountain, Charlie took two of his strongest field hands and rode in the wagon down the hill to the stables and dragged Snow down from the loft; they tied his hands and feet with rope and put him in the back of the wagon with the green corn they had gathered that day. When the wagon came over the hill, the crowd parted like the Red Sea to let it pass. Snow struggled to his knees to talk to them.

"Repent, repent, the end of the world is at hand, for I have seen the burning fires of hell."

He looked into the eyes of Lottie, dark with hatred of him, then he fell back down and heard the singing and calling of the Negroes as they went back home.

He cried great, sorrowful tears that welled and bubbled from his eyes, ran down his nose and splashed onto the gray, dusty boards of the wagon.

2

It was mid-afternoon and Snow lay on his bed, his hands and feet tied to the bedposts. After five days of screaming and begging someone to get the rats and bugs off him, suddenly, two days ago, he had become lucid. Still Charlie would not untie him, had told him that tomorrow he was taking him over to Milledgeville to the state hospital for the insane.

Snow lay without moving, without thinking. Long-ago happenings came to him, floating in and out of his brain like dreams he could not hold on to. He was down in the bottoms with Roy and his daddy, and he was ten years old and had found the skeleton of his dog Sam. The faded red rag he had soaked in turpentine was still tied around his neck. Sam had gone off by himself to die and Snow never did know what had happened to him until that day he found him way up under a bush. That was the only animal he'd ever loved in his whole life, and he'd knelt there in the gray dirt crying. *Berryhills don't cry, son,* and his father's hand on his shoulder urged him to his feet to finish plowing under the potatoes.

He saw himself and Callie at the edge of the woods in Seddon at the white frame church getting married, Callie in her white dress with the bunch of purple violets pinned to her shoulder; she laughed as she ran down the steps with the rice falling around them, the people laughing and calling to them. They'd run through the graveyard at the side of the church to where he had the buggy waiting, and he'd felt sorry for all the poor dead people who couldn't be happy the way he was that day.

He heard crying, and he thought the girls were all babies again, and then there was the clanging of the supper bell, his mother calling him from the field.

Sounds came to him faintly, the faraway rumble of thunder, the wind slamming the barn door closed, the Negroes singing in the fields; remembrance in a bright burst pierced his brain and he saw Lee Rose standing at the foot of the steps the afternoon she came, smiling up at him. It was the past come back to haunt him, destroy him, and he cried out and lay thrashing against the ropes that held him until, mercifully, thought faded away and he slept again.

When next he woke, there was a shadow in his bedroom doorway that moved to stand silently beside his bed. He turned his head and looked up into the spotted face of J.T.

"You know who this is?" J.T. asked, leaning close to him.

"Skewbald," Snow answered.

There came the faint, far-away sound of someone humming, and J.T. nodded.

"God don't love ugly, Mista Snow." He raised his new sharpened ax and, neatly as chopping a block of wood, split Snow's head straight down the middle.

He dropped the ax there by the bed and went out the back door of the house, slipping along the edge of the woods to the stables; he rubbed warm axle grease from the wagon wheels over his face and arms, then hid deep in the woods back where the hogs rooted until after dark. Traveling only at night, he turned up a week later in the town of Sweetwater.

294

He got a job chopping cotton for an old farmer and his wife who didn't have any children. After a day or two the farmer became suspicious of J.T. being so black and glistening and, holding the shotgun on him, made him come up to the barn to the watering trough and scrub. When the axle grease came off he saw the spotted face and arms of Skewbald.

"Why, I know who you are," the farmer said, "you're that nigger over in Clement that killed that white man. It's been all about you in the papers. Boy, there's a posse out looking for you and a thousand-dollar reward for you, dead or alive."

Holding the gun on him, the farmer made Skewbald drive the wagon over to Clement and when late in the afternoon they turned the corner onto the main street, just after they'd passed the First Baptist Church, he poked Skewbald in the back with the barrel of his shotgun and made him drive the wagon standing up so everybody could see who he was.

People shouted and ran up and down the street; somebody threw a rock at Skewbald, and when at last the wagon turned onto the main street square some men were waiting. They dragged Shewbald off the wagon and took him into the woods at the edge of town and built a bonfire. Some who followed them there said the flames reached higher than the statue of General Robert E. Lee in the court-house square.

The men threw Skewbald into the fire and everytime he crawled back out, screaming and begging for them to kill him outright, to shoot him, they threw him back into the fire again. After he was dead, some of the people who had been watching cut off his fingers and toes to take home for souvenirs.

Buddy came and got J.T. and took him home. They buried him the next Sunday in the cemetery back of the church down at the quarter, but he never did have a name on his headstone except the one Buddy lettered there with black paint. There wasn't a stonecutter in Georgia who would chisel the name of the white man's murderer into the stone.

Lottie took Ophelia and Ophelia's boy and left Clement. Some people thought she went back home to Waycross and others said she went to her brother in Detroit. But nobody knew for sure because she wouldn't talk to anybody, not even Charlie when he came to her house begging her not to go. She kept Ophelia and Ophelia's boy inside the house with her, until late one evening she unbolted the door and they left. They cut across the cotton field with their clothes bundled up inside white sheets that they carried on their heads.

Months later, when the newspapers had stopped writing editorials about the tragedy over in Clement, when people had mostly even stopped talking about it, the all-white all-male grand jury was dismissed because the prosecutor couldn't find anybody who would testify to what they'd seen that afternoon outside Clement.

The old farmer who brought J.T. in went down to the sheriff's office then to collect his reward.

3

LEE ROSE LAY on her back on top of the dark green spread of the hotel bed. She seemed relaxed because she lay so still, her eyes closed. But she was not relaxed; her body was heavy and lethargic, sunk into a jellied mass of apathy so that it was hard for her to move; her fingers were curled loosely around Snow's hog-killing revolver. She clasped the gun lightly, as if it were a lover's hand.

She had come here last night straight across the street from the train station and checked into the cheap hotel called the Caswell. Her suitcase sat unpacked in the corner. She was fully clothed except for the high-heel ankle-strap shoes she had tossed carelessly to the floor; the hem of her pin-stripe skirt was pulled down to cover her knees, her slim legs were crossed at the ankles.

She drifted in and out of sleep, but then about the middle of the afternoon there was the shrill whistle of the mill a block down the street, its shriek finally piercing the hazy recesses of her dreaming, pressing into her brain. She awoke completely, thinking the scream came from her, that the dry metallic taste on her tongue was from the barrel of the gun in her mouth. She pushed the gun away from her until it fell with a thump onto the bare boards of the floor; soon she would take it up again, but not until she remembered for a while, as if in remembering she could make her twenty-three years seem long.

It was hot, she was drowning in the heat of the room and she left the bed and went to raise the window. The air was acid with the fumes from a bus parked in the street below; it was emptying itself of its load of men who walked laughing up the sidewalk, calling and joking to one another, heading for the big wire gates of the mill. A woman, a waitress in a white uniform, hurried across the street to the station restaurant.

Lee Rose pressed her forehead against the wooden edge of the raised window and was aware suddenly that her stomach was empty, growling with hunger. Since she had not eaten since noon of the day before, she thought she might go to the restaurant and buy a cup of coffee from the waitress who had just walked across the street, might even talk to her for a while. But why? What use was there in talking to some stranger, what need to nourish a body that was soon to die? She wished her heart would not beat so hard, that her bodily functions would stop, would at least slow, so she need not notice them; she wanted the parts of her body that filtered and manufactured and pumped to know somehow that there was no longer any need for them to continue working with such efficiency.

She went back to the bed, but before she lay down, stripped off all her clothes, her girdle, damp with sweat, her stockings, her suit, everything. She left them lying in a heap on the floor and when she lay down she ran her hands lightly over her naked body, felt the hard muscular tightness of her youth, and knew that if she did not kill herself she would live to be an old woman. She would grow thinner and tougher over the years like her father's people. Some of them lived more than a hundred years and often her father had said proudly "My people don't die, they just dry up and blow away."

Because she felt so old, she was surprised at the smoothness of her skin, and when she touched her face, thought she should feel there the deep ridges of age. She thought that if she went to look in the mirror over the dresser, there would look back at her from the shadows a wrinkled old woman with white and stringy hair.

She lay her arm across her eyes to blot out the weak rays of late afternoon sunshine. Thoughts darted in and out of her mind like mayflies that are born and almost as quickly die. In her stupor she felt that she had grown wise, that she knew many things, but she was not certain what it was that she knew. She thought it had to do with people not talking. If her father had talked to her, there was a point when he could have changed her life, could have stopped what was about to happen.

That last night in Clement when she had sat late with him on the porch, when she had said to him, *there was to say you loved us,* he could have said: *but no, it isn't possible, I don't love you, I don't know why,* or he could have said, surprised, as if he thought she always knew: *why, yes, I love you, and your sisters too. How could you doubt it?* Then she would have caught the train the next morning and come on home, the question she had gone there to ask him settled in her mind. She could have come home and accepted him as he was and not been tormented any more. If he'd spoken, if only he'd turned to her and told her what was the truth.

She thought of Maribeth who so innocently loved everybody, who was doomed always to believe the love poems she read, and who would always give too much of herself; never did she hold back some secret part that belonged only to her.

But in the end, both of them were rejected; Maribeth by the soldier and she by Norman who came home smug and smiling with a black-haired wife who clung to his arm when they walked into church on Sunday mornings. *The fault in us is the fault of our father who is cruel and insensitive and who never really loved anyone—*

This, then, was what she knew, and she was elated with her wisdom. But quickly the joy faded, the knowledge she had gained had come too late, what she had learned could not save her. And even if it were not too late, she was too tired to try any more; she could never go back to the way things were; now she wanted only the peace of surrender, of giving up.

Already, in her mind, she heard the explosion of the gun, the sound crashed through the flimsy walls of the hotel, echoed through the dimly lit hallways and into the lobby where the worn and faded people sat waiting, listening. They sat straight when they heard the shot, interested, alert for a time. The desk clerk, leaning on the counter, jerked his head up sharply from reading the afternoon newspaper, then, faintly, across the street in the station restaurant they heard the sound. Diners stopped chewing their food, their eyes widening with alarm; but the waitress, who had worked there for many years, stopped her work only momentarily, shrugged and went about pouring coffee and wiping clean the tables. She had heard that sound many times before from the Caswell hotel.

Lee Rose lowered her arm from across her face and when she opened her eyes saw that the room was nearly dark, the shadows bold and looming. She closed her eyes again and thought that in a few minutes she would get up and go home to sit on the porch in the dark with her mother; there would be the perfume of the roses that bloomed so reluctantly, so briefly, this time of year, the buds scarcely opening before they shattered in the heat. She wanted to sit in the cool evening on her mother's porch and rock and listen to the sounds of children playing and in the living room the drone of the radio that played on and on, that nobody ever thought to turn off.

She lay in a half-sleep, and the years of her life slid by so fast, the people walking and running so fast, like in the movies when the action is speeded up, people and places and voices all mixed up: Jo Anna was running after her down the lane, her feet slapping silently in the dust, her voice calling to her, *wait, Lee Rose, wait for me,* her voice mournful like a child lost in the woods; her own self running away from her little sister; fleet and loose she ran and passed her older self squatting in the alley at the new house, picking among the gravel for bits of colored glass, the rocks cutting into the winter softness of her feet not yet grown tough from going barefoot. Her father came from the field hurrying past her to pick up the baby, tossing the baby into the air and catching her, laughing and laughing, both of them laughing; as she watched them there in the lane, the sun filtered down through the leaves of the trees, dotted the shade like swarms of yellow butterflies that fluttered and swooped when the wind blew.

She was in Clement and she sat with her back against the tree, the rough bark of the tree cutting into the thin cloth of her shirt. It was the time of day the whippoorwills sang, and the flat, peaceful surface of the pond was gold with sunset; around its banks the shadows crept and frogs began to sing from the marsh grass. They'd brought a picnic there early in the afternoon, she and her father, and they'd sat on the pine needles at the edge of the pond and eaten biscuits filled with ham and drunk lemonade from a jar that had the yellow wedges of lemons floating in it.

Long after the picnic was over they'd sat on and on into the long twilight, sat there under the trees in the green shadows. Just at dark they'd gone back to the house and there was the sad smell of the wisterias, the blossoms hanging heavy and pendulous all around the roof of the porch.

That night her father had touched her finally, after all those years he'd put his arms around her and held her close to him, and afterward she was ashamed and hated him. And he hated her too; it wasn't just indifference any more like all the years when he had looked at her but didn't really see her. Now he hated her.

The mill whistle blew and, alarmed, she quickly sat up in bed, her head aching, throbbing; when the air stopped vibrating, she got up and picked up her clothes from the floor. She turned the skirt right side out again, shook the wrinkles out of her stockings and her blouse, folded her suit coat neatly and lay them all across a chair. She set her shoes side by side under the bed. Then she picked the gun up from the floor and lay down.

She thought of them all once again, whispered their names: *Mama, Jo Anna, Maribeth.* She ought to leave them some message, some explanation of what she was doing, but she would not; she had never liked to write letters.

She turned on her side and bent her legs slightly, curled her arms around the gun, cradled it to her. She pushed the barrel down her throat and closed her eyes and she was back at the farm and it was just before dark, the time of day she loved best. She was alone in the gray field and the chimney swifts with their bow-shaped wings were circling high, outlined against the dusty blue of the sky; through the thin woods at the edge of the road she saw the outline of the old house. Her mother was calling to her, her voice faint from so far away.

—Lee Rose! Lee Rose! Lee Rose!

302

She turned away from the sound; she would not let her call her back. She ran cross-grained to the furrows and the wind was in her face, she was running and running until her blood vessels burst, only this time there was no scary Jo Anna screaming, *Mama, make her stop, make Lee Rose take the gun away.*

4

IT WAS a muggy, sultry day the first part of August when the two policemen knocked on Callie's front door. All morning long it had tried to rain, the clouds rolling across the sky dark and threatening, the wind blowing the dead leaves off the trees so that it looked more like fall than summer. Already some of the trees were bare, having shed their leaves during the long drought of June and July. There had been no rain to speak of all summer long.

The policemen knocked on her door around noon and they were polite and called her ma'm. "Do you mind if we step inside, ma'm?" they said, and when they were just inside the front door they showed her Lee Rose's billfold with the identification that said Callie was the one to contact in case of emergency.

The blood left her head and she was freezing cold when they told her about Lee Rose, but she wouldn't sit on the couch like they asked her to because she was calm suddenly; she didn't believe what they said. She kept shaking her head and telling them no, that wasn't her daughter they were talking about; and no, there was nobody she wanted them to call to be with her. My daughters are away for the day, she explained, and then she dressed in her best voile dress and wore her brooch with the glass sets to go down to the police station with them; they took her in the patrol car and the streets in the white glare of midday were mostly deserted. All the buildings that were so familiar to her now looked strange and oddly distorted, misshapen.

The police station was ugly inside with the dirty, pale green paint peeling off the walls; the electric fans on the wall and on the floor blew her dress tight around her legs and fluttered the papers the policeman wrote on. He finally had to weight them down with an ashtray that had painted on it drooping palm trees and the indigo blue Gulf of Mexico. Across the bottom was written, "Souvenir of Panama City Beach, Florida."

Callie sat in a chair by the side of the policeman's desk and through a haze saw the sweat that beaded on his forehead; she thought the stiff yellow bristles of his mustache looked like the bristles in the tiny vegetable brush the Fuller Brush man had given her last week as a free gift. He asked her questions, and once she thought she would laugh because they sounded so much like true and false questions from school days.

Your daughter was despondent when she left home?

No. *False. Lately she'd seemed happy, she talked more and there was a boy she'd begun dating from the church that she seemed to like a lot—*

The gun we showed you belonged to your husband?

Yes. *True. It was to kill hogs with; every winter when he shot the hogs, all of us ran to hide in the closet so we wouldn't hear them squeal; we put our hands over our ears—*

Your daughter went over to Clement the first part of July?

Yes. *True. And I was mad at her when she left. The last thing I said to her when she left was why don't you just stay over there since you love him so much, don't bother to come back. I wouldn't care. I watched her walk away down the sidewalk. I stood on the porch waiting until the bus came, but she never looked back toward the house. When the bus passed by—the buses come right by the house now—I waved to her. I wasn't mad any more, but she didn't see me—*

On and on she answered his questions, through stiff lips she answered him, sure that soon he would look up at her and smile and put down the pencil. He would smile at her and lean back in his chair and tell her to go on home, there'd been a mistake after all. I can see now, he'd say, this woman isn't your daughter, she's someone else's daughter—

They took her in an elevator down to the basement to look at Lee Rose. They kept calling her the deceased and when they said they didn't think she'd suffered at all, Callie wanted to scream at them but no sound came. It was like in dreams when she'd try to cry out and she couldn't make any sound.

It really was Lee Rose, only it wasn't her either; it was just somebody who faintly resembled her; all the vitality was gone, her neck was arched back in a twisted way, but there was no mark on her that Callie could see; her white skin was darkly mottled.

"No, that's not her, that's not my daughter," she said, shaking her head in a definite way so they would believe her.

They took her back upstairs to the desk and she sat down and signed some papers in the places they told her to. Then they gave her Lee Rose's purse and her suitcase and they told her there wasn't any suicide note; they'd already searched through all her things. The blond-haired policeman took her by the elbow, and as he led her to the door someone asked him if he needed any help and he said, no, it was just a routine suicide.

He walked Callie to the door when they got back to her house and he kept asking if there was someone to call for her, did she want a neighbor lady to come and stay with her, or was there some relative. She kept shaking her head at him, and when he left she sat on the front porch and Mrs. McNabb from across the street hollered to her, wanted to know if there was anything wrong, she'd seen the police car. But Callie wouldn't answer her. She turned her chair so her back was to the white-haired and skinny Mrs. McNabb; she sat there rocking until late in the afternoon when Jo Anna and Maribeth finally came back home from showing off Laurel June to one of Maribeth's old Sunday-school friends.

It was the hottest day yet in August when Lee Rose was buried. After the service at the Baptist church they went across town to the cemetery. Most of the people left after the church service because it was so hot, but a few people came to the cemetery. Most of them couldn't stand the fiery heat of the sun and went to stand in the shade of a big, black jack oak close by; all around the grave where they walked the dry grass was mashed into the dust. Now and then a yellow leaf fell; the tree could not support so many leaves with so little moisture. The red clay dirt piled to the side of the grave had turned gray and crumbly in the heat.

When at last the preacher finished reading his words of hope and redemption, when he had said that even the vilest sinner could be saved and had slapped his Bible shut, Callie sent Maribeth and Jo Anna to wait in the car with Norman and his Australian wife. She told them to stop pulling at her, she would not leave, she would stay until the dirt was put back and the flowers in place. There was a Negro man who shoveled the dirt, and when the clods hit the coffin with a hollow sound he shook his head at her in a solemn way.

"You ought to go home now, missus," he said, but Callie wouldn't leave. She had brought this child into the world and now that she was leaving it, would not desert her.

Through the horror of it all, though her face was gray and her eyes dry and dusty as the grass and leaves, after it was all done, the dirt spread smooth, the wilted flowers laid, there was the comfort of going home. When she walked up her front steps she saw insignificant things with great clarity: the red geraniums she had planted up close to the bannister were budding, and the paint on the foundation of the house was flaking off, it lay like a thin drift of snow against the bricks; in the fall it would need painting. A shingle was gone from the roof that she had not noticed before.

The neighbors came to her house and she saw that Jo Anna's eyes were red from crying; Callie's heart ached for the little sister who had tagged Lee Rose everywhere. The Tancretti boy was there with his arm around Jo Anna's shoulder; he never left her side; Maribeth was in the dining room white-faced and polite, pouring coffee. Callie saw all of them vaguely; in a mist they swirled about her, their soft flesh as they hugged her was not so comforting as the hard and bony wood of her house; her house was crystal clear to her, its shape in sharp outline. It seemed shining and radiant to her.

The season changed, the long summer ended. It was late fall, the time of bright blue October weather, of short days and small white butterflies that swarmed around the fall flowers. In the cool hush of early mornings Callie stood at her front window to watch the school children pass by, their book satchels bumping against their legs as they skipped along the sidewalk to the grammar school.

There was in the air the quivering edge of anticipation, and

sometimes she would stand dead still, stop whatever she was doing, to listen. Sometimes she suddenly stopped stirring the
food in a pot, waiting. But she did not know what it was that
she waited for, what it was she hoped to hear; she thought
perhaps she listened for the sound of the bus stopping at her
corner, or waited for the step of someone's foot on the front
porch coming home. But she didn't really know.

This afternoon, she sat late on the porch and in the west the
lonely red glow of the sun was setting; she thought that to anyone passing by she appeared as always, but she was not the
same; there were the changes. She recalled the summer only in
snatches, her memories as elusive as happenings in a dream;
thoughts came to her and faded almost at once, and she would
be confused, wondering what it was that she had remembered.

Yet lately things seemed better; she had struggled to bring
order to her life again, for there lay sanity and comfort. Every
afternoon, she worked for a while in the yard, moving this
bush or that; sometimes she forgot where she had planted a
particular bush and would have to hunt for it. When her work
was done in the yard, she bathed and dressed and sat on the
porch, angling her chair so she had a good view of the sidewalk, could see anyone who might be leaving or coming home.

At this time of day there was no one, not even a stray child
running home through the dusk. They were inside with their
families, gathered around the supper table or perhaps listening
to the radio. But then, far up the street, came the sound of
children's voices, and Callie started with alarm, leaned forward in her chair to peer up the sidewalk. They were still out,
Lee Rose and Jo Anna; she had called them many times but
they had paid no attention to her. She did not like them out so
late and, irritably, she rocked and thought that soon she would
have to call them again.

But there are no children, the children are all gone, and she knew that behind her the house was dark and empty. No one was in there, no supper cooked on the eye of the gas stove. All of them were gone; she had fixed up the house for them, but they had gone. There was new living-room furniture and tile on the kitchen floor covering the old boards that had ribbed the flowered linoleum for so many years. Finally, there was enough money, too; she had her retirement from the plant because of her perfect attentdance record and because she had worked there for at least ten years. There was also a small widow's pension from the government.

After Lee Rose died, the changes came all at once, one after the other; everything that happened, happened within a few weeks. First there was Snow, murdered by the race of people he'd always loved so well; Charlie had called her and asked her what he must do and she'd told him to bury him over there in Lone Oak with the rest of his people. In her sorrow for Lee Rose she tried to find out from Charlie what had happened over there in Clement. But he didn't know anything, or else he wasn't telling.

A week after that Jo Anna came home from a date late one night—she'd been gone all that day too—and told Callie that she and the Tancretti boy had gone over to Georgia and gotten married and that she was pregnant. She packed her suitcase and left that night to go live with him in the back of the grocery store his father owned. Maribeth stayed on with the baby for another month and then she left too.

"It's no use, Mama," she'd said, "I can't stay here and sleep in the bed where Lee Rose and I used to sleep. I can't stay in this neighborhood either with people staring at me when I get on the bus and asking questions about Lee Rose and Daddy too. I have to get away from you, Mama."

At the shock on Callie's face, she said, "I love you, I really do, but you've taken over Laurel June and it seems like she belongs to you, not me. I'm going to share an apartment with the girl I told you about that I met at work, that way it won't cost so much—"

She put her arms around her mother.

"Oh, God, Mama, I hate to leave you here by yourself, we've all had so much trouble; let's start somewhere new. Leave this neighborhood where you've been so unhappy. You can get an apartment close to me—"

"No, I won't do that, Maribeth," Callie said. "I'll never walk off and leave this house that I've put my blood into. You go on to your apartment. I'm staying right here; I'll never leave."

She knew that one day she would leave, but it would be feet first and only across town to the big cemetery called Valley Haven. A busy highway ran alongside it and the whole avenue was bright with streetlights. When the sun went down at night, instead of dark and the lonesome singing of crickets, there'd be cars going by, with laughing people on their way to parties or off on trips. She would lie next to Lee Rose through all the sunrises and sunsets of eternity, but she would never know what had happened over there in Georgia to make her want to die—

"Good evening, Mr. Cox," Callie called, nodding to Chester Cox as he passed by. He was coming home from his evening walk and she pulled her chair close to the bannister to talk with him, hoped she could hold him there for a while. "How's Mrs. Cox?" she asked.

He tipped his hat to her.

"Good evening, Mrs. Berryhill," he said, and his lips twitched at the corners; he seemed on the brink of laughter as he always did. "Mrs. Cox is doing fine, just fine," but he did not linger to talk; he continued on down the sidewalk and turned in at his walk, disappearing into the shadows of his screened front porch.

Callie leaned back in her chair, disappointed that he was gone, the sidewalk empty again. Birdie Cox had had a stroke and was paralyzed down her right side. Some said her mind was gone, but still she was someone to talk to on lonely evenings even if she didn't make a grain of sense.

Callie shivered and pulled her sweater closer about her; it was cold, the sun almost down; when dark came, it would come quickly as in the dead of winter. There would be no more long twilights when people sat late on their porches and the sound of their voices were friendly in the night.

A flock of birds flew over and Callie half rose to watch them, hated to see the birds leaving. The golden days of October did not fool the birds, they knew winter was near and that it was time for them to leave. Already there had been frost; only this morning the roofs of the houses and the last of the zinnias in the back yard were coated gray with it.

It was dark, she had sat on the porch far past supperttime. The moon was up, its light silvering the sidewalk and the grass; up and down the street patches of electric light shone from windows onto porches and yards; it was time to go in and turn on her lights. But then a bus stopped at the corner and a man stepped into the square of yellow light that shone from the windows of the bus onto the sidewalk. When the bus pulled away she saw a dark figure in the night and Callie thought that it was Snow coming home late again, drunk for all the neighbors to see.

Jo Anna, turn off the porch light so the neighbors can't see your daddy stumbling up the steps, but then the man crossed to the other side of the street and Callie went into the house.

But she did not go to the kitchen to cook supper; instead, she locked the front door and went into the room where Maribeth and Lee Rose had slept together. The moonlight flooded through the window and the solemn gray ghosts of her children hovered around her, their fingers, insubstantial as gossamer, clutched at her.

If I could, I would have frozen time and kept all of you with me, Jo Anna sleeping next to me in my bed and Maribeth writing letters to pen-pal boy friends that she would never meet; Lee Rose could have stayed a child forever, turning cartwheels, rolling and spinning across the grass in the summer twilight. But I could not stop time and all of you are gone.

"Well, house, it's you and me now." She was startled at the sound of her voice. "I'm the last one, house," she called, and the sound carried through the rooms, echoing into the dark corners.

She went into the back room and undressed, and when she had on her gown, pulled back the covers and lay down. Since she did not need a blanket, it was not yet winter; her father once had told her that as long as he could still lie on top of the cover at night there was enough warm weather left to get in his winter crop.

When her eyes had adjusted to the dark, she saw across the room the outline of Snow's bed, the bed that Jo Anna had finally slept in the last year she was home. For a moment, she pretended Jo Anna still slept in that bed and that she heard her breathing. But she stopped herself: there was no one there, she would not fool herself, she was completely alone. Next year she might try to rent out the front room, might get it fixed up and run an ad in the paper. But she would not do this until she had proven to herself that she could live alone. Her children would visit her, she knew that, but they would always leave again and in the end there was only herself to rely on.

She thought that since she was not sleepy, she would plan

her garden for the spring; thinking of the flowers soothed her, and, as always, the marigolds flashed first in her mind because they were her favorites. Their odor was bitter and unpleasant; there were dozens of other flowers that had a sweeter smell, but none had caught the yellow and bronze of the sun in their blossoms as had the marigolds. Now that Birdie Cox was bed-ridden, it would be her own yard that was the showplace of the neighborhood; there would be arbors and trellises and narrow pathways winding between the flower beds.

She lay in the dark and was pleased that she no longer had to leave a light burning for herself. She had not had the night-mare dream of Lee Rose for many nights; the wax Lee Rose, walking slow and stiff-jointed as puppets do, had not come to her trying to tell her something, the words gibberish.

She turned on her side and closed her eyes, and beyond the golf course a train climbed the hill and crossed over the trestle, the long cry of its whistle echoing through the valley. The wooden arms of her house cradled her, then, all at once, as lately it sometimes happened, she remembered Lee Rose the way she used to be, running up the sidewalk, her black hair flying in the wind—